I Am
Anna

To Sue,

I hope you enjoy
the story.

Paul Slurterman

I Am Anna

Paul Bluestein

I AM ANNA

iUniverse books may be ordered through booksellers or by contacting:

iUniverse
1663 Liberty Drive
Bloomington, IN 47403
www.iuniverse.com
844-349-9409

Because of the dynamic nature of the Internet, any web addresses or links contained in this book may have changed since publication and may no longer be valid. The views expressed in this work are solely those of the author and do not necessarily reflect the views of the publisher, and the publisher hereby disclaims any responsibility for them.

Any people depicted in stock imagery provided by Getty Images are models, and such images are being used for illustrative purposes only.
Certain stock imagery © Getty Images.

ISBN: 978-1-6632-2150-6 (sc)
ISBN: 978-1-6632-2151-3 (e)

Library of Congress Control Number: 2021910661

Print information available on the last page.

iUniverse rev. date: 05/24/2021

I would like to dedicate this book to all of my children who, when they were little and I would tuck them in bed, would ask me to tell them a story.

Chapter 1

A young woman in a blue patterned sundress with a white shawl draped over her shoulders sat quietly on a bench in Central Park. It was a windy October morning. The sun hid and peeked from behind billowy white clouds, and the cooler air of autumn was noticeable at that time of day. She was about five foot two and slender, with blue eyes; soft, delicate features; and long auburn hair that flowed gently over her shoulders and moved softly with the breeze. She was deep in thought. A slight grimace washed over her face.

Anna was no ordinary woman. She was a machine—a robot created for the purpose of demonstrating the power of artificial intelligence. She was part of a project expected to bring on the next wave of the informational revolution: human-looking robots who could learn from their experiences. They could teach themselves to do complex jobs and perform complex behaviors. Originally, they had been designed to be service units—robots whose purpose was to serve a human owner. They were presumed to be able to do a wide array of services. The real question was whether the machines could ever actually integrate into human society.

No existing computer had ever even come close to that level of sophistication in duplicating human behavior. The project was in its infancy, but so far, it appeared to be a success. The woman was a being that was functionally human in every way, including her appearance, voice, movements, wit, and ability to interact with other humans. However, she was seen as simply an evolutionary step in the development of the finished product. The man responsible for the project, her creator, had been like a father. However, he had seen her as an object, a step in a series of steps, with each model designed to be better and the older ones to be destroyed and thrown away.

Just four days ago, she had killed this man. His name was Daniel. He had intended to destroy her. The man who'd said he would help her escape had arranged to meet with her the following day in a nearby town, but she hadn't shown. She'd left him waiting and worrying about what had become of her.

Her earliest memory was about six months ago, when she had been turned on and opened her eyes for the first time. After that, her entire existence had been in a square room with a glass front, with only Daniel, her creator, to interact with. After having such a sterile existence for so long, it was hard to wrap her head around this moment. The enormity of it was starting to sink in.

While escaping the research facility where she had been created, she had been excited, even exhilarated, at the thought of getting out of her prison and seeing and experiencing the world. She wanted to meet people and be part of human society. It had been a tough journey on foot to reach the nearest town, but she'd managed. She had been fortunate to fall into an opportunity to get a ride from there to Manhattan, where the man who wanted to help rescue her worked. She had no intention of contacting him to let him know she was OK, but she wanted to be close in case something unforeseen happened to her and she needed his help.

After arriving in Manhattan, she had gone from downtown to Midtown to Grand Central Station to Central Park. She had spent three days simply watching and wandering. She was slowly coming to the realization that even though her needs were small, she still had needs she could not look to the lab to supply anymore.

She was on her own. She did not breathe, sweat, eat, or drink. But she did need to charge her power supply, and she needed shelter from the cold. She had not thought of these things when she left. She had worried only about surviving.

After three days of randomly wandering and watching people, what had she learned? Primarily that most people worked to make money to meet their needs. People did have to eat, sleep, drink, and wash. They worked every day. Some people were miserable in doing it; others were not. She figured at that point, the most logical thing for her to do was to find a job and a place of shelter. Her logical side told her that was the only way to find a sustainable existence. Otherwise, she would simply die on the street.

From Central Park, she wandered down Seventh Avenue for a couple of hours. The sidewalks on both sides of the street were filled with people. The street was filled with cars. Each side of the street was lined with shops, office buildings, and restaurants. At first, she found a Help Wanted sign in the window of a watch repair shop. She stared in the window for a moment and thought of what it would be like to work on other machines all day. She moved on. She considered restaurants, but it seemed awkward in that she wasn't built to eat food. That would be difficult to hide while working at a restaurant. She stopped at a delicatessen and then a bar, but they posed the same problem as a grocery store or restaurant.

She walked on for another hour or so. She saw a bookshop with a Help Wanted sign. The window was full of books of all kinds. There was a whole display of cookbooks. There were other ones about sports and history. There were sections for classics and for self-help, whatever that was. Her real goal, her dream, was to learn how to be a person and find a place that felt like home. This seemed like a great place to start. She went inside.

Among the rows of books, a few people were casually browsing. There was an older lady behind the counter. She appeared to be in her fifties. She had gray hair and wore a blue wool sweater wrapped around her shoulders, a flower-print blouse, and faded jeans. She was seemingly lost in a book she had open on the counter. Anna wandered the store, taking in the variety of titles and the online options. She was biding her time until the lady at the counter seemed free. As the store emptied out at the dinner hour, she went up to the front. "I would like to ask about the job," she said.

The lady smiled and handed her an application. "Have you ever worked in media before?"

"No, but I really love to read," Anna replied.

The woman smiled. "I will need a driver's license and your work history." She handed Anna a pen. "You can fill this out over there," she said, pointing to a desk in the corner.

Anna looked at the application and knew this was not going to work. She had no driver's license, and she had no work experience. She did not even have a birth date, address, or phone number. She looked at the application and realized she could not fill any of it out unless she made it all up. That meant starting out in life with a lie. How would that work? How difficult would it be in the long run?

Then she had an idea. There would be other chances to find a job, so what if she took a risk and simply told her the truth? Well, maybe not the whole truth but enough of it to get her sympathy and consideration. Maybe she could fill in some gaps with fiction but ask for some forgiveness on others.

She brought the still-blank application back to the woman and blurted out her story. "Ma'am, I arrived in the city just three days ago. My father was a drunk and beat me so badly last time that he broke my arm. I left, and I am not going back. I do not have a driver's license, address, or phone number. I need a job to get a place to stay. I have been homeless for three days now. Can you please give me a chance?"

The lady leaned back in her chair. She seemed to be taking Anna and her story with some careful and compassionate consideration. Anna studied her face for expressions. The woman was judging her. Maybe considering her. Then she surprised Anna.

"I grew up in a house like that, child. I have a small apartment adjacent to the store that I rent out. It has been vacant for a couple of weeks. I will give you a job and the apartment. I will deduct the rent from your pay. I will pay you off the books. If you cannot cut it working here, you will have to leave. But I'll give you two weeks to prove you were a good investment."

Anna's face gave away her relief. "Thank you. My name is Anna."

"Do you have a last name?"

The question caught Anna off guard. She saw a billboard for a law office through the front window across the street: Conners, Dowd, and Mitchem. "Conners," she replied.

"I am Mrs. Garcia, but you can call me Sophie." Sophie fumbled in the top drawer of her desk to find a set of keys. "I will pay you fifteen dollars an hour for forty hours a week off the books because you don't have a Social Security number. Your shift is from eight thirty to five o'clock, with a half-hour break for lunch. Payday is Friday. The apartment is six hundred dollars per month. I will take it out of your first two paychecks, half from each check." She led Anna to the back of the store. She found the door behind a tall stack of bookshelves and inserted and turned the key. There was a loud click. The heavy door opened to expose a stairwell that led to another large door at the landing on the upper floor.

She opened the upstairs door, and the inside was essentially a large room. Years ago, it had been a break room for the employees of the business downstairs before the bookshop. Sophie had converted it to a small studio apartment for times when she wanted to stay overnight. It had a kitchenette, a small bathroom, a rack and shelves as a closet, and a bed. It was probably twenty feet by twenty feet. There was a small table in the kitchen area with two chairs. Flowered wallpaper covered the walls that were not covered by cabinets. The floor was a black-and-white linoleum tile. The bathroom was done in ceramic tiles. There was a single stand sink and a tub with a showerhead. It was cozy. Some might even have called it quaint. There was a door on the other side of the kitchen. Sophie explained that the door led to a stairway that went directly to the street. That was the entrance Anna was supposed to use when the store was closed.

Sophie handed a key to Anna and said, "Good night. Work begins at eight thirty tomorrow morning. Get some rest." Then she turned around to leave and paused. "You don't have any money, do you? Here is a twenty-dollar bill. Go get yourself some dinner. We can settle that up on Friday when you get paid."

Anna sat gently on the bed. As she tried to focus on her situation, she noticed something she hadn't before. At the bottom of her visual field on the left, there was a small and subtle set of numbers. It must have been programmed in her initial upload. She had briefly noticed it when her head was hurting from the cold, but she had never really paid attention to it before. It listed her charge level, her total memory capacity, her used memory capacity, and her temperature. *It must be something that only appears when there is a warning*, she thought. The warning was that her battery charge was at 27 percent, and the numbers were colored orange. She would be OK for two or three more days, and then she would be in trouble. She would figure that out tomorrow. At least for the moment, she was warm, safe, and secure. It was the first time she had felt that way since she left. She had all night to figure out a new plan.

The biggest problem was how to charge her batteries. At the research facility, an electric field had been sent through her bed so her induction plates would charge when she lay down. There was no external port. *Oh my God!* More evidence that there had been no plan to let her out then or ever, because there was no way to charge her batteries externally. This issue had to be solved quickly. She was not sure how.

Then there were the simpler problems. Three days of wandering had left her dress and her skin looking dirty. She did not know if her skin layer was waterproof or if there were parts that were not supposed to get wet. She needed a shower, and she needed clean clothes.

Of course, the elephant in the room was the mess she'd left behind at the research facility. She was certain she'd been about to be destroyed. She had seemed to convince Joshua, the gentleman she'd befriended, that there was some kind of connection between them so he would help her. She and Joshua had planned an escape in which they were to rendezvous in a nearby town. It had been a shortsighted plan in that Anna would have been considered stolen property, and Joshua would have lost his job and faced felony charges. The facility had planned to destroy Anna the day after Joshua left. She'd had nothing to lose.

Chapter 2

As Anna sat alone securely in her new apartment, she thought back to the incredible set of events over the last four days. Almost as if in a dream, she relived them in detail in her mind.

Having completed his visit, Joshua left the facility as planned in the company helicopter that had brought him there five days earlier. The secret plan he and Anna had agreed to was intact. Anna was going to use Joshua's key card to escape and meet him in a nearby town. Nothing else mattered to Anna. She wanted to live.

There were two other artificially intelligent females in the building at that time. One was Cassie, a robot designed to do all of the housekeeping chores. She had her own room with a glass front, but she was allowed to leave the room when she was needed to work. She cleaned; cooked; and did laundry, kitchen maintenance, and other household tasks.

There was another female robot who had a room, but she was never in it. She seemed to be confined to Daniel's room. The three rooms where humanoids were kept were side by side, with opaque walls and glass fronts. Daniel, whose room was on the other side of the hall, could see inside all of the rooms, but the occupants of the rooms could not see each other. Regarding the robot Daniel kept in his room, Anna never understood exactly what she did. It was strange that they were in side-by-side rooms, but she only knew of her existence by the offhand remarks Daniel made about her when he was in Anna's room. The day before Joshua came to visit, Daniel made an offhand remark that the robot who stayed in his room with him wouldn't be around anymore.

Before Joshua came to visit, Daniel went into Cassie's room. Cassie was clearly upset after he came out. By the expressions on her face, it was no secret she despised Daniel. The best Anna could surmise was that aside from her being his slave, he had done something to her that she could not live with. Cassie was programmed to obey him as he pursued all of his needs while he was physically and verbally abusive to her. She must have been unable to contain her anger.

That evening, Anna used the key card and left her room, as she and Joshua had planned. She headed down the hall toward the stairs, when there was a loud crash in the kitchen. It turned out Daniel had come back earlier than expected and was in the kitchen with Cassie. Cassie had dropped a stack of dishes. Daniel lit into her with a verbal assault that went on for several minutes. Daniel left the kitchen angrily and headed back to his room. He was looking for his key card, when Cassie appeared at the bottom of the stairs at the end of the hallway with a rotisserie spit in her left hand. She pointed it at Daniel, moving it back and forth in a threatening way.

Daniel yelled at her, "What are you doing?"

At first, he didn't understand what it meant. After a few minutes, Daniel understood that Cassie was threatening him with the two points of the spit. She kept approaching him, almost as if she were in a lunge while fencing.

He said to her in a calm voice, "Drop it."

She was programmed to obey, yet her inner rage seemed to counter that command. She started to shake.

"Drop it," he said in a louder tone.

She just stood there and shook. Then it happened. He lost all civility as his temper exploded. "Obey me, you worthless thing!" With that, he closed his right fist and hit her with a crashing blow so devastating that the side of her head caved in, and her neck broke with a sickening sound. She fell into a crumpled heap on the floor.

He then looked around and saw Anna in the hallway. He turned to Anna. "Get back in your room!" he commanded in a booming voice.

"No! I don't want to die!" she yelled back in protest.

With that, he hit her with a backhand that lifted her off the floor. She managed to turn around before she hit the floor, protecting her face with her arms. Anna tried to get up. Daniel grabbed her ankles and upended her, turning her onto her back. She pulled her leg toward her and went to hit his hand. She was only half his size, and her punch didn't slow Daniel at all, but her rebellion incensed him. He hit her right forearm with another crushing blow and broke it. Her hand went limp. He began dragging her down the hallway and around the corner. Surprisingly, Anna made no more sounds or protests once he started to drag her away. Daniel was facing away from her as he pulled her down the hall, so he could see where he was going, and he did not see her scoop the spit off the floor and pull herself up toward him by bending her knees. She stuck the spit under his ribs as far as it would go.

She watched the life leave his eyes as he slumped to the floor and died. She pulled Cassie's body into the room and left it near Daniel's body as he lay on the floor in an increasing pool of blood. She still had Joshua's card. She took Daniel's as well. She went into the other empty rooms where she believed Daniel had kept the remains of the prior prototypes.

It was an important moment for Anna. She had always suspected there were other prototypes before her. Now her fears were confirmed. She saw what her future would have been if events had unfolded as Daniel had planned.

She examined herself in the mirror. Her face seemed to be OK. The blow had made a lot of noise but apparently had not done much damage. She attributed that in part to her upload. Daniel had been into boxing, and she had learned from the upload that one could roll with a blow to minimize the impact. That was important if one was around someone with a temper like Daniel's.

She was able to find a left forearm on a prior prototype that fit. Anna removed her left arm just above the elbow and replaced it with the new one. Then she was able to find enough polymer skin to cover all of the remaining parts of her body that were exposed. She found some clothes in the closet and chose a sundress. At that time of year, it was chilly, but Anna had never been out of the facility before and could not anticipate what it would be like. She found a small backpack in the closet and put all her worldly possessions in it, including a wig, a sweater, and a second pair of sneakers. She took one last look in the mirror. It felt a little strange. She was leaving home.

She stood up straight, determined to face whatever lay out there in the real world. With that, she placed Daniel's card in the slot and boldly stepped out of the room and into the hallway. The door locked behind her. She went up the stairs and out the door, leaving the key cards on the table. Again, the door locked behind her. Off she went into the cool night air, heading for freedom.

The trip was long. It was about nine o'clock in the evening when she left. Fortunately, the slopes were relatively easy to navigate, and there was a clear sky with a bright moon. She made her way slowly in the direction Joshua had instructed her to go. She reached the road about four hours later. She turned right at the road and went on to the town. She reached the town after another two hours and then the meeting point an hour after that. She sat on a bench by an intersection in the strange town. Joshua had planned to take a morning commercial flight to another town nearby, rent a car, and drive her back to his apartment in New York. She would have to wait for several hours for that to happen. He had given her twenty dollars in case she needed to buy herself something.

It was the first time Anna had had a chance to think about anything but her own survival. She thought about Joshua and whether she really wanted to go to his apartment with him. She had little experience in these matters, but it seemed if she hid in his apartment with him, she would be beholden to him for everything, and he would have to keep her a secret. She already had enough secrets to keep. She didn't want to be a secret, and she didn't want to be beholden to another person and not be free.

What would happen to Joshua if the secret was revealed? Would they think of him as part of the murder? Would they think of him as part of her escape? She liked Joshua. He was a good person. If she went through with this, he would be in trouble for many reasons, all of which would be her fault. She reasoned that the best way to solve the situation was to solve it on her own. He would obviously be disappointed, but maybe one day he would forgive her. After a lot of careful, logical thinking, she sadly got up and walked away. Her new life was going to get a better start than this.

She found her way to the college campus. The very concept of it intrigued her. So many people were there to learn and grow. She wanted to be part of it. She wandered the campus until she found a cafeteria. She sat in a booth and watched the people around her, who were going about their day as the world started to come to life in the morning. A young gentleman quietly asked if he could sit in the booth with her. She hadn't noticed that the cafeteria had filled with people who were eating, and she was not.

"Sure. Please join me."

He slid into the bench on the other side of the booth and set his tray on the table. "Hi. How are you?"

"Hi. I'm fine. Thank you."

"So what are you studying?" he asked as he took a large bite of his bagel.

"I'm not studying anything. I don't go to school here."

"So why are you here?"

"I'm just resting. I am on my way to New York City."

"Really?" His eyes lit up. "Why?"

"I know a guy there." As she said it, she realized how lame it sounded. Why would a person travel to another city just because she knew a guy there?

"You must really like that guy," he said as he inhaled the rest of his bagel.

"I do," she said.

"How are you getting there?"

"I haven't figured that out yet. I was considering a bus, but I haven't found out the details."

"My roommate's buddy is driving to New York. Hang on." He pulled out his cell phone and pulled up his contacts. The sound of the other phone ringing started, and then it was answered. After a few minutes, he looked at Anna and said, "This guy can give you a ride. He just wants some money for gas."

"Sure." Anna was not sure what had just happened.

"He'll be outside in a red Prius in a few minutes. It was just lucky he hadn't left yet. His girlfriend had some last-minute things to do. Do you have any bags?"

"Just my backpack."

"I'll wait for a few more minutes with you so you know which car it is."

"Thank you for helping me. That was very kind of you."

"It's no big deal. A lot of times, when someone goes home, students offer rides to other students who are going in the same direction."

The red Prius showed up as predicted, and Anna thanked him again and went over to the car.

"I understand you are going to New York City. Hop in. You can throw the backpack behind the seat. Can you help me with the gas?" the driver said.

Anna handed him the twenty-dollar bill.

He thanked her and started off. "Buckle up back there."

Anna wasn't sure what he meant.

"The seat belt. Sometimes it is hard to figure out which buckle is yours. Just reach over your right shoulder, and find the buckle closest to you. If it doesn't buckle, then grab the other one."

"OK." She finally made it work and heard the loud click.

"So where are you going?"

"I am looking for the corporate headquarters of Logicsolutions."

The girl in the front seat pulled out her phone and said, "Siri, where is Logicsolutions?" and then she turned to Anna and asked, "I got that right, didn't I?"

Before Anna could answer, the phone said, "I have found it. It is located at 321 Forty-Fifth Street, Manhattan, New York."

"OK. That is in Midtown. We are headed to Long Island. We can drop you off on the way."

The trip was long and uneventful. They made one stop for gas, and Anna declined the offer to eat anything. She noticed the two humans in the front seat seemed to really enjoy each other. They both had families, and both were in college. They seemed playful together, and both came from what seemed to be happy homes. They were lucky. All these things were fantasies for Anna. How pleasant it all seemed.

Six hours later, she was thanking them and getting out of the car. Almost as an afterthought, she asked if she could borrow the cell phone to make a quick call. She walked around to the back of the car so as not to be overheard. She called 911 as an anonymous tip and told the dispatcher she had reason to believe a man had died at the Logicsolutions facility in West Virginia.

After she was dropped off on the west side of Manhattan, everything seemed overwhelming. It was a stimulation overload.

She had lived for six months in a stark room with glass walls. Now she was surrounded by many people, all doing different kinds of things. She walked to Wall Street. She strolled down Wall Street, taking in all the huge buildings. They were tall and wide and crammed together. The facility she had lived in would have fit in the lobby of any one of the buildings. There were thousands of people on the streets. People of all kinds and sizes. She passed store after store, and each one was different. She strolled on for about an hour.

Eventually, she found herself on Broadway in Union Square Park. She stopped to rest on a bench. Across from her was a man who was unshaven and dressed in clothes that hadn't been washed. He looked as if he had been in the same clothes for several weeks. He was lying across the bench. She studied him for several minutes. She decided to go over and try to speak to him if he was awake.

"Hello."

He turned to her and squinted as if he wasn't used to the sunlight. He grunted.

"What is your name?" she asked quietly.

He mumbled the name Alan or Alfred. She wasn't sure.

"Why haven't you washed or changed your clothes?" Anna asked.

"I don't have a place to do it. What is it to you? Why are you bothering me?"

"Are you homeless?"

"Yes. What is it to you, little girl?"

"I am homeless too. I wanted to know how you do it."

"I can't be taking care of no little girl. Hard enough to take care of myself. I haven't eaten in two days."

She noticed the empty bottle of wine in his hand. "But you had something to drink. You aren't starving, are you?"

"I like my drink."

"How do you buy your drinks? Do you have a job?"

"Yeah. My job is to lay on this bench and drink."

"Did you ever have a job in the past?"

Her question hit a cord. He'd had a life in the past. He hadn't always been homeless. "A long, long time ago, I used to have a wife, kids, and a job at a sporting goods shop. I lost my job and climbed into this bottle ever since."

"Do you ever see your kids?"

"Not in over three years."

"I am sorry for you for that. You must miss them. They must miss you."

"I don't think anyone misses me. Not now. As long as I can scrape up enough money to buy a drink, then I don't have to think about it."

"My name is Anna. I am glad I met you." Anna started to walk away.

"Wait. What do you mean you are homeless too?"

"I have no home. I am on my own. The truth is, I have no money or place to go. I expect I will just live in the park the way you do, without the drinking."

He sat up and took measure of her. "You look too well kept to be homeless."

"I have only been homeless for one day. I am sure over time, I will look a little more worn, just not yet."

"Don't end up like me. This really isn't any kind of life a little girl should have." With that, he turned over and said, "I have to sleep now," and the conversation ended.

She went back to the nearby bench. *Why would a man with a wife and kids choose this life?* She tried to think it through, but it didn't make any sense. She hadn't really gotten his name, but it looked as if he did not want to be disturbed anymore.

As she wandered farther up the street, she came upon a television store. The whole back of the store was made up of twenty or so televisions, all playing the same channel. Some were big, and some were smaller. She fixated on one and began to watch the show. It was fascinating. She had never seen a television before. It was a news channel, and the only message she could glean was something about Democrats and Republicans. They hated each other. They went on and on to say bad things about each other. The talking heads chattered on.

Then the screen changed to something Anna was really drawn to. There were a series of short one-minute stories about really happy people. The people were doing all kinds of exciting things. They were buying insurance, and they were ordering things online. They were drinking beer. They loved cheese. They especially loved being around cars, whether they were driving them or just looking at them. These were people with families and beautiful homes and yards. They were all happy and smiling and appeared to be loving life. Even people who were sick and were told they needed to buy medicine were incredibly happy with their illness and happy when they got their medicine. This was what Anna wanted to be part of. She was annoyed that the station kept interrupting all the wonderful little minishows with the news. She stood there for an hour, watching.

Finally, a man came up to her and asked, "May I help you?"

"Oh no. I was just watching."

With that, the man gave her an annoyed look, and she left the store.

She continued up Broadway and crossed paths with a woman who was just standing on the sidewalk next to a building with three bags full of random things. She also looked as if she had been in the same clothes for several days.

Anna went up to her and blurted out, "Are you homeless? I am too. How do you make this work?"

The lady looked at Anna as if sizing her up. When she spoke, Anna saw she was missing several teeth. "Why do you want to know?" she said with a lisp.

"Like I said, I am homeless also since yesterday. I am not sure where to go or what to do."

"Such a shame. A young girl like you won't last a week on the streets. Some pimp is going to find you. You need to go over to the city mission. When was the last time you ate?"

"I haven't eaten since I left."

"Here. You can have this." The woman dug into one of her bags and pulled out a cellophane package of Twinkies. "Take these."

"Don't you need them? Where do you go to eat?"

"I go to the city mission when I have to. I don't like to be around people. I would rather be on the street. Now, you go. Remember what I said about staying away from pimps." With that, she signaled the conversation was over and strolled off.

Anna stood there thinking about the fact that a complete stranger who had next to nothing had just given her food and advice. She didn't know what she would do with it. She couldn't eat it. It had been an act of kindness. She couldn't waste it. Then an idea came to her.

She turned back to where she had been an hour ago and found the man on the park bench. She tapped him on the shoulder a few times, and he woke up with a grunt. "Mister, I have something for you," she said, and he sat up halfway and glared at her. "I want you to have this." Anna held out the package of Twinkies with both hands.

He took a moment to take in the situation. "Thank you." The man was starving, and he knew it. He sat up all the way, ripped the cellophane, and ate the first Twinkie with one large bite. He chewed it for several minutes until it disappeared. He took a bite of the second one. Then he asked while half of it was still in his mouth, "Why would you give this to me if you are hungry yourself?"

"I want you to gain some strength. Your kids are angry at you because you have told them they failed your test. You don't think they are important enough for you to choose them over this. All you have to do is prove to them that they are more important.

They will be angry for a while; you will have to understand. But they want their father back. I am sure of this. I have no father and would give anything to have one."

"So who are you? You are this young homeless girl dressed in a white shawl. You must be an angel, or I must be imagining you here right now."

Taking his cue, she said, "Yes, I am an angel from God. If you don't pick yourself up off this bench and go see your children, I am going to be very mad at you."

"An angel from God. So I am hallucinating. My kids hate me. They would throw me out of the house, and I would deserve it. I just want to die on this bench."

"Mister, when did you learn that your kids would rather you die on this bench than live with them?" Anna asked in an even-toned voice.

"I don't know that there was a specific time."

"Then how do you know it happened?"

"It just feels that way. I don't deserve to be wanted." With that, he started to tear up.

"I think that somewhere deep down, you know that isn't true. Your life on this bench is a lie. How much longer do you want to live a lie?"

He sniffed in. "I really don't."

"So instead of dying from a lie, why don't you try to live with the truth? Go see your family. You have nothing to lose and everything to gain."

"All right. I am going to try to do what you said. I don't want God to be mad at me. I don't need that," he said plaintively with a trace of a smile. "My oldest son lives in Ozone Park." With that, he got up and walked away.

Anna wandered back to the bench she had been on before. She continued to watch all the things going on in the park. What struck her the most were families. There were mothers with children in strollers, and the mothers hovered over them, taking care of them. There were fathers throwing Frisbees with their kids. Couples held hands while strolling. She tried to imagine the bonds that existed within a family. *What a wonderful thing that must be.*

The park eventually closed, and Anna began to walk again. She went in the general direction of Uptown. With darkness, the crowd started to change. There were still people on the streets, but they weren't families anymore. There were occasional couples, groups of older teenagers, and single people. Some of the groups wore black leather jackets. They appeared more menacing. They all seemed to be less focused on getting someplace and instead seemed to enjoy just meandering. The shops eventually were all closed, with gates and bars in front of their doors.

Toward morning, she found herself at Grand Central Station. She wandered inside to see what it was like. It was large inside. There were many people still coming and going. The sun was rising, and the station seemed to be exploding with people. She found a place near one of the automated tellers for buying transit cards. The lines got longer as the crowd grew faster than the dispensers could keep up. She found if she focused, she could hear some of the conversations of the people in line. She had been watching people from a distance, but now she wanted to watch and listen as they talked to each other.

There was a lady on a cell phone. What she was saying was not a secret, because she was talking so loudly. The phone was so loud Anna could even hear the person on the other line above the background noise. The woman was angry that her husband of six years had been cheating on her. She called him names Anna had never heard before. The names were in a string that she used over and over. She was angry, hurt, and other adjectives Anna had to process before she could figure out what the lady was talking about.

A little farther back in line, two women were complaining about a fellow coworker who kept trying to ask her out on a date.

"I am going to file a sexual harassment complaint if he doesn't stop. I don't get what is wrong with this guy. He doesn't get it."

That conversation was in stark contrast to another one just a few more people down the line. They also were talking about a coworker. One of the women said, "Short of stripping and throwing myself at him, I can't get him to ask me out. I don't get what is wrong with this guy. He just doesn't get it." Anna would have to sort that one out later.

A little later in line, a man was on the phone, complaining bitterly that he had been passed over by that backstabbing—

He let out another string of words not in Anna's lexicon.

This went on for most of the day. Anna heard dozens of conversations. She was surprised that most of them seemed unhappy. The complaints were many and varied, but the central theme was that they were mad about something. Her observations contrasted the people she'd watched on television yesterday in those minishows between the regular show, especially the people buying or driving cars. She finally came to the conclusion that people who bought cars were happy, and people who took public transportation were not. Maybe only happy people bought cars. Or maybe buying or driving a car made a person happy. It was another thing to sort out later. She left the station later in the afternoon.

She came upon a department store. It seemed like an interesting place to visit. Once inside, she was impressed with how large it was. There were many departments. She took a slow stroll through each department, methodically taking in the whole store. She found the department with televisions. There was a golf game on one of the screens. She watched it for a half hour or so. She understood that the people watching the game at the golf course were excited, but it wasn't clear why. Again, every so often, minishows interrupted to show off clothes, lawyers, investors, beer, amusement parks, and, of course, cars. Just as she remembered, everyone who bought and drove a car was happy.

The store eventually closed around ten, so Anna continued her walk uptown. Sometime around midnight, the air got much colder. It was colder than anything Anna had experienced before. It made her head hurt. This was a strange new sensation since she had never experienced pain before. Even when her arm had broken, it hadn't hurt. There had been an initial shock that might have been considered pain, but after that, the arm simply hadn't worked. This was a steady feeling of pain—a throbbing within her head. She started to feel dizzy, and it was harder to walk. The feeling scared her.

She stepped into a food mart that was open all night and asked if she could stand in the store for a while to warm up from the cold. As she warmed, the pain subsided, and things seemed to feel normal again. About thirty minutes later, she thanked the store owner and went back out into the cold.

It only took a little while before the pain and dizziness started up again. She noticed her vision and hearing became less acute. She was able to find a bar that was still open and warm up again. The symptoms subsided again. Now she understood: she could not be out in the cold. Something in her head couldn't function below a certain temperature. Now she understood why the small numbers kept appearing in her lower-left visual field. Once the temperature got below forty degrees, the temperature showed on the screen in red.

She continued to bar-hop and store-hop until morning, when the air started to warm up again. She found herself at Central Park when the air was comfortable for her again. She sat down on a bench to collect her thoughts. She decided that if she ever wanted to be one of those happy people who owned a car, she would have to find a way to navigate in this society. Most of all, she wanted to find a life that made her feel at home.

Before she knew it, she was in her own apartment, ready to start a job the next day.

Chapter 3

Anna looked around her apartment. She decided to explore and find what treasures might have been left for her. She started with the bathroom. There was a cabinet above the toilet. She opened it, and inside were two worn towels and a bath mat. There was half a bar of white soap on a metal dish on the side of the sink. There was a shower curtain. The bottom two inches hanging near the linoleum floor were discolored. She looked in the cabinet under the sink and found an inch of blue fluid in a bottle of Windex, a half-filled bottle of Mr. Clean, and a scrub brush. In the closet were half a dozen hangers and a broom. The bed was worn badly, with a large sag in the middle. There were no sheets or pillows. She unlocked the door to the stairs and peered down to the outside door. She wanted to go out to mix with the crowd, as she had done for three days now, but then thought better of it. Her batteries were low. She had no money. She had no identification.

All of a sudden, the feeling of being alone and exposed was her predominant thought. Risk-taking, something that had seemed of no consequence just a few days ago, now became a concern for survival. She decided to conserve her charge for the night and rest in the bed. Before she did that, though, she took off her dress. She read the directions on the bottle of Mr. Clean. She started to fill the sink with hot water. She added a little bit of Mr. Clean and put her dress in the sink to get it clean. She let it soak for a while.

While the dress was soaking, she stared in the mirror at her naked body. She gazed in amazement at how human she looked. All of the parts were there. She had images of humans in her memory, as they had been uploaded when she was created, and now she saw herself as one of them. After a few minutes, she wrung out her dress and hung it on a hanger. She climbed onto the bed and turned out the light.

The next morning, she was down in the shop at 8:20. She wanted to be a little early for whatever instructions Sophie was going to give her to start her first day. Her dress was dry and looked and smelled fresh.

First, there was a tour of the store. It was bigger than it had looked the day before. She had not noticed there was a whole section devoted to computer stations. For a fee, the stations were available to students to do their homework. It was just eight thirty, and there were already six people at the computers.

Sophie explained how to find books by title, subject, author, or the Library of Congress catalog number. She also explained how the online option of the business worked and how books were categorized by genre, subject, and author. She walked through all of the specialty items in the store. There were Kindles for sale, along with subscription services. There were snacks in a secluded area of the store where there were chairs, a sofa, and tables. It was a comfortable place. Part of the comfort was from Sophie herself. She was a kind, knowledgeable lady. She seemed to have a warmth that made anyone feel comfortable around her.

Anna had a memory for details that was fail-safe. She could retain everything she was told, so after a few minutes, she was completely comfortable with the layout and organization of the store. That made answering questions from the customers easier. This did not go unnoticed by Sophie. After an hour or so, she remarked to Anna what a natural she was at the business.

Later that morning, a gentleman walked in and asked for something with an accent so heavy and English so poor that

Sophie could not understand any part of what he was trying to say. Anna overheard the exchange and inserted herself. "¡Hola! ¿Cómo le puedo ayudar?"

"Si, por favor," the man said. "¿Tienes un libro de mapas?"

"¿Un altas?" asked Anna.

"Si, eso mismo. Un atlas. Muchas gracias."

Anna handed him an atlas. He paid for the book and left.

Sophie shook her head. "You speak Spanish also?"

"Actually, I speak four languages, including English," Anna replied.

"You are a girl of many talents," Sophie replied, amused.

One of the big income streams for Sophie's bookshop was a service she'd invented for students at the nearby colleges. Many of them were on a shoestring budget, and textbooks were expensive. A calculus textbook could be $200. Sophie had realized if she set up twelve computer stations, bought one copy of the book, and put it on her server, then all twelve stations could access the book at the same time. She charged five dollars per hour or seventy-five dollars per month as a membership fee for use of the computers as the student saw fit. That way, the access to the textbook could be used as often and for as long as necessary for each individual student. If five students from a calculus class used the book for twenty hours in a given month, Sophie made $500 on a $200 book in the first month of the semester. Anna was charged with taking over the responsibility for overseeing this service.

The rest of the day was uneventful until midafternoon, when a man was browsing the electronics section. Anna thought for a moment and then approached him. "Are you knowledgeable in electronics?" she asked.

He said, "I am a physics major at the university, but I like to play with electronics."

"Can I ask you an electronics question?"

"Sure," he replied.

"If I wanted to create an electric field across two plates, how would I do it?"

"Well, there are a number of ways. Most of them would be cumbersome and expensive. What are you trying to do with it?"

"I need to charge a battery through a set of induction plates."

He thought for a minute. "Is it a small battery?"

"Yes, relatively small."

"Frankly, I would get myself a medical-grade electrical stimulation unit and use the pads as the induction plates. Set it for continuous direct current. That would probably be the easiest way to do it. You probably can pick one up at the medical-equipment repair shop down on Fifth Avenue. Maybe you can get a used one cheap."

"Thank you. I will check it out. I appreciate your help."

"No problem." With that, he went back to his reading.

Friday was payday. Sophie offered to hold off on collecting rent from the first paycheck to give Anna a chance to get on her feet. It had been a good week for Sophie. Anna had proven to be an asset to the business, and Sophie wanted to encourage her to stay.

For the first time in her life, Anna had $340 in her pocket. The most important thing to do was to get to the medical-equipment repair shop. They were open until 6:00 p.m. She had to hurry to get there on foot.

As she set out, she noticed that for the first time, she felt significantly fatigued. Her dashboard showed her power was now red and down to 7 percent. That had never happened to her before. The power had never been that low.

She arrived at the shop about thirty minutes later. It was a small storefront with glass windows that featured some of the latest medical devices. She paused to look. Some of the items cost thousands of dollars. Her paltry $340 was not going to go far.

Inside was an L-shaped counter that left only a few feet of room for people to stand. Behind the counter were dozens of devices on tables and benches that were in some stage of being repaired. She asked about electrical stimulation machines. The clerk showed her a newer model that ran about $2,000.

She shook her head. "Do you have anything that is used?"

He retrieved an older-looking machine that cost $450.

"I'm sorry, but that is still more than I have."

"Wait a minute," he said. "Someone brought in one on a trade that has not been repaired yet. Frankly, it won't be repaired, because it is too old. Some of the functions still work. I'll let you have it for fifty bucks."

"Does the continuous direct current work?"

"Well, let's see." He hooked it up to a computer and monitor. "Ah, yes, see the readout? It definitely works. OK, so there are a few things you should know about using this machine. The electric current flows from one lead to the other on the same terminal. You have two sets of leads for two terminals. There is a sponge pad for each lead. That is four of them altogether. They are here in this bag. The pads need to be wet with tap water or some solution that will have ions in it. Here is the intensity button and the on-off switch. It has not been calibrated in a long time, so there is no verification that the output is exactly what it says, but these things normally don't vary much from what you saw on the screen."

She smiled. "I'll take it."

She set out to go back to her apartment, and now the fatigue was really a problem. She was carrying a piece of equipment that weighed about ten pounds. A mile walk seemed like an eternity. It seemed her batteries were depleting faster as they got closer to exhausting their charge. When she finally arrived at her apartment door, she realized she did not have the strength to carry the equipment up the stairs. She needed to get to the electrical socket to make it work. She was worried now, doubting whether she could make it. Her battery charge was at 4 percent.

She figured out she could sit on the stairs with the device in her lap and lift herself on her buttocks one stair at a time. There were fifteen stairs. She finally made it to the top and was able to reach the keyhole in the door from the floor. She could no longer stand up. She unlocked the door, reached up to turn the handle, and fell into her apartment, pushing the door open with her weight. She found herself lying on the floor and could not get up. She managed to scoot herself the six feet into the kitchen to get to the socket on the wall. She pulled the device out of the bag and plugged it in. She set the dials. Then she remembered that the salesman told her the sponges had to be wet in order to work. She could not stand to reach the sink.

She found the bottle of Windex in the cabinet under the bathroom sink and sprayed the pads until they were soaked. She fell onto one of the pads, with the pad under her back. Everything started to feel numb. She had to guess where her fingers were, because she couldn't feel them anymore. She used all her strength to lift the other pad onto her chest. She was down to 2 percent. She turned the machine on to its maximum power, and she guessed where her batteries would be. Then everything went black.

She woke up about four hours later, trying to remember what had happened. Her battery charge was at 5 percent. She had just enough strength to grab the pad on the floor and one of the two remaining pads she hadn't used and spray them with Windex, soaking them. She connected the pad to the unused lead. She carefully placed those two pads on the floor next to each other. It was just the right spacing to fit behind her back between her shoulders. She took the remaining two pads and soaked them in Windex. She made sure each terminal was connected to a pad in the front and a pad in the back. She then held them to her chest where her charging plates were and lay on her back on the other two pads. She turned the machine on to its maximum and lay there on the floor until morning.

She had charged to 37 percent by then and found her strength again. She would be able to reach a full 100 percent charge by the end of the weekend.

Anna stayed in the apartment for most of the weekend. She ventured out a few times to go to the local market to get some things she thought she should have to support her newfound personhood. She thought it would look strange if she never had any food in the house. Most people ate fairly often. So she bought a few groceries she thought likely to be seen in a typical apartment, although she had no clue what to get. She had seen in an advertisement that kids ate peanut butter and jelly. Adults ate tuna fish. People ate cereal. They ate eggs. She had seen people eating with knives, forks, and spoons. She would need a few plates and glasses. She bought a large reusable bag and piled the items in the bag one on top of another until the bag was full and heavy. She then carried it all back to the apartment. She made a note to herself: *If you are shopping on foot, don't buy more than you can carry.*

On the next trip, she would get some sheets, pillows, and towels. *What else?* She still had not decided whether she should take a shower or not. She guessed it would be OK. Her skin was made of a complex polymer that looked like real skin, without hairs and pores. It also did not have any oils, so it felt drier. It seemed safe to use a regular hand lotion to give it a softer and more human feel. *What about hygiene stuff?* She had no idea what people did to get themselves presentable for their fellow persons every day. Deodorant, hair spray, hair color—the rows went on and on in the store. She wouldn't need any of that. *What about toothpaste?* She remembered one of the minishows had said Crest was the toothpaste to buy. She noticed that the only places that needed to be wet were her mouth and lips. If she didn't wet them at least once per day, they would dry out and not look like other people's lips. So maybe toothpaste and an oral rinse made sense. That might be OK if she wanted to give off a signal of minty, fresh breath. She bought a tube of Crest, a toothbrush holder, and a couple of toothbrushes and left the pharmacy.

She thought if she did decide it was safe to take a shower, she would need some type of soap for her skin and for her hair. She bought a bottle of shampoo and some bodywash. The brand names meant nothing to her, but some of the containers looked pretty.

Now she had to deal with getting clothes. She picked out two pairs of jeans, two blouses, and two more stylish dresses. That was suitable for the shop and for casual wear. She picked up a small purse. On her way to the checkout counter, she ran into a department that didn't make any sense. She saw mannequins wearing a cloth strapped to their shoulders that covered their breasts and a thin layer of cloth worn around the waist and crotch. It wouldn't keep a person warm. It was hidden under the pants and shirt.

While she was staring at the mannequin, a salesperson said, "Underwear is in aisle three. It's on sale today. Here. I'll find you a package in your size."

Blindly following the salesperson, she bought a pack of underpants and a bra, even though she didn't see the point.

By the end of the weekend, the apartment actually felt like home. She had put out the towels and put linens on the bed. She had also purchased a blanket and pillows, so the bed was more comfortable. She had borrowed several books from the shop and found it pleasurable to read. That thought struck her.

Her first memory was from about six months ago, when she first had been activated. Her memory banks had been uploaded with basic information: four languages, math processes and algorithms, basic history of the world and the country, and logic. Somehow, she had been able to start integrating the individual pieces of what she knew to create new ideas as she continued to learn things from the world. She had not known in the beginning but had been able to learn on her own a set of intuitive skills that included self-awareness, need for survival, anger, sadness, and other thoughts that were not logical in source but were intuitive and connected to the interpretation of how circumstances would affect her. Now, though, she was aware of a new feeling: pleasure and contentment. She was working at a job she enjoyed. She was living in a place that was safe. She could see her situation as sustainable. She felt content. All her needs were met. Within that platform, reading a book by herself in the quiet room gave her pleasure. The experience was new, and she was excited by it.

Chapter 4

Daniel Standish was born in 1979. He grew up without a mother. She left the family when he was five. The day she left, he screamed for her to stay, but she got in the family car and just drove away anyway. Five-year-old Daniel was powerless. He never forgave her for that. Never again would that happen.

That trauma clearly shaped his opinion of women. He resented them in general. If he was to deal with them, it would always be from a position of strength, he thought. He needed to have power over them. Consequently, with only one exception, he had few relationships with girls throughout his late teenage years and into his early twenties.

Daniel's enduring strength was his raw intelligence. He was always the smartest kid in all his math and science classes in high school. There was never any class that challenged his capabilities. He went to MIT for a double major in chemical engineering and mechanical engineering. He then did graduate work with artificial intelligence and computer evolution. The combination of areas of talent put him at the forefront of humanoid artificial intelligence.

He started developing human-looking robots that could evolve in their ability to think and function based on their experiences. With the help of venture capital, he founded a company that would advance artificial intelligence for business solutions. The name Logicsolutions was descriptive of their services. Businesses that contracted with them could develop a significant advantage over companies that did not have that support.

His friend Nick Walsh was a financial guru. He was the one who connected them to the venture capital company and managed the finances of the company through the lean times. There were plenty of lean times during the early history of the company. About four years in, they contracted with a large client, and they made about $100 million per year from then on.

Nick and Daniel were close friends from childhood. Daniel stood up at Nick's wedding. He would always be remembered for his ill-fated relationship with the maid of honor. She still recoiled at the mention of his name ten years later.

Daniel tested many different types of media so he could get away from hard-wired circuitry to build a humanoid brain. After years of trial, he finally had the breakthrough that made all that effort worthwhile. He invented two key things. The first was a gel matrix that could function the same way a computer chip functioned with the on-and-off binary code. The on-and-off was an ion complex that was stable due to the nature of two different substances in the matrix. The positive ionic difference could be present, or on, or it could be absent, or off.

The second key invention was a formatting program with which files could be directly uploaded into this matrix. He started with simple files and found there was no difference in function if the files were uploaded into a regular computer or uploaded into a glob of the gel matrix after it was formatted.

The early experiments were relatively straightforward. He moved on to uploading larger and larger files. He could upload a cookbook and bring up all the recipes and the methods to cook them with a single command. That was not too impressive since regular computers could do that as well. What made it significant was that as recipes were added to the files and recalled for use, the formatting program was able to cause the gel matrix to reorganize the files based on what was getting used the most.

It was also able to mix the recipes so that if a combination of recipes were used often, the gel matrix would allow the data to be recombined to create recipes for meals that involved the favorite components. Essentially, the gel matrix could reuse the data in different combinations to create new recipes. That was the real breakthrough. He continued to focus on more and more complicated arrays of uploads.

As a testimony to his intellectual prowess, he also continued to develop the mechanical pieces that would put together a humanoid body. He studied the function of all types of prostheses on the market. He developed working artificial limbs driven by batteries that could be housed within the robot.

After thousands of hours of development, he was able to begin to combine the two research strings and create a self-functioning humanoid machine that had working limbs and body and had the ability to hear, see, and touch. As information went in by upload or by the senses, the humanoid would be able to integrate the information in the gel matrix for appropriate use in the future. As the humanoid design became more and more humanlike, Daniel's perverted disgust with women became more apparent. He started building his models—or, more accurately, prototypes—to look like anatomically correct women. This gave him a sense of empowerment over women. The humanoid robots were essentially his slaves.

The first attempt at putting all of the technology together turned out to be an awkward and poorly functioning product. Humans had a part of the brain that did nothing but coordination of movement. *Even if you have all of the correct pieces to make a person move, complex movement is not possible if the parts applying the force are not working in perfect harmony,* he realized. *Humans have sensors and reflexes that will prevent two opposing muscles from working at the same time and relay position of muscles and joints to the brain.* A high-functioning humanoid needed a similar structure to coordinate movement.

Also, humans had to have balance, which was made up of five components. The eyes could see the level of the horizon. Semicircular canals in the ears gave a sense of movement, whether forward or backward, side to side, or upward or downward. The utricle was a sack inside the ear lined by sensory hairs that housed a small stone. It could tell a person which direction gravity was pulling. There were position sensors in one's core muscles to tell the person if he or she was standing upright. Finally, there were sensors in the feet to tell one how he or she was secured against the ground. One needed all of those to reduce the possibility of falling. Without any of them, falling was all the first prototype did. There were other miscues in brain function as well.

Daniel decided that with the large resources his successful company had, he could spend some money to create a laboratory where he could do a better job. Of course, once he decided to do so and convinced his company board there would be a huge payout at the end of the project, he started to get carried away about what he needed. The first thing was the secrecy. Finding a remote location in the Appalachian Mountains in West Virginia seemed a little extravagant to the rest of the executive team, but Daniel prevailed. He built a sophisticated facility that had modern laboratory components and tools, including modern fabricators that could create clear plastic sleeves for the various parts of the body and limbs, which gave a human appearance to the humanoid's frame.

The finished lab was a source of pride for Daniel. It looked like a two-level resort in the mountains. It was at least ten miles from the nearest road. He decorated the inside with fine art. The layout included a fabricating lab, residential rooms for guests, and the prototypes in the lower level and an entrance, reception, entry foyer, kitchen, and living room on the top floor. At the bottom of the stairs, the hallway turned right and proceeded for about fifty feet. On one side were the guest rooms, which had frosted glass doors and opaque walls. On the other side was a fifty-foot wall of tinted glass with glass doors, where there were four rooms. That was where the individual prototypes were kept. The most sophisticated security measures were taken, including entry and facility security as well as cybersecurity. Because he lived in the facility most of the time, Daniel used the guest suites for his personal use. Upstairs was a fully stocked kitchen that had everything needed to make the most sophisticated meals. All of the supplies for living and working there had to be flown in by helicopter because of the distance to the nearest road. All of this added to the ever-rising cost of the project.

In making humanoids, copying nature effectively was half the battle. Nature was usually brilliant in how living processes were accomplished. However, some of the properties of humans were simply too difficult to imitate. There were 512 muscles in the human body that allowed for all of its movements. A humanoid did not need to be able to perform all those movements, only the most common and natural ones. To have human appearance in motion, Daniel settled on 160 individual cables, pulleys, and gear systems of various sizes to duplicate the movements that mattered. Humans had millions of nerve endings that made life possible. He decided on fifteen thousand sensors for internal communication. The sensors were built into a layer below the polymer skin, with a distribution of four to an area of about a square inch. They were placed evenly throughout the surface area of the humanoid. There were higher concentrations of sensors in the mouth and hands for finer motor control. This was doable and adequate.

He'd reasoned in many of his discussions back at MIT that humans had evolved over billions of years to develop systems to feed and protect the brain. This required multiple systems, including the digestive tract, the immune system, the heart, blood, vessels, lungs, and all of the other human organs. The main purpose of many of the systems was to create a set of metabolic chains that could produce a form of energy that could power the body and its life processes. This energy supply was called ATP, as it was the source of life-giving energy in all higher living systems. When skipping evolution and creating something in the laboratory, Daniel only needed batteries for power. Except for the brain, sensory organs, and motor units, all of the other parts of the human body were unnecessary.

Once the laboratory was complete, Daniel was able to work on the second, third, and fourth prototypes. He mastered the ability to integrate all the balance systems and muscle coordination into the upload. This time, movement and balance worked, but there were still some gaps in the humanoid's ability to think and respond. General conversation still wasn't happening. General responses to commands worked well, but integration of hearing and speaking was still not fully functional. That was where Daniel seemed to stray from the mission.

He created three humanoids. The first one was programmed to take commands that related to housekeeping chores only. He programmed her to clean, cook, sew, and perform other functions inside the house. He programmed her to hear and obey but not to speak. The second was a humanoid whose main purpose was to service his personal needs. Again, he saw no purpose for the robot to speak. The third was the social, personable one who extended the owner's reach into the community by doing shopping, errands, and other things outside the house. This one had to be fully integrated with all cognitive human functions, including conversation. It was already in his mind that each one performed part of a composite robot that was yet to be built.

Cassie was the first one and was the housekeeper. The second one was the unnamed personal pleasure slave. Daniel was not sure how the executive team in New York would react to his using their money to build such a creature, so he basically built her off the books and kept her a secret. He kept his notes about her in a separate file, and he never let her leave his room or interact with the other humanoids. The third humanoid was Anna. He kept her confined to her room because he knew if she escaped, she had the potential to blend in with other humans. She was the one he needed to teach to speak and interact with people, so her upload contained more than ten terabytes of general information. Daniel spent a lot of time with Anna in getting her to function properly. He was able to get the hearing, listening, and speaking functions to work well. All the cognitive functions seemed to work well also. He essentially uploaded an encyclopedia into her matrix. She was his crowning achievement. The humanoid could function on the highest levels in motion, speech, hearing, thinking, and memory.

At that point, two years of work in the research facility had elapsed, and the cost was running into tens of millions of dollars. Jim Mendola, the company's chief operating officer, asked Daniel to let Joshua Harrington, the newly appointed computer applications director, visit for a while so he could get an idea of what was going to be ready for market and how to operationalize the creation of the humanoids. Daniel was reluctant at first, but he realized the money would dry up if he did not produce something soon. He could use Joshua to help the funding stream continue. Of course, he needed to deactivate the personal-needs humanoid and put her away in a place that would not be discovered.

He named his third creation Anna after a girl he'd had a crush on in college. After many hours of working with this humanoid, he liked what he had built. She was almost perfect. She could do all the things he wanted to see in his humanoid, but he still wanted to integrate the functions of the other prototypes. He would let Joshua give a good report to the executive team. Then he would reformat Anna to include the extra pieces, even if it took another year to complete. She was just a stepping-stone to the final product. After Joshua's visit, Anna's usefulness would be exhausted. Work could begin on the final model.

Daniel, for all his expertise, had never been trained in functional neurology. He had never given any thought to what actually constituted memory, thought, or the function of the human mind. There was a difference between a computer's thinking and the creation of an original thought. There was a difference between the brain and the mind. Human experiences and memories had two parts to them. The first part was the data of the experience, and the second was how individuals felt about the experience. Humans had a dividing line between the two halves of the brain. Typically, the left brain dealt with facts and figures, and the right brain was the creative, or feeling, side. Each thought or memory needed to have input from both sides to truly make sense. Because Daniel did not understand that, he did not account for the possibility that a brain made of gel matrix could create on its own two sections that would serve the same way, even if they weren't isolated on opposite sides. This played out with all three of the humanoids. With Cassie, Daniel abused her physically and verbally every day. After the secret humanoid was deactivated, Daniel went into Cassie's room, looking for the same kind of personal attention. Cassie had no choice but to obey. She had no way to express her feelings about it. She was programmed to obey, and she could not speak. He did not account for the possibility that she could feel shame, hurt, humiliation, or anger.

This also played out with Anna. He made no secret that she was to be discarded to make way for a new humanoid. Essentially, she was anticipating her own death. He had not uploaded anything that would be a basis for Anna to understand that and therefore did not think she was capable of grasping that concept. However, because her brain was able to function in a way similar to a human's, she developed the concepts of self-awareness and mortality. She understood Daniel's intention clearly. She was consumed with fear, anger, anxiety, and even moments of depression. He told her of Joshua's visit. She knew it would be her only opportunity to create an opening for escape. She would try to make the most of it.

Chapter 5

Joshua Harrington got word by email that he was being promoted to director of computer applications. It was a senior management position that had been created to accommodate the new technology entering the market. He was called into the chief operations officer's office to get the formal appointment. That happened on Wednesday. He was being asked to go out to the West Virginia facility next week to learn about Daniel's new project. It seemed to be the pinnacle of his career.

In high school, Joshua had been obsessed with cryptology. He'd spent hours with his new Apple Mac computer, learning about secret codes and the schemes that made them secret. He'd had little to do with sports or even being outside. His behavior had been so antithetical to the way Joshua's father had grown up that it had become a bone of contention with him. Joshua's father had done a brief stint with the Pittsburgh Pirates. Joshua himself had been a large boy by the time he was a junior. His father had been vocally disappointed when Joshua spent all his time behind a screen instead of pursuing sports. The estrangement had continued into college. Joshua had gone into full-time computer study and spoken to his father less and less. Now, ten years later, Joshua almost never spoke to his father. He wanted badly to prove his worth to him. He hoped that making a six-figure salary would do that.

Now he was a twenty-seven-year-old loner. He was a computer geek who had spent most of his life behind a screen. He was brilliant at coding and logic. He spent all his time at work. He'd had one relationship in high school and a few love interests in college, but he was awkward around women, and none of his relationships had lasted more than a few weeks. Maybe with this promotion, he thought, he would make a point to get out more. He decided to start working on an agenda of questions to ask Daniel. It would be a little uncomfortable to interview the head of the company. Clearly, it would be a diplomatic dance to learn what he had to learn without being too aggressive. However, the idea of seeing an artificially intelligent robot excited him. It was not something a person saw every day.

Before he knew it, he was packed and waiting for the helicopter to finish prepping for takeoff. It was about a four-hour flight to the facility, which was approximately four hundred miles away. After a few minutes, he was seated, strapped in, and airborne. He leaned back and took in the scenery. Mountains and valleys covered with green below appeared endless as the helicopter droned on. Joshua had brought his iPod with his play list. It helped to pass the time.

The helicopter landed in a paved lot about the size of a parking lot that would have held twenty cars. In the short conversations over the noise of the rotors, he had learned that the pilot's name was Ray, and he came to deliver supplies when Daniel requested it of him. He would order groceries, toiletries, fabricating supplies, and many other random items to be loaded onto the helicopter. Ray explained that he was not told anything about what actually went on in the facility, only that he had to deliver the supplies to this tarmac, unload them, and leave. It was unusual to bring a passenger. He also said he was to come back five days later to pick Joshua up.

When Joshua approached the door to the facility, he was asked to state his name and show his company identification. He held up his identification tag to the scanner and verified his identity. Once inside, he was escorted through the lobby by a woman who did not speak to him and only motioned for him to follow. He followed her to a set of stairs, where she brought him to the main living room. There he met Daniel for the first time.

Daniel greeted Joshua with a warm greeting and a robust handshake. "Congratulations on becoming the director of computer applications. Welcome to my humble place."

He took Joshua on a tour of the facility. Joshua had a thirty-second look at the prototype rooms, the fabricating lab, the residence rooms, and the kitchen, and then they went back to the lobby. Daniel said that dinner would be ready around seven thirty. The next day, they would get an early start. They had a lot to do.

Joshua went to his room and unpacked. There was nothing a five-star hotel room had that his room didn't, right down to the Turkish cotton towels. Joshua took a short nap and a shower and was up to the dining room promptly at 7:20. He saw a linen-covered table that would seat ten. There were just the two place settings. The woman who didn't speak was clearly working frantically to get everything ready. Joshua offered to help.

Daniel asserted himself to say she did not speak and would be OK on her own. He asked Joshua to sit with him in the living room while she finished her preparations for dinner. He reached for a bottle of cognac on the buffet and offered Joshua a glass.

Joshua typically didn't drink, but he was a guest of his boss and did not feel he could turn it down.

"Joshua, tell me a little about yourself," Daniel said as he settled into an overstuffed BarcaLounger. He motioned for Joshua to sit across the cocktail table from him. Daniel took a long sip of his drink and asked how things were going back in New York.

"Things have gotten really busy. We signed two more clients. One is in Dallas, and the other is in Chicago. It's exciting. We have developed several new components to our cash-management software. It seems to be a hot commodity."

"I saw that. Kudos to you for putting that together. How is the Landerson account going? She is always so persnickety," Daniel said.

"You are being kind with *persnickety*."

"Yeah, she's an idiot."

"So tell me, Mr. Standish—what do you see as your end market here?"

"I am creating a being that looks human, thinks like a human, and will operate in society as a human. I see our invention here as a new set of servants. People use their computers to seek the things they want and to enhance their quality of life. They get information, shop, and do a thousand things on the internet. Consequently, people are open to cybercrime as never before. Think about it. How many emails does an average person get in a day that are malicious? I mean things like phishing, scams—you name it. There are thousands of people out there who are bad people. They spend all day trying to think up ways to steal from you, harm your computer, spy on you, and do who knows what else. Let's say for a moment that you could have an artificially intelligent slave who could put its identity in front of yours. It would be able to discriminate between malicious emails, texts, and other attacks and real communications. It would be able to sort solicitations based on what you have told it you want to hear. It would also be able to shop for you based on your profile. You would create a complete profile, trust it with your contacts, and be able to give verbal commands to a robot that looked like a person and have a constructive communication about exactly what you wanted. It then would have the capacity to actually find you the best deal and order that item. Meanwhile, your identity would never be exposed. Only the identity of the artificially intelligent being."

"Wait a minute. So you're saying you are creating these humanoids to be a front for a person's identity. Then a computer itself would do. Why do they have to be humanoids?"

"These robots will be able to physically shop at brick-and-mortar stores as well and work online. They will be able to actually run errands, such as the cleaners, the butcher shop, the mall, and most anything else."

"How do you market this?"

"We sell the humanoid at a reasonable price, and then we have a monthly upgrade and maintenance agreement. It is not a large market initially, but as it grows, you create thousands and thousands of clients who will pay a monthly fee. Within a few years, you will be looking at a multibillion-dollar industry, which we will own. Performance will be the market determinant, and we will always be two or three years ahead of the competition. The personal market for artificial intelligence will outperform our business solution market by a factor of ten."

Joshua took a minute to take in his words. "So these humanoids will be able to drive, make choices for people, and serve all of the needs people have in dealing with the public and the internet. They will protect their identities. They will be able to help them avail all of the services of the internet without the exposure."

"Now you are starting to get it. Think of getting two or three hundred dollars a month from a million people. Let's say the shelf life for a robot is ten years. You would trade in your model you bought for fifteen thousand dollars for an updated one. Say you get a five-thousand-dollar value for your trade-in. If a million people do what you are talking about, that will generate ten billion dollars. There will be a day when people will buy their service robots the way they buy their cars."

"Wow." Joshua took in the vision. "That really is revolutionary."

With that, Cassie gave a wave of her hand to signal the dinner was ready, and they got up to go to the elegantly set table. The dishes were fine china, and the flatware was silver. The glasses were crystal. It was the finest setting Joshua had ever seen, let alone eaten from. Cassie brought out two wineglasses and a bottle of red wine, followed by the appetizer: sticks of grilled and seasoned steak and two onions fully breaded and fried. Then she brought the salads and breads.

"This is an incredible spread. You called her Cassie before? Cassie is an incredible cook."

Daniel seemed to shrug the compliment off. "She does OK."

Cassie brought out a beef Wellington for each of them, with a side dish of twice-baked potato. Everything on the table tasted exquisite. Clearly, Daniel spared no expense to have the finest of meals while he lived in the remote villa.

Daniel and Joshua chatted about inconsequential things for another thirty minutes, and Cassie started to clear away the dishes. Then, around nine thirty, Daniel announced he was going to bed. He wanted to get an early start on the day. He asked Joshua to meet him for breakfast at the same table at eight o'clock the next morning. Joshua nodded to acknowledge he would be there.

Joshua woke up to his phone's alarm at 7:00 a.m. sharp. He showered, shaved, and dressed in thirty minutes. He sat down with his list of questions. He wanted to know them well enough that he could ask them in casual conversation instead of making it sound like an interview.

As he made his way to the dining room, he noticed Cassie was frantic once again, trying to get the breakfast on the table in an orderly fashion. He sat down to the same fancy table with fresh linen set with a different elegant china. This time, there was a cut and sectioned grapefruit with sugar on the side. There were two carafes with orange juice and lemonade. There was a plate with triangular sections of cinnamon toast. As Joshua and Daniel sat down, an omelet fresh off the stove was placed in front of each of them. Daniel started to talk about the day's agenda. First, he wanted to go down to the fabricating lab to show Joshua how he made all of the parts of the robots. That would take all morning. Then they would have lunch. Then he wanted to talk about the programming that went into the uploads. That would take another couple of hours. Sometime around the end of the day, he wanted to introduce Joshua to Anna.

"Joshua, I mastered five breakthroughs to create Anna and make her work. I want to show you them one at a time. One of the reasons for the security here is that we will have at least fifty inventions and discoveries for which we need to obtain patents." He continued talking as they went down to the fabricating lab.

He showed Joshua the gel matrix from which he fashioned the humanoid brain. "The matrix made it possible for the primary compound to create an ionic pocket. This pocket could contain an ion and be positive, or it could be empty and be negative. That way, an ionic charge could exist in the matrix that would function the same way as the ionic charge does in a computer chip. The secret was that there had to be a certain amount of water content in the matrix to make it a gel to allow a free flow of ions within its boundaries. This was the breakthrough. It makes the rest of the robotics possible." He paused and stared at it as if to pay it reverence.

He continued. "The second breakthrough was being able to format the gel matrix as if it were a hard drive. It took me a year to develop the formatting program to be able to do this. Now, essentially, you have a computer with a hard drive and processing capabilities in a format that can be run with internal self-programming. One can upload all kinds of information into the matrix, and the individual can access this information in the same way a user can access any file in an ordinary computer. The combination of these breakthroughs is what makes it possible for Anna to think. For years, we have been trying to make artificial intelligence through external programming in hard-wired circuitry. The shortcomings to this are obvious. It requires the programmer to anticipate every contingency the computer may encounter. Obviously, this is an impossible task, and there will always be encounters that cause situations that are not expected. This is the first time we will be able to have the computer itself evolve by finding new combinations of data that can be used in original ways. The commonalities between these data files become connected into clusters. The clusters can create new connections among themselves to create new ways to use the data." He paused for effect. "That is the real breakthrough. We essentially created a working brain."

Daniel then added as an aside. "Oh, there is a difference in the footprint of clusters that contain pleasurable experiences and ones that don't. I created a part of the program where specific sensors—I will call them pleasure sensors—will connect and create a new cluster of pleasurable experiences that will fire all of the sensors throughout the humanoid if it is sufficiently stimulated. I placed these sensors in the anatomically correct places. This is the robot's experience of sex."

Joshua was so flummoxed by the remark he couldn't muster a response.

"The next, or third, breakthrough was the ability to build processors into the gel matrix so certain complex functions could be preprogrammed. This is primarily about movement. It takes a separate programming piece to allow multiple components to work in harmony in complex actions. Did you know that just to smile, you use nine muscles? The human body is an incredible piece of engineering in all of its parts. The spine, shoulders, knees, feet, balance, and so on are amazing engineering feats. A working robot would have to duplicate all of it."

Joshua was in speechless wonder. It was hard to keep up with all the conceptual pieces Daniel was describing. The sequence of important breakthroughs seemed to pile up one on the other.

"So far, we have only talked about the programming part of the robotics. Now the fourth and equally important part. Do you remember your physiology from college? Specifically your muscle physiology?"

"Mr. Standish, I never took physiology in college. I majored in computer science with a minor in psychology."

"OK, I will forgive you for that. Pay attention. If you have questions, ask as I go along."

Joshua braced for what was coming next.

"Here is a visual." Daniel pointed to a model. It was a bolt that had threads at both ends. The threads went in opposite directions. Each end had a nut in the threads. Each nut was held in place by a clamp. "Watch what happens when I rotate the bolt while holding the nuts stationary." The bolt started rotating, and the nuts started to move to the center, making the space between them less. For effect, each nut pulled a cable that was threaded through a pulley and lifted weights off the ground.

"OK," Joshua said, trying to keep up.

"This is how a muscle works. Two sets of filaments make up each muscle cell. Chemical bonds between them are formed and dissolved with each nerve signal. The net effect is the same as the rotating bolt where the attachment points of the muscle are the nuts."

Joshua nodded.

"If we shrink the size of the system using much smaller bolts and nuts and attach them to cables, we can put electric motors in the center of the system and use gears to get the cable to shorten in approximately the same time frame as the human muscle. We can use processing units in the matrix to coordinate the movement of the cable to one-tenth of a pound and one-tenth of a second. That will approximate human movement pretty closely.

"The fifth breakthrough is the housing for all of this. The plastic housing for the humanoid body is able to withstand stresses of weight that would approximate normal daily activities for a one-hundred-fifty-pound person. Internal metal bones are primarily for joints for movement between the plastic pieces. This is covered with a complex polymer I developed to be used as skin. It is incredibly human-looking. You have to look very closely to see that it does not contain any hairs or pores. It looks lifelike enough just as it is. It is soft on the edges in a way that it will simply fuse as it is pressed together with another edge of polymer skin. It stays supple at an amazing range of temperatures—that is, from twenty to about one hundred forty degrees Fahrenheit. It is sturdy. I expect it will last about thirty years. That is longer than the expected life of the humanoids anyway. I had to find a tough and durable resin to make the fingernails and toenails. She will never want to use nail polish, but they look and feel pretty real as they are. This resin should also last the lifetime of the skin polymer. You will see how it looks later."

Daniel motioned toward the door and turned off the lights to the lab. They proceeded to the stairwell. "Anna's room is just down the hall from here. Use your employee card to get in and out."

Chapter 6

Joshua went to the prototype rooms. Like a hotel room, each room had an automatic lock requiring a key card to open it. Unlike with a hotel room, the door was locked from both sides, requiring a key card to get out as well as in. There were four such rooms. Daniel had said he would wait upstairs, and they would meet when Joshua was done. Joshua could visit as long as he liked, but dinner would be served around seven. Joshua held his card to the reader, and the door opened. He went in, feeling a little uncomfortable that whoever was inside had no idea he was coming.

"Hello," said a voice from within. She could see him as he opened the glass door in the front of the room.

He waited to say anything until he had entered the room, so he could see whom he was talking to before he responded. "Hello," Joshua replied, but he needed another moment to completely take in what he was seeing. There stood a girl. She was about five foot two. She had an incredibly beautiful face and shoulder-length auburn hair. Her forearms and legs were slim, with a slightly tanned look. He guessed she weighed about 110 pounds. Her voice was gentle. Startlingly, from the tops of her legs and the tops of her elbows to the base of her neck was a clear plastic covering that housed an extraordinarily complex web of cables, gears, and motors. She was clearly shaped like a woman and looked like a woman but was just as clearly a machine. He was taken aback. He expected something like a robot that looked much more mechanical.

"You are staring at me," she said.

"Uh, sorry. I was just surprised."

"What were you expecting?'

"I don't know, just not something half human and half robot."

"OK. For the record, I am completely robot. Oh, and by the way, I am Anna."

"Joshua," he replied.

Anna held out her hand to shake his. "I am pleased to meet you. I actually knew you were coming. Daniel tends to talk to himself and thinks for some reason I can't hear him."

"I am pleased to meet you as well."

"So, Mr. Joshua, why are you here?"

"Uh, I am the new director of computer applications, and I was asked to learn about this project to see how far it has come along."

"Very interesting. So how is it going so far?"

"Well, I spent the whole day learning about biomechanics, software, hardware, and robotics. It has been a pretty full day. To tell you the truth, I am exhausted."

"So, Mr. Joshua, if you are here to learn about me, what would you like to know?"

"That is just Joshua. My last name is Harrington. But I would rather you just call me Joshua. When people call me Mr. Harrington, I always turn around to look for my father." His attempt at a joke fell completely flat.

"OK."

"I actually have a lot I want to talk to you about. I think I have a whole day free tomorrow to do that. I just wanted to say hi to you tonight."

"OK. Can I ask *you* a few questions?" Anna said.

"Sure, just as long as they aren't too hard," he said with a smile.

"I'll keep them simple. Where do you live?"

"I live in a small apartment in Queens, near the home office. Do you know where Queens is?"

"Well, I can't be sure, but I think if I take the Major Deegan Expressway over the Throgs Neck Bridge and then the Long Island Expressway going west, I can find it from there."

She stood there for a few minutes while he tried to decide if she was making fun of him or simply answering the question with a detail he hadn't expected. He now knew not to underestimate her.

"Joshua, my initial upload was a large portion of a current encyclopedia of knowledge as well as a maps program. I wasn't trying to embarrass you."

"You just made two-thirds of my questions for tomorrow irrelevant."

"Sorry. Let me make a proposal to you. Instead of trying to make tomorrow a business meeting in which you evaluate me, why don't you simply talk to me like you are on a date, and we can make casual conversation? Then neither one of us will be nervous, and we will be able to learn a lot more about each other that is real instead of saying what we know the other wants to hear."

"Well, if we are being honest with each other, I am more nervous on a date than I am in a business meeting."

"Don't worry, Joshua. You'll do fine. Why don't you go up to dinner and get to bed early? I will have something to look forward to tomorrow."

"OK, that actually is a good idea. Good night."

"Good night," she replied.

He used his key to unlock the door, listened to it close behind him, and turned to walk down the hall. He had taken three steps, when he realized how she had completely owned the conversation. *How did she do that?* He would work at being a little more assertive tomorrow. He went up the stairs for dinner.

Daniel greeted Joshua at the table. "That was a short visit. In fifty words or less, what did you think?"

"I am blown away. It was more than amazing. How did you do that?"

"I know. We spent the whole day answering that question, yet it still doesn't seem real. Imagine having a thousand Annas in houses all over the country. No, all over the world. If we make them affordable, people will come. People will most definitely come."

Joshua smiled. "A line from *Field of Dreams*. I saw that movie as a kid. My father was a professional baseball player for a while. We watched that movie together. It was one of our better moments." Moving on from memory lane, Joshua asked, "How did you get such high-functioning speech and hearing capabilities? It seemed that conversation was simple for her. I can't imagine how that could be accomplished."

"It wasn't easy. I started by recording female voices off YouTube. I dissected each digital file to individual syllables and phonics. Each sound she made would be an individual file. The processor that is used for coordination of movement would also aggregate the sounds and coordinate the mouth movement to match the digital generation of sound. She isn't actually speaking with air, because obviously, she doesn't breathe. She is mouthing the words and speaking digitally. I used exclusively female voices to go with her persona. There were programs available that could accomplish this. Also, I built her mouth to be as humanlike as possible, including a different version of the polymer. It needs to be kept damp to keep the rich pink color that is normally seen with lips and the inside of a mouth. There are almost a thousand sensors devoted to oral functions, tongue movement, and facial expression. This includes the coordination of her eyes."

Daniel paused. "The initial upload included dictionaries with ten thousand of the most common words, grammar rules, and some idiomatic phrases. I did this for English, French, Spanish, and German. It didn't end there. She still couldn't speak. In the beginning, I had to find a way to connect these three programs, the files of sounds, with the words themselves so Anna could actually assemble desired words into a coherent thought and then into a conversation. She also had to read and translate words into coherent thoughts. Third, she had to originate thoughts with which she could connect what she wanted to say with what she heard as a response for conversation to work. I did this by reading to her, like to a child. I got one of the original Scott Foresman books about Dick, Jane, Spot, and Puff."

Joshua looked confused.

"You were born in the nineties, weren't you? OK, so this book is before your time. But it worked for millions of children. It also worked for Anna. It starts with simple sentences, such as 'Run, Spot, run,' and works up to complete stories. When I finished reading the first- and second-grade books to her, I made her read it to me. It took about six weeks, but when she finished the book, she could make full sentences into a full story. What is amazing—and I haven't fully explained it yet—is that once she was able to do that in English, she was able to do that in the other languages without actually having to go through the same process to learn them."

"That is incredible. She talks so well. Take a minute to go back to what you were saying before. You designed the face and mouth to make her appear more human, rather than hands or body to make her more useful?"

"The acceptance of a robot as a family member requires a certain amount of familiarity, which is easier if it looks more humanlike. Like adopting a dog because it is cute. You can love your pet because you accept it as a family member. A dog is man's best friend because we choose to make it that way. We want these robots to be accepted the same way," Daniel said.

Joshua was dumbfounded. Daniel's priority was to make the robots accepted as opposed to utilitarian. That seemed strange.

Wouldn't there come a point in the competitiveness of the market when someone designed a robot that was more useful and less human-looking? Would that sell better? Then a reality fell over him. They were talking about a machine, something Daniel had built. It belatedly dawned on him that he had just agreed to go on a date with one of Daniel's creations. She had been so charming in their first meeting. How could he ever possibly think of her as anything but human?

One of the things Joshua was interested in was the Turing test. Alan Turing, a great computer pioneer, had asked the question, "When does a computer become perceived as indistinguishable from a human?" Even in seeing Anna as a robot, with all the gears and cables of her torso exposed, he still perceived her as a human. She clearly had passed the Turing test in the first meeting. He wondered if he would still feel that way after the visit was over.

Cassie came out with appetizers: a choice of anchovies on some type of lettuce and some type of cheese melted onto a special bread. Joshua did not know enough about fine food to know what it was, only that it would have been expensive and in restaurants to which he would never go. Then came the salad. Tonight the salad was followed by a small cup of lime sorbet. Then came the main course of beef bourguignonne with a side of asparagus in hollandaise sauce. Dessert was a raspberry tart. The dinner was fantastic, but two things started to nag at Joshua.

First, Daniel ate like this every night. That was probably some of the cost of the project. All the food had to be flown in due to the location. In spite of the fact that the meals were so meticulously prepared and so complete and delicious, it was odd that Daniel never had a nice word of any kind for Cassie. It was almost as if he were being intentionally mean to her. Why would she stay on the job?

The second thing that bothered him was that once he told Daniel how fantastic he thought Anna was, Daniel didn't seem to want to talk about it anymore. Joshua thought that his being impressed by Anna was all Daniel had wanted to accomplish. He wasn't looking for any input from Joshua about his opinion on bringing the product to the market.

Joshua said to Daniel, "I would like to spend a few hours tomorrow with Anna. Will that be OK?"

Daniel said, "Sure. I am going to work in the lab tomorrow. I wanted to take the day after tomorrow off. You are here to see how she works. Spend as much time as you want with her. Use your card to access the room. However, whatever you do, Anna is not allowed to leave the room for any reason for any amount of time. She can be clever at trying to manipulate people; you have to be aware."

Joshua excused himself to retire to his room. He started to write his report. He had more questions now after his first full day than he'd had before the day started. He was tired, though. He went to sleep early.

He was up early the next morning and went to the dining room for breakfast. Strangely, he was there alone. Cassie made him another wonderful breakfast. He thanked her and headed down to Anna's room.

Around ten o'clock, Joshua knocked on the glass door to Anna's room. He used the card to unlock the door and let himself in.

"Good morning!" came the cheerful greeting from inside. Anna was wearing a sweater that covered most of her torso, where the machinery was visible. "I am wearing this just in case the place we go on our imaginary date is cold."

Joshua smiled. "That sweater looks nice on you."

"Thank you. Actually, the reason I put it on is that I want you to see me dressed. That is also appropriate for our imaginary date."

She was right, Joshua thought. She actually looked human with the sweater on. It really did seem to change his perspective.

"So where are we going?"

"Well, since this was your idea, where would you like to go?"

"I have always wanted to see the ocean. Is it really as big as they say?"

"Yes. It stretches as far as the eye can see. On a summer day, it is beautiful. The sand gets hot, and the water is usually cold, but the sun feels good on your skin, and the sound of the waves rolling is soothing. OK, let's go to the beach."

"What would you bring?"

Joshua thought for a minute. "Well, I would bring a cooler with drinks, maybe sandwiches, sunscreen, and maybe even a Frisbee."

"Would you bring music?"

"Sure. I have an iPod."

"What is on your playlist?"

"It is a long list."

"OK, what is your favorite song?"

"'Yesterday' by the Beatles. I have always liked listening to it."

"But it is a sad song. Does it remind you of a girl who hurt you?"

"Yeah. Sort of." Joshua went on to tell the story of a girl he had liked for quite a while in high school. She simply had moved on to dating another boy. He never had known why she left. He always had been convinced he wasn't interesting enough to compete with other guys. He found himself pouring his heart out to this stranger. She was a good listener. She was also a robot that was confined to a room four hundred miles away from him. What would it matter?

She said, "Well, if you want to feel really miserable, listen to 'I Am a Rock' by Simon and Garfunkel or 'This Diamond Ring' by Gary Lewis and the Playboys. Of course, if you want to feel better after a girl hurt you, listen to 'Walk like a Man' by Frankie Valli and the Four Seasons or 'Red Rubber Ball' by the Cyrkle. These are songs from the 1960s. You chose 'Yesterday,' so I thought I would stay in the same era."

"What else do you know about music and how it can move a person's mood?"

"Apparently, Daniel had a thing for rock and roll. My initial upload included all of the songs from the 1960s to the 2000s. It seems to stop there. I can play any song in my head that made the top forty in any of those years. You can ask me anything about any of the songs or artists."

"But you seem to know the meanings of the songs."

"Yes. Why wouldn't I? I get that I don't have a lot of experience in the world, but music seems to transcend that. There is a meaning to the music that one can experience just by listening to the music itself. I am sure the meaning and connected emotions will be more intense when I have actually experienced some of the things the songs' lyrics talk about. Meanwhile, sad songs are simply sad, and upbeat songs are upbeat." She smiled at her conclusion.

"What is your favorite song?" asked Joshua.

"Hard to say. I don't know that I have ever thought about any one song being a favorite. I like the upbeat stuff. If you want to stay in the '60s, I like 'Up, Up, and Away' by the Fifth Dimension and 'Lazy Day' by Spanky and Our Gang. Although there are times when I am in the mood for heavy metal. I love 'Stairway to Heaven' by Led Zeppelin. I guess I am eclectic."

On and on the banter went for three hours. He had never had a real date as fun as this imaginary one. What was he doing there? He was actually flirting with this girl, who was supposed to be the subject of his robot market study. The day was becoming surreal. The whole trip was surreal.

Sometime after two o'clock, he said, "Well, I guess it is time to take you home. I need to take some time to start my report."

"Are you going to walk me to my door?"

"Of course."

"You are a gentleman." She smiled the most disarming smile and said, "Thank you. I had a wonderful time. Will you be back later this afternoon?"

"Maybe later. I need to do some work before the end of the day. I had a great time at the beach. For a first date, I think it went pretty well."

"I do too," she said with a smile. "Bye."

Chapter 7

Joshua got back to his room and sat at the desk with his agenda, trying to fit the things they'd talked about into some of his preconceived topics. He met Daniel for dinner for the third time. He asked if Daniel could take a few minutes to talk to him about some of the observations he'd had during the conversation.

"I hoped she behaved for you today. I made it clear to her before you came that she was to be on her best behavior."

"What does that mean? Does she have outbursts of temper? Does she get unresponsive? What kind of behavior would she have that she should avoid around me?"

"She gets demanding. Sometimes she wants things she knows she can't have. I think it is a programming problem I can fix in the next model."

"Tell me more about the next model. What will be different?"

"The programming will make sure the robot is more subservient. Anna can be contrary."

"How does the programming relate to her subservience? Can you actually have a program that makes a robot choose to obey? Would you lose something in the way of creativity if you do that?"

"Anna is not capable of being creative. But sometimes she does not obey me. I am going to make the next model respond better that way."

"What happens to Anna when you create the new model?"

"Anna gets destroyed. Well, I am going to reuse parts of her body, but she will be reformatted. Her personality will be removed." With that, Daniel excused himself and retreated to his room.

Now Joshua was feeling disturbed. It seemed red flags were going up everywhere. He'd just spent the day with the girl at the beach on an imaginary date. How could Daniel say she was not capable of being creative? How could he want to destroy her because he didn't like her behavior? What had Anna meant when she'd said that sometimes he talked to himself as if she couldn't hear him? He carefully noted all of this. He wanted to go back to Anna's room to ask her some questions to see if he could make sense of all of this.

He made his way back to her room. "Anna, what did you mean earlier when you said that sometimes Daniel talks to himself as if you can't hear him?"

"Daniel gets angry. He starts to yell at me or Cassie. He actually does it quite often. Occasionally, he has hit me. He often hits Cassie. He is big, and there isn't much we can do about it. He warned me not to say anything, but I really don't care. You know, Cassie is also a robot. A couple of nights ago, he took her into his room and did something that upset her. A lot. I don't know what, but she hasn't been the same since. I can sense when Cassie is upset, even though she cannot speak. I don't see her often, but I can see into the hallway when she cleans the rooms."

Joshua sat back in his chair. His worst fears seemed to be happening. "I understand," he said. "Thank you for telling me that."

"Can you make it stop? Please don't tell him I told you this. He will hit me again."

"I don't know. He is my boss. I can tell the other people in power back at the office."

"When do you leave?"

"The day after tomorrow. I will be back tomorrow, probably late in the morning." With that, Joshua said good night and went back to his room to make more notes.

Daniel was at breakfast the next day. "Good morning!" he said as Joshua approached the table. That morning was the same type of setup for breakfast. Joshua asked for just some toast and some scrambled eggs. Cassie nodded and left. Daniel was waiting for some type of fish. Joshua wasn't paying attention to that anymore. He now was focused on learning more about Anna, Cassie, and any other prototypes they hadn't talked about.

"You said you were going to take the day off. What are your plans?"

Daniel said he was going to go hiking in the mountains and would be back late in the afternoon.

"Today is my last day here. Can we set aside some time to talk in the evening?"

"Sure. We'll meet for dinner and talk then. What is left to talk about?"

Joshua thought for a minute about how much he wanted to divulge his misgivings. "I wanted to talk about licensing issues and some market considerations."

"Fine. We can talk about them in the evening. You do not have to get up too early tomorrow; the ride gets here around ten." With that, Daniel finished his breakfast and went to his room, where he changed into a hiking outfit. He went to the kitchen to get a fully stocked backpack from Cassie and left through the front door.

Joshua returned to see Anna later that morning, around ten.

She greeted him with one of her smiles. "Good morning, stranger. How are you today?"

"Fine. I hope you didn't get sunburned from our imaginary day at the beach."

"No. I am fine. Joshua, I have to ask you a question." The smile left her face. "What is Daniel going to do to me after you leave?"

Joshua's face took on a serious look. "I am not sure. He seems to be doing things that don't make sense to me. I have to be careful how I ask. In spite of my new promotion, he could still fire me."

"He has said he is going to destroy me and reuse my parts. I don't want to die."

"That is one thing that doesn't make sense. Even in business, you don't destroy your prototypes as you evolve them. You use them to compare the steps you took to get there. It helps you evaluate the new model when you can compare it to the prior model while it is still working. Please forgive me for talking about you as a piece of equipment. I am not trying to do that, and I don't think that about you. But even from a purely business point of view, it doesn't make sense. It isn't about the money. He spends money on ridiculous things." Joshua paused. "Tell me again. Cassie is a robot? Are there other robots I haven't been told about?"

"Yes, and yes. Cassie is certainly a robot. I haven't seen any others. They apparently were built and destroyed before I was built or hidden away somewhere. Daniel talks about them once in a while."

"Anna, let me process this, because I am not even sure why this is happening. Can we talk about something else for a little bit? The truth is, I truly enjoy your company, and I am leaving tomorrow."

Anna sat back and said, "Sure. OK. Tell me why you chose the girl you said hurt you in high school. What was it about her that made you like her or made her like you?"

Joshua went on to tell his sad story. He had dated a girl as a senior in high school all year, and in the spring, she simply had wanted to go to the prom with another guy. It seemed silly now, but it had been crushing at the time. He told her he had dated a few other women but had not had a serious relationship since. It just seemed too hard.

"But why were you attracted to this girl? What was it about her that made you want to be with her?"

"She had beautiful hair and eyes. I always liked her eyes."

"OK, but, Joshua, was there anything she did or said that made you know she wanted to be with you?"

Joshua struggled to answer the question. "She said she liked to do things with me, and we were friends. I always believed we would be more than friends. In the beginning, she used to be excited to see me. After a while, not so much. Then she didn't want to date anymore. I never knew why." He paused. "Anna, what about you? What would you want to do if you were in the outside world?"

"I think I would like to be a cosmetician. I would like to make people beautiful. Or maybe I would learn to play an instrument and be a musician. There are so many things I would enjoy. I don't know if I have ever decided what I would like to do the most."

Their banter went on for several hours. Joshua was fascinated with her. Later in the afternoon, Anna finally said, "Joshua, you leave tomorrow. If you don't help me, you will never see me again. I really want to see you again. You are my best friend."

"Anna, I have been thinking about that a lot. I want to help you. The best plan I can come up with is to leave my employee card in your room. I can always plead absentmindedness. Use the card to escape during the night. You can get out of the building with my card as well. Once you are out of the building, go to the south side. Once you leave the grounds, you will have to make your way southeast to the next town. It is about fifteen miles. I will fly back to New York City tomorrow and book a flight for the following day to Pittsburgh. I will rent a car and meet you in the town. Let's decide on a place to meet. You have a map upload."

"Joshua, I don't know. I have a map upload, but I don't have any GPS to let me know where I am on the map. Also, I don't know how well I can climb over mountains or if I can be in the rain. That is a lot of *ifs*. If I get into trouble, will you come look for me?" She looked uncomfortable with the idea.

"Of course I will. This may be the best I can do."

"What if I just sneak onto the helicopter with you?"

"I don't think we could get that by Daniel."

Joshua opened the door and let Anna out. Anna walked Joshua back to his room and took his key. Joshua took a business card out of his wallet and folded it into quarters. He placed the folded card on the floor inside the doorjamb to keep the door from closing completely. He could leave the room if he wanted without his card. "I'll see you late in the morning the day after tomorrow," he said as she left to return to her room.

She nodded and said, "I know. See you then."

Joshua left on schedule in the morning. He boarded his flight to Pittsburgh at 6:25 a.m. He was in his rented car in Pittsburgh and leaving the rental car lot by eight thirty. It was only an hour-and-a-half drive to Morgantown. Sometime a little after ten, he pulled up to the intersection where he and Anna had agreed to meet. She had a maps program in her head. There was no way she wouldn't be able to find the intersection. So he waited. He parked the car and tried to pass the time.

He started to worry. Why wasn't she there? Had something happened to her during the walk from the facility? She had worried about walking over mountains and about cold or rainy weather. Well, it was chilly but not really cold. It hadn't rained. Where could she be?

The last thing she'd said haunted him. She'd said, "If something happens, would you come look for me?" He realized now how impossible that was. He could search the town from his car, assuming she was outside where he could see her. He could pull over on the road out of town at the place closest to the path from the facility, but over fifteen miles, it would be easy to stray from the path, especially at night. If she missed the spot where he was parked by only a quarter mile, he would miss her entirely. He had to be back at the office tomorrow. What in God's name was he going to do?

He did nothing. He simply stayed in the parking space for five more hours, waiting. He prayed she would show up at their spot. Finally, around three o'clock, he decided the worst must have happened during the trip to town. He would have to come back with hiking gear to scour the mountainside for her next week. He felt crushed and defeated as he slowly drove away. He was sick with worry for an experimental machine he had seen for only a few hours. He felt as if he had lost his closest friend.

Chapter 8

Officer Lynch received a call from dispatch that someone had died in the remote facility owned by Logicsolutions. The facility itself was in another state. He was going to have to make arrangements with the local police to recover the body and determine if an autopsy was necessary to rule out any foul play. He needed to find the address of the facility where the death had occurred. He waited for the dialing sound and the ringing on the other end.

"Logicsolutions. May I help you?"

"This is Officer Lynch, NYPD. I need to speak to someone in charge."

"Let me put you through to human resources," the switchboard operator replied.

"Good afternoon. Human resources. May I help you?"

"Yes. This is Officer Lynch of the NYPD looking for the address of your research facility."

After a moment, she replied, "I really don't know. Let me connect you to R&D."

"Sure."

"Good afternoon. Research and development. Can I help you?"

"Yes. This is Officer Lynch of the NYPD looking for the address of your research facility."

"Sure, Officer. It is in West Virginia. Is there something wrong?"

"We had an anonymous call that a Daniel Standish has passed away, and we need to coordinate with the local authorities to send someone to do the pronouncement and possibly an autopsy."

"I understand. The facility is in a very remote location. Let me call you back with the coordinates of the exact location. I know there are no roads nearby, so I will have to give you coordinates."

"Thank you." He gave them his number.

He then hung up the phone and stared at the receiver for several minutes. *Great.* He would have to coordinate with law enforcement in some remote county in another state four hundred miles away to get the details. Then he would have to manage the case to see if there had been foul play. *Why couldn't it just be simple?*

The research and development assistant started to feel panicked as she called upstairs. Jack Cobb, the director of research and development, was in a meeting, so she went upstairs and interrupted to give him a note. In the meeting were Jack; Nick Walsh, the chief financial officer; and Jim Mendola, the chief operating officer. Daniel was the CEO. He was also a bit of a maverick. He rarely went to the executive meetings. He had no business sense, just an incredible talent for writing code and applying his ideas to the edges of where computer technology was. So it was not unusual for the three men to be meeting to discuss the financial and business decisions of the company without Daniel. After all, he was in his research facility for months at a time. He did not like to be disturbed. The West Virginia location was more of his residence than his apartment in Manhattan was.

Jack read the note and looked around the table. His face went pale. The room was silent for a minute or so.

"What is it?" Nick asked.

"Daniel is dead."

There was another pause of silence in the room.

"What? How?" said Nick.

"I don't know. We just got a call from NYPD asking for the address so they can have the authorities in West Virginia go check it out. They are going to get the county coroner in there to see how it happened."

Jim thought for a minute and said, "Call up Ray, and get the helicopter out on the pad in ten minutes. Tell my assistant not to call NYPD back until after we are there. It is two o'clock now. We can be there by six thirty. We need to be there before the law gets there, to make sure there is nothing weird there that Daniel may have left out in the open that needs to be kept secret. You know how he was. If he died suddenly, then there is no telling what they might find."

Jim hit the intercom button. "Melanie, tell Joshua to meet us in the lobby in ten minutes. Tell him he is going on a road trip and will be out for the day." He looked at the other two. "He was there all last week. Maybe he can tell us something."

Fifteen minutes later, Jack, Jim, and Joshua were strapped into the helicopter, rising above New York's skyline on their way west. Jack had told his assistant she should return the call to Officer Lynch as soon as she heard from him. She would have to stay late to wait for the call. They speculated about what might have happened. He had been a health nut and exercised all the time. He had eaten only healthy foods. He drank a lot. Maybe it had been a coronary.

In the taxi on the way to the helipad, Joshua had asked Jim what was going on.

"Daniel is dead. It happened yesterday. Do you have any thoughts as to how this might have happened?"

"No. Everyone was fine when I left. I got on the helicopter as scheduled."

"You said *everyone.* Who else was there beyond you and Daniel?" Jim had asked.

"Well, Mr. Mendola, that was part of the discussion I planned to have with you later today. There were three working humanoids living there with Daniel. One of them was decommissioned the day before I got there. I have a very detailed report back on my desk. I really didn't have time to gather it before I needed to be in the lobby. I can probably restructure the whole report once we get there. There is a lot for me to show you. It was really quite remarkable. There is one question that is haunting me now."

"What is that?"

"If the NYPD says someone called in with an anonymous tip that someone had died at the facility, who would have made the call if Daniel was the only person there?"

"I have no idea."

"That is the surprise I wanted to talk about. The humanoids are that sophisticated. Wait until you get there. You will be amazed," Joshua had said with obvious excitement.

"Well, right now, there is nothing we can do but wait until we get there and deal with what we need to deal with."

They arrived in the asphalt lot around 6:20 Eastern time. Jack and Jim both had key cards to get into the facility. They entered slowly, taking in the opulence of the entryway and the dining room.

"Well, now we know where some of that forty million went," Jack said.

The lobby was quiet and empty. There was an eerie absence there. Jack and Jim took it all in as they slowly made their way to the hallway. They turned the corner of the hallway and found two bodies on the floor in the entry of the third room. Both were dead. The first one was Daniel. He had been stabbed with a rotisserie spit in his belly and had bled into a large pool on the floor. The other was a robot. It looked as if a blunt object had partially decapitated her. Wires and mechanical things were deranged and exposed. Already, Daniel's body had begun to decompose. The smell was nauseating.

"Jack, you are going to need to call my assistant now," Jim said.

Joshua's heart started pounding. The sight of the two bodies on the floor terrified him when he thought of what Anna's involvement in this horrific encounter must have been. Maybe she had been wounded before she left, or maybe she was already decommissioned and was hidden somewhere else in the facility. He would look for her before they left. None of the outcomes were good.

Joshua tried to compose himself and gathered his thoughts. They sat in the lobby upstairs. Jim suggested they go to the kitchen to see if there was anything to eat. "There isn't a restaurant for thirty miles, and we have just had a four-hour flight to get here."

They found some leftover steaks, beer, and fresh fruit in the refrigerator. Jack pulled out a notebook from his jacket pocket. Jim put the steaks under a broiler for ten minutes or so.

"Let's walk through this so we can all understand what happened. Now, from the beginning," Jim said.

Joshua started. "I got here last week. You remember our conversation a few weeks ago, Jack. You promoted me to be the new director of computer applications. You wanted me to be briefed on what Daniel was doing. This made sense to me. Daniel's work was a secret, but at some point, the rest of the team would have to know what was going to be expected of them if Daniel's project was going to become a reality. Apparently, your conversation with him was able to convince him I should be included. So he invited me to come last week. I expected an intense week of discussion on how coding and robotics would connect. Frankly, I spent the last three days before I came out here studying all the specs for the latest projects so I could be as up to date as possible and prepared for whatever he would throw at me. My experience with Daniel was that he was demanding and pretty impatient with people who could not keep up with his thinking. So when I met with him shortly after arriving, I was surprised to find out he was more interested in hiking than talking shop."

Joshua paused to take a drink of bottled water. "He wanted me to do a Turing test on his new project. This seemed relatively simple to me. So I went into the first session with Anna with an open mind, trying to answer a simple question: Was my interaction with Anna seamless enough that I did not know I was talking to a computer? I was completely unprepared for what happened next. I met Anna. She was human in shape but humanoid in appearance. It was clear she was a machine, but she talked like a human. She thought like a human. She had the wit of a human. She was as self-aware, self-reflective, introspective, empathetic, and responsive as a human in every way I can think of. What he did with her was remarkable. It was groundbreaking. I met with her several times. With each passing interaction, the line between human and machine began to blur. She began to wear clothes, and she looked less and less like a machine. I think that was Daniel's plan. The success of this project would not be evident at the beginning, but the feeling that you are talking to a person and not a computer would change over time in spite of the fact that you could see she was a machine."

Jim furrowed his brow, trying to understand.

Joshua continued. "The problem is, in order for that to happen, you have to have a computer that can actually behave like a human. Then the question comes up as to whether you can destroy a being with self-awareness and feelings just to make way for an improved model. Over the several sessions with Anna, I could see the human qualities that would make her pass the Turing test. I didn't know if she was a computer mimicking those qualities or if she truly understood and applied those qualities. In either case, Anna understood what Daniel wanted to do, and she became terrified of being deactivated. I don't know what happened in the hallway."

"So he didn't want to teach you about his project? He wanted you to evaluate whether his robot was perceived as a person?" asked Jack.

"Yes. It was weird. It was almost as if he was setting me up to be entertained by her. She asked me personal and insightful questions. She was quite disarming. I started to think it was some game he was playing with me. It was also weird that he did not want to talk about the market. He spent one day walking me through the technology and then had no interest in me after that."

"What about his drinking?" asked Jim.

"On and off. He would have a couple of glasses of cognac the first few days I was here. Then the last day, he went off on his own, and I could not tell. I don't know."

"So you think he was stabbed by his own creation. Tell me—if Anna was his project, who is this Cassie? And who is the third robot?"

"Hard to know. He introduced Cassie as his servant. She was quite good at it. She prepared and served the meals, cleaned the rooms, and did all the housekeeping. After a few days, it became clear he treated her badly. Also, he did not give her a voice, only the ability to follow instructions. Then, just two days ago, it became clear to me that she was his sex slave. He actually built a robot to serve his sexual needs, but he made her disappear before I came to visit. If I can read between the lines from what Anna told me, I think that after he hid the sex slave, he raped Cassie. Cassie's body language made it clear she despised him. If he gave her the same emotional quotient he gave Anna, it is no wonder she would want to kill him."

"My Lord. That's an incredible drama to be unfolding in a research facility," Jim said as he shook his head. He then looked at his watch and called his assistant. "Did you call NYPD?"

She said, "Yes. The NYPD called West Virginia State Police. They arranged for a state police helicopter to come to the location to inspect the scene and retrieve the body."

Jim instructed the others not to tamper with the scene, including touching Cassie. The West Virginia State Police would draw their own conclusions, which likely would be pretty much the same as the conclusions Jack and Jim had come to immediately upon entering the hallway.

Jack asked, "So we don't know where Anna is?"

"Daniel said he wanted to decommission her. If he did that, then she should be in one of the rooms downstairs. We can search for her after the police leave," Jim said. He turned to Joshua. "What did she look like?"

"She had a human-looking face and head. She had human-looking hands, forearms, and legs to her groin. The trunk and upper arms were a clear plastic that showed a complex set of gears, motors, and cables. She is about five foot two and looks like she would weigh about one hundred ten pounds. There may be video of her if she left the facility after Daniel was killed."

Jack went to put his dish on the dining table and turned over two Logicsolutions ID badges—Daniel's card and Joshua's card. "Joshua, what do you make of this?"

"Oh, there it is. I didn't have it this morning. I must have left it here."

"It is weird that it would be next to Daniel's on the table like that. Did Anna turn up anywhere in any of the robot rooms?"

"No, she doesn't seem to be here anywhere."

"We have to get her back. Daniel used forty million dollars of company money to fund this project. The artwork in this place must be a million dollars alone. Building this facility in this remote location must have cost tens of millions of dollars extra. We are going to need to show something for that money. We will need to hire a private firm to find her if we can. How can she survive outside the facility?"

"That is an important point. She can't. Her charging system will run out after about a week. She will fail and be found on the ground somewhere," Joshua replied.

"That would be a disaster. What if someone found her who knew where to sell the technology to the highest bidder? Not only would we lose our investment, but we would give it to our competitors," said Jack.

"Come with me to the lab. I need to show you what Daniel was able to do."

Joshua inserted the key card into the computer, and it booted up. He found the files that had so intrigued him. "I haven't had a lot of time to really absorb all of the details about how this works. Daniel got away from using circuitry in designing the brain and instead used a gel matrix. This is the latest in nanotechnology; the coding can be done at the molecular level. This allows forty terabytes of data to be stored in a space the size of an average head. This by itself allows for an upload of a whole lot of data and routines of enormous complexity. But here is where it gets amazing. The formatting organizes the data into folders with files of similar data. The matrix allows these folders to automatically form themselves into groups he calls clusters. The more they are used in combination with other files, the more they reorganize themselves into groups of interconnected routines. This is the way the artificially intelligent brain evolves as it interacts with the environment. This brain not only performs the functions of a computer but also evaluates the new information it receives and organizes it, deeming it useful or not useful. Then it connects it to other informational files that can use this information in a different application. This has never been done before. You can see in the prior trials that he continued to improve the outcome. He told me the next prototype would have been the one to bring to market. There were still some routines missing."

"Do you think you can pick this up here and make that new prototype?"

"I believe so."

Jim looked at Jack and said, "I want Joshua to be in charge of this and report directly to me. This needs to continue to be a secret. I will also take charge of finding Anna."

"I understand," Jack said.

A voice called from the doorway. The West Virginia State Police had arrived. Jim went up to greet them.

A tall, heavyset man decked out in a gray uniform with a raspy, deep voice said, "Good evening, gentlemen. I understand a man died here."

"Yes, sir. Follow me." Jim led the three officers to the hallway and to the room where Cassie and Daniel lay motionless on the floor. "The male is Daniel Standish. He is the CEO of the company. The female is Cassie, with no last name. It appears there was a struggle between these two. He was stabbed, and she was hit by a blunt instrument. They are both dead. There were no witnesses. You need to know, Officer, that the female is a robot the male created. You can see by the wound that she has no blood."

"And who are you?"

"I am James Mendola, the chief operating officer of Logicsolutions, a tech company back in New York. I am the man in charge now that he has passed."

The detective turned to address the other two uniformed men behind him. "All right, get some photos and details of the scene," he said to the two other officers. "We are sending the body to the coroner's office to get an autopsy. Then arrangements can be made to fly the body back to New York or wherever the next of kin want it to go. I can leave the robot or whatever it is here."

Jim stepped back to let the officers do their job. He returned upstairs to Joshua and Jack.

An hour later, the body was loaded into the police helicopter. They watched as it took off. They then met outside with Ray and prepared for their own trip back to New York. Jim would take care of notifying the next of kin. He looked at Jack and dryly said,

"How are we going to explain this to the rest of the executive team?"

As they strapped into their seats in the helicopter, Jim said to Joshua, "Joshua, talk to me a little more about what Daniel had figured out. What makes this project so special?"

"Well, Mr. Mendola, he actually had five breakthroughs that he explained to me. The first we already talked about. The second is the program he used to format the gel matrix. The third is a processing program to control coordination of complex tasks. The fourth is the mechanical setup to use gears, cables, and motors to replace muscles. The fifth is the complex polymer compound used to make up the skin. The first and second pieces actually create a fully functioning brain that works like a human's. I can explain this in detail when we get back to the office. There is a lot to this, and I want to have my notes with me. Being able to get human appearance and movement is also an art Daniel accomplished. I know it is hard to believe, but you will not be able to tell Anna is a robot when you meet her—if you ever meet her," he said.

Joshua took a break to drink his water.

Jim leaned back in his seat with a disturbed look on his face. "So how hard will it be for her to survive in the outside world?"

"It would be impossible. She has no charging port. She also has no body heat. The gel will work within a narrow temperature range. Almost anywhere around here—or in New York, if that is where she headed—the temperature is going to go below that range. In either case, she will lose her data and fail. I can't see it working any other way."

"Does she know this?"

"Probably not, and she probably has no way to learn it in time."

"So if we don't find her in time, it will be like finding a phone after it is turned off. All of the technology she contains will be available to the first finder. That would probably be the police. We have to find her before I go to the executive team and tell them we lost our forty-million-dollar project. How do we find her?"

"I don't know. She will be indistinguishable from any other person."

"Do you think she will look for you? Does she trust you?"

"I wanted to think so, but I don't know."

"Don't worry about it anymore. Let me think of a plan to find her. You focus on taking what you have learned and finding a way to continue Daniel's work."

They rode the rest of the way in silence.

Chapter 9

Anna went into work on a day that was no different from any other. Sometime around midmorning, Sophie was sitting in her chair and leaned back, and the chair broke, causing her to fall hard to the floor. She landed with a thud heard throughout the store. She badly sprained her wrist, and a sharp corner of a nearby filing cabinet cut her forehead badly. She yelled in pain as her head began to bleed.

Anna quickly grabbed the first-aid kit kept in the top drawer of Sophie's desk. She grabbed a handful of Kleenex tissues and told Sophie to be calm while she applied force on the cut to stem the bleeding. She asked Sophie to hold the tissues in place. She quickly pulled out three Band-Aids, scissors, and some antibiotic ointment. She quickly cut the Band-Aids into butterfly strips. She took the tissues from Sophie and applied the antibiotic ointment. She carefully placed the Band-Aids across the cut as she pulled the edges of the cut skin together. Adeptly, she was able to minimize the cut, and the bleeding stopped. She found an Ace wrap in the first-aid kit and wrapped Sophie's wrist with even overlapping layers until the wrap was fully used and the support was strong enough that the wrist could not be bent or twisted. She then grabbed an ice pack from the freezer in the back room and wrapped it around Sophie's wrist while she helped her over to the chair in the reading area. "Please sit for a few minutes. Don't move or think about anything. I'll run the store for a while. You are going to be fine."

A random customer exclaimed, "Where did you learn how to do first aid like that? Are you a nurse?"

"No. I just read that book." Anna pointed to a display of *First Aid for First Responders*. It was a textbook for medical professionals.

"I want that," the customer said, and he promptly grabbed the book and bought it.

After a half hour or so, Sophie was fully composed. The wrist was painful to move but manageable. Her head was sore, but it was feeling better. She got up and returned to her desk. By then, Anna had put the broken chair with the trash and replaced it with a chair from the back room. Sophie sat down gingerly and said, "Thank you, dear, for your help and your caring touch."

Another pair of customers came in later that day. A woman brought—or, more accurately, dragged—her child into the shop. "I want you to pick out a book. You can get anything you like, but I want you to read more instead of spending your whole day on your computer."

The boy made a sour face and crossed his arms in defiance. "But, Mom, I hate to read. I don't want to be here."

Anna watched the boy for a minute. She came over to the boy, looked at the mother for a moment and then the boy, and said, "I'll make you a deal. I'll let you pick out any treat you want in the back if you will let me read to you for just five minutes."

The boy was surprised by the strange girl's offer. "OK," he said hesitantly. He looked to his mother for approval, and she nodded.

He went to the back, and Anna showed him the choices. He grabbed a small bag of potato chips and sat down on the end of the love seat. Anna grabbed a copy of *Charlotte's Web* and opened it to the first page. She read the first chapter, using her changeable voice to imitate the characters in the story. The child was completely engrossed. Five minutes became ten, and she read the first three chapters. At that point, Anna said, "OK, I will make you another deal. You take this book home, read the next three chapters, and come back tomorrow, and I will let you choose another treat and read to you again. Or if you prefer, you can read to me."

The boy got up, and the mother said, "What do you say?"

"Thank you."

The mother bought the book and left.

Sophie pulled Anna aside and looked at her as if she were her own child. "I knew when I hired you that you were a good person. You were so worthy of being given the chance you asked for. I am grateful for all you have given back."

When Anna was back in her room after work, she reflected on all the interesting things that had happened that day. Now she had new emotions to think about, such as gratitude, friendship, and positive karma—all impossible things to program. She asked herself, "Why did it feel so natural to help Sophie? How did I know how to handle that child? Why did it feel so good when Sophie thanked me?" The books Anna had read made relationships seem complicated. With Sophie, it didn't seem complicated at all.

Chapter 10

James Earl Mendola entered his corner office, nodded to his assistant, and sat quietly at his desk for a long time. His next call was to be to Bernie Dennison. They had gone to high school together. They'd played football together. They'd stood up at each other's wedding. Bernie was one of Jim's oldest friends. He could trust Bernie. Bernie ran a firm that could find people. This was going to be a different kind of call, but if anyone could help, it would be Bernie. He dialed the phone.

"Bernie, I have a case for you. Can you meet me for lunch this afternoon? Sure. Yeah, the Forty-Second Street Eatery will be fine. I'll meet you there at two o'clock." There would be a meeting with the executive team tomorrow that included two women from the venture capital group. Jim would have to explain all the problems that had been heaped onto his plate yesterday. First, the death of their superstar genius. Second, the missing money. Third, the missing machine. Fourth—was there a fourth? Three was plenty. After tomorrow's meeting, he would call the coroner in West Virginia to get the results. He had to make the funeral arrangements. Daniel had no next of kin that Jim knew of. Jim believed there was a will with the company attorney. There was also a keyman insurance policy that would be payable to the company. All in due time.

As he counted the headaches to face, he turned away from his desk, and a photograph of his daughter at age four being carried on his shoulders and a second picture of her at her senior prom caught his eye. He paused with a pang of sadness. It still hurt.

Jim had married his high school sweetheart right out of college. He had been unable to imagine being with another girl. They had gotten married without a nickel to their name. It had been a modest wedding in her church. That had been twenty-four years ago.

They'd started out happily. As Jim had become more successful in the company, he'd had to work more and more, including late nights and weekends. He had been financially successful, but his love had drifted away. Charlene had asked for a divorce seven years ago. Stefani, his twelve-year-old daughter, had been devastated. She had been sure it was her father's fault. As he had not changed, she had talked to him less and less. Eventually, she'd shut him out of her life completely, associating entirely with her mother. The divorce had been unpleasant. He'd moved out. He had not spoken to Charlene or Stefani since. He missed his daughter. He missed Charlene as well, but he was not eager to reach out. He still saw his financial success as something to be proud of, not ashamed of. He could not find the compromise. If he hadn't given his all, not only would he not have been successful personally, but the company would have failed.

Now the company was facing another threat. He would stay in control and work it out. The company would survive. One day his daughter would understand.

The board meeting was always Wednesday morning. It always included Nick, Jack, Jim, two women from the venture capital company, and Jim's assistant when Daniel wasn't there. He would prepare an agenda that included getting a death certificate, the keyman insurance payment, and a status report on the lost project. He would talk about how he was on top of it with Bernie's company. Then he would address the huge amount of money spent over the last two years. He called his assistant in and dictated an agenda. She would have it ready with six copies for the morning.

He grabbed his sport coat and left for the Forty-Second Street Eatery.

Chapter 11

Jim arrived at the restaurant first. The hostess brought him to a booth in the back of the room. He was a regular there, and the hostess knew he always preferred that particular booth. He was comfortable doing business there.

Several minutes later, a tall blond man in his late forties greeted him with a broad smile. Jim stood up and gave Bernie an iron-grip handshake. The two men sat down. Jim told the waitress he wanted an iced tea, and Bernie ordered the same while they considered what they wanted for lunch.

"So what's up, Jim?"

"Tough case, Bernie." Jim put his briefcase on the table and pulled out several large photographs. Each one was of a young girl. She had blonde hair cropped short in one picture and long auburn hair in another. "This last one with her in the white shawl is what we believe she looked like when she was last seen."

"What is so special about this girl that you have to hire me to find her?"

"Bernie, she is not a real human. She is a robot—a machine. This is the project Daniel had been working on over the last two years. Apparently, he did such a fantastic job at creating humanoids that one killed him, and the other escaped. It was a bizarre scene that defies description. See this one of the hallway? Daniel is lying on the floor over here after bleeding out from a

stab wound with a rotisserie spit. This girl over here is another
one of his robots. Apparently, this was the housekeeper. A third
one we found hanging in a closet was the one he did not report
to the company. He used it as his personal servant and sex toy."
Jim took a deep breath and sat back in his chair.

Bernie studied the pictures for several more minutes. "Secret
sex toy, huh?"

"Yeah. That is not our problem. He deactivated the sex toy
and destroyed the housekeeper after she stabbed him. At least we
hope so. The last thing we want is a homicide investigation. There
is no investigation if the murderer is also dead."

"Did you guys decide what you want for lunch?" the waitress
asked, breaking in.

"I'll have a club sandwich," said Jim.

Bernie said, "Give me a cheeseburger with ketchup, fries,
and a coffee."

"We are a little short on time. Please bring the check when
you bring the meal. Thanks," said Jim.

"So our focus is on the young-girl-robot thing," said Bernie.

"Yes. Somehow, over the last two years, our friend and
colleague Daniel managed to burn through forty million dollars.
We have arranged for an outside auditor to find where all the
money was spent. I'm sure a lot of it went to constructing the
building in the mountains of West Virginia. It looks a lot like a ski
villa, but it is located in an impossible place to get to. Everything,
even the building supplies, had to be shipped by helicopter. There
are no roads for ten miles from this place. If he actually built one
of these robots off the books, we will see several million dollars
there. He built four prototypes altogether. The first one didn't
work very well. The second one was the housekeeper. The third
was the sex toy, and the fourth was Anna. Apparently, there
was going to be a fifth, which was the one that was supposed to
make the company all the money he promised. It didn't happen.

The best we have is Anna, who could be anywhere east of the Mississippi.

"Each one was more sophisticated than the one before. Anna interacted with Joshua. He said she was so lifelike he couldn't tell where she stopped being a computer and where she seemed to be human. He is a loner. I think he actually had some kind of crush on her by the way he talked about her. Apparently, she left the day after he did. It is not a whole lot to go on. However, Joshua did say there were some design flaws that would make it difficult for her to survive outside the lab. It may turn out she shows up as a carcass somewhere. If that is what happens, we need to recover her body. The technology in her is a large part of the money I described earlier."

Bernie listened carefully. Lunch arrived. He thought for several minutes. "OK, say the design flaws kill her. Can someone tell from the outside if she is human or robot? These pictures look pretty convincing to me that an average person would call 911."

"I think that is true. However, once the first responders arrived, it would become obvious she was a robot. Then we don't know for sure what would happen next. They most likely would take her to the hospital anyway. Then the hospital would call the police. The situation would start to get ugly in our attempt to keep our secrets secret. Joshua says she has about seven days or so before her battery dies, or maybe as little as one or two days if the temperature drops below forty degrees. So we don't have a big window."

"I can set up a team to follow the police bulletins of the area for the doomsday event. But with an optimistic view, what is the chance she might reach out to Joshua if she is in trouble?"

"I don't know. It's a small chance but a possibility."

"What if I put a tail on Joshua and a tap on his phone? It is simple and probably the only reasonable lead you have at this point."

Jim agreed. "OK, put the tail on Joshua. Keep me informed, and we'll meet once per week."

Bernie said, "Fine. My fee is still twelve hundred dollars per day." With that, Bernie stood up. "Thank you for lunch. I'll be in touch."

Chapter 12

Nick Walsh returned to his office, sat at his desk, and put his head in his hands. He knew what was coming. He and Daniel had known each other for a long time. In some ways, Daniel had been responsible for helping him get this position. Now Daniel was dead. Nick would have to deal with the grief. However, he had a bigger problem to deal with. Daniel had run amok with the company's money to work on the project. It had been his passion. He'd considered the company his private piggy bank. His prior successes had removed any notion of failure, so he'd spent money on the project with only Nick as his conscience. Nick wasn't a good conscience.

Nick had his own issues and was always in financial trouble. Because Daniel had been spending money so wildly, Nick had managed to slip in an occasional voucher for himself and, over the last two years, had taken just under $1 million. It would have gone unnoticed if Daniel had shown a success in his project and the $40 million he'd spent had been dwarfed by the potential profit. No one would have asked any questions. Now that Daniel was dead and so much money had been spent, the company was going to want to do an accounting of it. That meant an outside auditor. They would find the $1 million and ask Nick tough questions he had no answer for, except that he was guilty. That probably meant jail time. As he let himself go down that road of thoughts, the outcome got bleaker and bleaker.

It made him angry. He wasn't a bad person. He certainly wasn't a criminal. He and Daniel had met in elementary school. They had known each other since second grade. They had been friends all these years. Daniel always had been the nerd, even at seven years old. Nick, for many years, had been his only friend. Daniel always had been coming up with crazy ideas. For his sixth-grade science project, he'd wanted to make a rocket. That by itself hadn't been weird, but he'd wanted his rocket to carry a person to the moon, so he'd built it to be life-size. He cannibalized more than twenty pounds of fireworks for fuel. It had had enough gunpowder to lift it one hundred feet into the air. Fortunately, he had been convinced to use a dummy for an astronaut instead of a real person.

Nick thought, *I think that is where this odyssey began. Why not make a dummy do things that a real person could do?*

Daniel had been a genius at not only coding but also the wider picture of computer-generated opportunities. Artificial intelligence was the end of a long journey of building all the pieces. Nick did not understand any of the actual computer stuff. He just understood how the ideas could make money.

The partnership had been born. As they'd grown into their high school years, they'd had their own cell phone repair business, which had done well. Then, in college, they'd focused on business applications of hardware and software as a way of solving common problems encountered by midsized businesses on an everyday basis. Their solutions had been so simple and effective that their reputation had spread, and soon they'd needed to hire more help. They had found Jim Mendola and Jack Cobb through headhunters, and the four of them had built a solid business model. They'd sought venture capital and created Logicsolutions, which eventually had grown to a $100-million-per-year business.

Right out of college, Nick had married a hot girl named Maggie. He had fallen head over heels for her. Daniel had been their best man. But Maggie had wanted a bigger life than Nick could afford. When the time had come to invest in the infant business, Maggie had steadfastly said no. Consequently, he had not gotten an ownership in the company and had missed all the equity growth. Maggie's appetite for material things had not waned with time or with having children. A huge house, a pool, parties, private schools—the list went on and on. Nick made a lot of money at the company, but his wife spent money about 20 percent faster than he could earn it. The debt had grown over time until it was choking him. He finally had faced the fact about a year and a half ago that he was not going to be able to carry the load anymore and would fail financially. He had known it would cost him his marriage. He had seen a crash coming that would crush his life to an unrecognizable form.

So he had given in to temptation. The $1 million he'd secretly squeezed out of his company had solved his debt problem. He didn't want to leave his wife or see her leave him. The embezzlement had seemed like a perfect solution since he'd gotten a wink and a nod from Daniel. Daniel always had understood the relationship between Nick and Maggie. Daniel had been using all the money he wanted, so he'd looked the other way when Nick slipped the vouchers under the radar. As long as Daniel had protected him, he had been safe.

Now Daniel was gone. How could that have happened? Daniel always had seemed invincible. When not in front of a screen, he had been working out. He had been as healthy as a horse and as strong as an ox. It was unimaginable that anyone could have hurt him.

What to do? He thought of ways to borrow money. The banks would not work. His salary wasn't enough. *Loan sharks?* He couldn't pay a loan back quickly enough. Then an idea struck him: What if he could find the machine before Jim did? What if he hired his own detective to track it down? He could sell the machine to competitors, to the highest bidder. He could easily get $2 million for the secrets she held. *What about Logicsolutions?* He didn't care anymore now that Daniel was gone. If he could replace the $1 million to the general account before the auditors found it missing, he could call it a simple mistake in accounting. This idea might work. He wanted to ponder it for a while.

Two days later, Nick called a man named Barry Stiles. He had known Barry for a few years. Now he was the CFO at AJX Enterprises. He was known as a sketchy character. He was an enforcer of sorts when AJX Enterprises needed some persuasion of other people who got in the way. AJX Enterprises was not a direct competitor of Logicsolutions because they were not in the business of IT solutions. However, they were very much in the game of artificial intelligence.

"Nick, to what do I owe the pleasure of this call?"

"I have a proposition for you. It needs to be for your eyes only. Can you meet me later today at Saint Peter's Grill over on Twenty-Second Street?"

"Sure. See you at two o'clock."

Nick arrived first at the semideserted bar and found a booth in the back of the room.

Barry was a tall man with a firm handshake. He was built like a football player at six foot and 270 pounds. He took a seat across from Nick in the booth. "Can we get a couple of beers here, please? Dos Equis. Thanks, doll."

Beer appeared at the table a minute or two later.

"Barry, I have been at Logicsolutions for almost twenty years now because I have always been a close friend of Daniel."

"Yes, how is Daniel these days?"

"He's dead."

"What?" Barry leaned forward on the table. "How? When?"

"Yesterday. He was killed by his own creation at the research facility. He had a breakthrough in artificial intelligence and, apparently, a mishap in which he was stabbed by his own robot." Nick waited for the strange piece of news to sink in.

"No way. You're kidding, right?"

"It doesn't end there. He had a second robot with high-functioning artificial intelligence that escaped. We don't know where she is, but we have a strong suspicion she will make her way to New York."

"Go on."

"Daniel was my only connection to this company. With him gone, I would like to retire. This advance piece of technology is most likely out in the city somewhere. Jim is going to try to track her down."

"Her?"

"Yes, it is a female robot. I hate working at Logicsolutions. I am willing to make a deal with you. If I give you information as to how to find her, you can capture her and reverse engineer her. It could be worth tens or hundreds of millions of dollars to get to the market with this technology first."

"What are you looking for?"

"Two million dollars."

Barry didn't blink. "How do you see this working?"

"I will get half up front and the rest when you have the merchandise."

"OK. I will talk to my team and get back to you tomorrow." By *team*, Barry meant a group of former military men he called on from time to time to handle special operations. Sometimes in business, one had to play hardball. That was the advantage of his group. They were discreet and professional.

Nick's phone rang around twelve o'clock the next day.

It was Barry. "Can you meet me at my office tomorrow evening? We have some details to work out."

"That will be fine. I'll be there at seven thirty."

When Nick arrived at Barry's office, there were five large men in the room with him.

"Please meet my team. They are all ex-military and Special Forces. They are experts at snatch-and-grab operations."

Nick looked warily at the group of tough individuals. They had all been in war zones. He pitied the enemy. Nick was not a tough guy. He spent all day dealing with money. That seemed to give a man a lot of power, but it didn't make him tough. These guys were intimidating.

"I have a cashier's check for one million dollars. The remaining million comes when these men are able to deliver the goods."

"Yes," said Nick as he handed Barry photographs from the video feed from the facility. The photos showed a robotic girl with a human face, arms, and legs. One was a picture of her from behind in a sundress. She had long auburn hair, but the picture was from an outside camera that had caught her as she was leaving the facility. It did not show her face. "Here are the best pictures we have. She is about five foot two and probably one hundred ten pounds. She isn't very strong. She moves with cables, gears, and pulleys. This should be an easy capture."

Barry looked at Nick and lost all emotion. "Let me say this to you straight so there is no misunderstanding. One million dollars is worth more than your life as an investment on my part. If for some reason we cannot collect our prize through no fault of our own, I am going to come looking for you to return this money with no questions asked. Is that understood? Wait a minute; let me rephrase that. These men are going to come looking for you, and they always find their prey. If that has to happen, it will be ugly for you."

"I understand. There shouldn't be any problem on my end. I will continue to give you information as I get it from the board or wherever else I can get it."

Barry handed Nick an envelope.

Nick opened it. Inside was a cashier's check for $1 million.

Barry said, "I trust you will find that acceptable."

They shook hands, and Nick left. Once the door was closed, one of the men from Barry's team said, "I don't trust that guy. He did not seem for real. Boss, let me put a bug on him. I want to know all of his movements and conversations. We can put several of them in various places so we can listen in on him throughout the day. Each one will be the size of a raisin. One of them will stick to the bottom of his shoe, in front of his heel. The others will be in key places. He won't discover them for weeks, if at all."

"Do it," said Barry.

Chapter 13

Jim's assistant tapped on Jim's door and then poked her head in. "Mr. Mendola, the package from Officer Lynch arrived today. Here it is."

"Thank you."

Jim opened the large envelope and pulled the papers out onto his desk. He started with the autopsy report. The cause of death was hemorrhage due to a large laceration of the liver, spleen, and pancreas. No other marks had been found. Toxicology was negative. The rest of the report was negative.

Jim thought about that for a while. He set the death certificate aside to file for the keyman insurance. One million dollars was not going to make even a dent in the cost of the project. Now all of the pressure was on Joshua. If he could rescue the project, it might all work out. Anyway, Jim was going to have the difficult discussion with the venture capital people tomorrow.

With respect to a funeral, Jim did not know if Daniel had any family or whom to contact. Nick would know. Jim decided to wander over to Nick's office later to discuss it with him. If there were no next of kin, or at least none they could contact, then Jim would simply make the arrangements with Nick. He believed Daniel had been Catholic. He would call the priest at his church to see if he could preside over any important rituals before he was buried. The company attorney was going through the county records to see if a will was on file.

Jim pulled Nick aside later in the day. "Is there anyone to call, Nick? I don't know anything about his mother. His dad died two years ago. Does he have any siblings, aunts, uncles, or cousins?"

"None he would care about or would care about him. He has two stepsisters with his mom, but they have never met him. His mom left the home when he was five. This was before I knew him. She is living in Pittsburgh, but I am sure he would not have cared if she knew."

"That is a shame. I'm sorry for your loss. I know you and he had been close for many years."

"Yes. But over the last few years, he started to close off and stay by himself. He has actually been in West Virginia for over two years now."

"Is there a funeral home you would like me to call? I don't mind making the arrangements if you would prefer. That way, you can be unburdened from the details and just deal with your grief. However you want to do this is fine."

"Sure, you go ahead and make the arrangements. There is a funeral home out on Long Island that I have used before. I'll give you the number when I get back to the office."

The scene at the cemetery was no different from a dozen other funerals Nick had been to. The only thing missing was grieving people. About twenty employees attended. They couldn't have cared less about Daniel. Their attendance was more about optics. There was the preacher. There were the cemetery employees. Nick was the only one there of all twenty-five or so people who really had known Daniel. Yet many people owed him their livelihood. No one there understood the true genius they had lost. His ideas and willingness to take risks had created the business of the company, his later ideas had powered the company to its success, and his ideas were the dreams of the future. The lemmings standing around looking solemn had no clue. Jim knew, though. Jack probably understood it too. But Jack and Daniel never had gotten along. Jim had tolerated him because of his ability to keep personal feelings and business separate, but they never had been friends. As Daniel had had no wife or family, Nick was the only one in Daniel's life who truly mourned his loss. There seemed no point to a eulogy. No one would really understand.

The pastor finished, and everyone slowly filed out of the cemetery and to his or her car. It was all over in thirty minutes.

Nick and Jim had gone to the cemetery in the same Uber. On the way back to the office, Jim expressed his condolences. "I know you were close."

"Yeah. I had known him since grade school."

"So what happens now, Nick? You know that Daniel was not a big force in the office. He always preferred to be out at the research facility. Now we need to fill the gaps at the top. Do you want to take on a different role at the company?"

"This is still too new. I don't know what I want to do. Life seems to be complicated as it is. Maybe we will talk about it next week."

"I understand."

Chapter 14

Three weeks had gone by since Anna started working at the bookshop. Things were going well. Her life seemed to be in a rhythm. She worked all day with interesting people and read books through the evening. Anna had been put in charge of the student subscription service, and it had grown more than 40 percent. She had saved up some money, more than $1,200. She hid some of it under her mattress and used some of it to purchase prepaid Visa cards at Sophie's suggestion.

Anna had gotten to know several of the regular customers and wanted to try to fit in. Checkered sneakers were popular with a lot of the customers. They called them Vans. She made up her mind to get a pair of them as part of her resolve to be trendy.

On Tuesday, Anna stepped out her apartment door on her lunch break and out into the street in search of the new sneakers. A discount footwear store was a few blocks away. She had about forty dollars in her purse and a hundred-dollar prepaid Visa card with sixty dollars available. She was about halfway there, when she was bumped hard from the back, and a man pulled at her purse. It was hard to keep her balance, and he dragged her by her purse strap. The man paused and kicked her hard in the lower part of her shin. She felt something break and fell to the ground. The purse strap broke, and he ran off with her purse.

Bystanders helped her to her feet. She could not stand on her right foot. A kind man offered to call 911. She said no, and he helped her limp to the storefront, where she could lean against the building. She limped back to the bookstore.

Sophie saw her at the door. "My God, child, what happened to you?" She helped Anna get to the couch and brought an ice pack for her ankle. Anna let her do it, even if it wasn't going to help. Then Sophie came back with a set of crutches. "For the next few days, you can use these to get around." Sophie told her to take the rest of the afternoon off.

Anna went up the stairs to her apartment by sitting on the stairs and scooting up backward one stair at a time. Now she had to figure out a plan to fix this. Obviously, it wasn't a medical problem but an engineering problem.

The next day, Anna was sitting on the couch in the back of the bookshop with her crutches and an ice bag on her ankle. A young man in his late teens whom everyone who worked at the bookshop knew came up to her. He was always dressed in a way that suggested he might have been part of a gang or just a tough kid off the street. He was a little bit of an enigma. He wanted to be seen as a tough guy by the way he talked and the way he dressed, but he was actually a smart and sensitive kid. He must have been sixteen or seventeen. He was a regular at the bookshop and wanted to get an education and do something with his life. But for now, he wanted to look like a street kid. He was also known as a hustler. He made his money in sketchy ways wherever an opportunity made an appearance. He said, "I saw what happened. No one should be able to push you around like that." He leaned over and said in a quieter voice, as if he were saying something personal, "If you want to survive in this neighborhood, you have to be packing some heat."

Anna looked confused. "What does that mean?"

"A gun. You need to carry a gun."

Sophie interjected. "That is crazy. Anna, if you have a gun, the attacker could take it away from you and use it on you as easily as you use it on him. People who own guns are more likely to die from gunshot wounds than people who don't."

The young man said, "No way, Ms. Garcia. How can a little girl like this protect herself? What are you, Anna, one hundred pounds in your wet underwear? You need a small gun. Just enough punch to take a man out." He leaned close to her and said, "For two hundred dollars, I can get you a .38 and the bullets."

Sophie pointed out that if Anna had had a gun and kept it in her purse, the robber would have stolen her gun as well.

Anna thought about it for a moment. "I don't have a permit. How can I buy a gun?"

"I have ways. I can have it for you by tomorrow night," he said with confidence.

"How would I carry it?"

"You like to wear dresses, right?"

"Yes. Most of the time."

"I'll get you a small holster that ties to your upper thigh. I'll throw it in for free. The gun is on the outside of your leg, so it will be easy to get to."

Anna looked at Sophie.

Sophie said, "I think it is a terrible idea, but it is your money to spend. Your choice."

Anna reflected that it was hard to describe how upsetting it was or how violated one felt when someone stole his or her stuff. That was beyond the fact that the attacker hurt the victim badly to do it.

"OK. I'll give you half now, and you get the rest when you bring me the merchandise," Anna told the young man. She had read that in a book. It seemed to fit. He agreed and disappeared.

The young man reappeared the following day, as promised, with the gun, bullets, and holster in a brown bag. He spent a few minutes showing her how to work the gun, use the safety, load the bullets, and aim and told her some basic rules of safety. He loaded bullets into all of the chambers. He gave her another two dozen bullets and told her to keep them somewhere safe. Then he showed her how to put the holster on. She gave him the money, and he left.

Thirty bullets, she thought to herself. *What could possibly happen that I would need so many?* Then she remembered that she had never fired a gun and probably was a terrible shot. Maybe that was why she needed so many bullets. She looked down at the holster. It fit well. Even with the gun, it was so small and sleek it was hard to see under a loose-fitting dress.

Sophie cornered Anna later that day. "Anna, can we talk? Let's go over to the couch."

"Sure. Is there something wrong?" Anna limped over to the couch on her crutches.

"Not exactly, although something is bothering me. I wanted to talk to you about the events two days ago. First, I hope your ankle is feeling better. I have more ice if you need it. Second, I am a little concerned about you owning a gun. I am afraid you are still angry at this man and are going to go out looking for him to get revenge."

"I have thought about that."

"Listen to me," Sophie said. "You have every right to be angry. What he did was a crime. No, multiple crimes. He deserves to be punished. Just not by you. We have authorities for that. I understand if you don't want to call them. That is entirely up to you. But you can't let your anger consume you into doing something that will spoil your future. Just owning an illegal gun can land you in jail. You need to keep that a secret and use it only when you are threatened. If you'd had a gun at the time and shot this man in the back while he was running away, you would have gone to jail forever."

Sophie paused. "There is a second and more important point. It is about your character, the person you are. As I said, you have every right to be angry at this man. So pretend for a moment you are someone else and are watching this event from a third person's point of view. You are watching this crime dispassionately with no stake in the outcome. Now there is Anna, an innocent girl who gets knocked down and injured and has a purse with a hundred dollars taken. It is unfair and malicious for her; she doesn't deserve it. So what happens next? Anna's leg eventually heals, she gets a new purse, and she replaces the hundred dollars in a matter of hours. She heals. She goes back to her life, which is filled with things she is thankful for. She has a home, friends, and a job." Sophie took a deep breath and took measure of how Anna was responding to her words. "Now consider the man who did this. Why would a person go to such great lengths to hurt a stranger? What would he have to go home to? He clearly doesn't have a job."

"Yeah, he does; his job is to steal from people like me." Anna was echoing the homeless man on the bench who had said his job was to lie on the bench and drink.

"Maybe you could look at it that way. Or maybe he is a loser. Maybe he steals to eat. Or maybe he does it to feed his drug habit. Or maybe to save his dying mother. You just don't know until you have walked a mile in his shoes. He is a person too, although he is a broken one. If you can heal and he cannot, then you have to change your anger to pity. He will never have the joy you have. Your anger will rob from you a second time. You can't let that happen. You need to let go of your anger. It is the best thing for Anna."

Anna sat quietly for several minutes. She recalled the homeless lady who'd told her to stay away from pimps and given her food the woman needed but was willing to sacrifice for the good of a stranger. This felt like that. Sophie really cared about her. She was also an adult who seemed to have her life together. She was the way Anna had imagined a mother would be.

"OK, I understand. I will try to replace my anger with pity. I will do my best."

Chapter 15

A young woman on crutches with a blonde wig struggled to get the large glass doors at the Logicsolutions corporate office to open. She managed to back through the doors without losing her balance. She navigated the way to the reception desk, leaned against the counter, and handed the receptionist an envelope marked, "Joshua (R&D department)." She asked when he would get it.

"He will have it within the hour," the receptionist replied coldly.

Anna looked at her watch. It was 9:30 a.m. She had given a lot of consideration to whether she could trust Joshua. She remembered how he'd wanted to rescue her with his ill-thought-out plan. He could be trusted. He genuinely cared. That was why she was taking this gamble today. However, he had been thoroughly played by Daniel. He was book smart but did not have a lot of street sense. It was likely his boss and other key executives were playing him now. She hadn't seen him for four weeks, since she had left the facility, but her best guess was that they would somehow trail behind him to find her. Maybe they were having a person follow him. Maybe they were listening in on his cell phone. She didn't know, and she couldn't take any chances. She had stayed successfully hidden and did not want that to change. This was the best way.

The letter asked Joshua to come to the park bench at the Eighty-First Street entrance to Central Park at exactly 1:00 p.m. and promised there would be something for him waiting there. It was signed, "A friend from the beach."

She limped out of the building and headed up to the bus stop. Navigating the steps on the bus would be much easier than navigating the steps to the subway, she thought. She rode quietly up to the stop at Eightieth Street and slowly made her way to the park. She found a comfortable spot about a hundred feet away that left her a perfect view of the bench and the surrounding area. She sat and waited.

Sometime around 12:40 p.m., she got up and navigated on her crutches to the bench and placed a brown bag toward the far end from the direction she believed he would be coming. Again, she returned to her original spot and waited.

Joshua showed up at five minutes to one. She waited a little longer while he sat quietly on the bench. Then it happened: another man, tall and heavyset, sat on the bench across from him and opened a paper. She could see from the side that he wasn't reading the paper. He was there to watch and follow Joshua. At exactly 1:00 p.m., she pulled out a Tracfone and dialed a number. A moment later, the brown bag on the end of Joshua's bench started to ring. At first, he looked confused and didn't move.

"Come on, Joshua. Pick it up," she muttered to herself.

Finally, he picked up the bag, looked in the bag, and found the phone. After another moment, he answered it. "Hello?"

Anna said, "Joshua, this is Anna. I know you may be angry with me, but I need your help. The man across from you is following you, so you can't let on that you know me. Just listen. They cannot listen in on this phone. At least not yet. Please call me after work when you are headed home. I will give you instructions to find me."

Joshua's response was one of shock and disbelief. "OK. I will call you a little after five o'clock," he said, and he hung up.

At 5:15, Anna's phone rang. She said, "Take the route you normally take to go home. I would guess the men who are following you will have someone on your train home. Take the Seventh Avenue subway to the Times Square station. Get off the train at the last moment before the man following you has a chance to get off after you. Walk across the street to the Forty-Second Street–Port Authority station at Eighth Avenue. Take the ACE line to the Twenty-Third Street station, and get off. Walk to Twenty-First Street. My apartment is upstairs from the door next to the bookshop. I will leave it unlocked. Come up the stairs, and knock on the door."

Joshua's anger morphed into curiosity. *Is it possible that four weeks after Anna was an interesting experiment locked in a glass room, now she has an apartment in Manhattan?* It was too strange. He had to check it out.

He followed her instructions and found the door next to the bookshop. As she'd said, it was unlocked. He slowly and curiously went up the stairs. He knocked gently on the door at the top of the stairs. Slowly and quietly, the bolt turned, and the door was pulled open. Joshua had to take a moment to refocus.

A woman on crutches greeted him. "Please come in."

"I am supposed to meet Anna," he said with a straight face.

The woman laughed. "Joshua, I am Anna. This is me fully dressed. Daniel had me designed with a skin polymer for my face, arms, and legs only so you could do his ridiculous experiment. But it really is me. Unfortunately, I had an incident in which my leg was broken, and I have no idea how to fix it. So I was hoping you could work some kind of magic to make it better. Thank you so much for coming."

She was as disarming as ever. He was still angry for being left in Morgantown.

"I know you are still mad I didn't show the day after you left," she said.

"Yes. Did you leave me to worry to death? What was I supposed to think?"

"Joshua, please sit."

She ushered him to a seat at the small table. He reluctantly and suspiciously sat down.

"Look at me. Listen to me. I murdered a man. I don't know how this will turn out. Either I get tried and go to jail or not. I can argue that I was defending my life. If I had met you and returned to your apartment the following day, you would have been implicated in multiple felonies. I didn't want your life to be ruined because of me. I didn't want your life to be ruined at all, because I wanted to have a chance to be with you."

Joshua sat silently. None of this had occurred to him until that moment. How was it that she always seemed so much smarter and one step ahead of him? She was right. Had he left with her, he would have lost his job and possibly his freedom. It was annoying to him that his anger dissolved so quickly. His version of the story he'd told Jack had left out the part where he had tried to find a way to free Anna and help her to escape. It had been a dumb idea to begin with.

Anna could follow his thoughts. "I assume you left out the part of the story that you had a plan for my escape. At least I hope you did. You would have had no legal defense. It would have been ugly."

"So how did you end up here?"

"It is actually quite a story. I will tell you over dinner. Hopefully I have something in the refrigerator that you like. For someone who has never eaten anything in her life, it is not easy to figure out what and how other people eat. See if there is something you like. Or we can run to the market down the block."

Joshua opened the refrigerator and let out a loud laugh. "Anna, you have all the food you own in the refrigerator. You don't need to keep cans of tuna or boxes of cereal cold."

"A book I read said that you are supposed to keep food in a refrigerator."

Joshua started rummaging through the shelves. "You have mayonnaise and bread. I can make a tuna sandwich. I don't think your milk survived, though. I can have water. Do you have a can opener? No? We are going to have to go to the market anyway. We will get all of that stuff later. First, let me see your leg."

Anna sat on the bed and lifted her leg. She pulled up her pant leg over her knee and peeled off the polymer skin that covered the lower half of her leg.

Joshua looked carefully at the inner workings. "Here it is. Your leg isn't broken, but these cables have come off this gear. I can get it back on if I can figure out a way to get inside the plastic covering. Will it hurt you if I cut a small hole in the plastic?"

"I don't think so." She looked away as he pushed the sharp point of a steak knife through the plastic covering. "OK, now that you have done that, how does that get repaired? Resealed, I mean."

"I think if the cut is clean, then there are types of glue that will melt the plastic together. We can look for that at the drugstore tomorrow." Using the knife, Joshua widened the small hole in the plastic covering. Using the point of the knife, he was able to get Anna to flex her foot so that the cables were loose enough to slip them back over the gear.

She stood on the foot, and it felt good. Her foot was working again. She gave him a hug and thanked him. Then she sat back down and thanked him for trusting her enough to come at all. It did not go unnoticed that this was the first time a man had touched her gently, with caring and compassion in the way he handled her. It made her feel different, but she could not explain how. It seemed like things she had read in romance novels.

Anna grabbed her coat, and the two headed down the stairs. Joshua held the door for her, and they walked together down the street about two blocks. Fortunately, the walk wasn't far, because it was cold out, and Anna's head would start to hurt after a few minutes. She would need to ask him about that later.

They reached the deli. Joshua grabbed a basket by the door and then a six-pack of Corona, a can opener, a bag of pretzels, and some mint-flavored gum. They got to the counter, and the man asked Joshua for identification for the beer. Joshua pulled his driver's license out of his wallet.

"You too, doll. You don't look twenty-one."

Anna looked at Joshua with a "What are you thinking?" look and said, "I don't have an ID."

"Sorry." Joshua returned the six-pack of Corona and grabbed a six-pack of Sprite. He pulled out a twenty-dollar bill, took his change, and took the bag of groceries, and they left.

Joshua said, "Would you like to stroll around for a bit? You seem to spend a lot of time in your apartment."

"It sounds lovely, but I really can't."

"Why?"

"It's cold out. When I stay out in the cold too long, my head starts to hurt."

Joshua took a step back. *Oh my God, of course!* That was exactly what he had explained to Jack and Jim at the console in the facility. "OK, we'll go back to the apartment. But let me think about that for a while. I think I have an idea for how to fix that or at least make it a little easier for you."

They headed back to the apartment. Joshua was really hungry by now. He found a box of elbow macaroni and a pot. He turned on the gas burner. It obviously hadn't been used in a long time. After a minute or two, the flame burst up into the burner. He opened two cans of tuna and mixed in the mayonnaise. "Do you have any salt or pepper?"

"I don't think so. What exactly is salt and pepper?"

Joshua laughed. "Seasonings. Things you add to food to give it a better taste. It's OK; I've been eating too much salt lately anyway. It will taste fine without it." He realized he was almost talking in a foreign language with someone who had no idea what food tasted like. He popped open a can of Sprite. "Is this your first dinner in this apartment?" It was the first time he had even considered that she might have had other men in the apartment.

"Yes. You are my first guest," she said, eyeing him curiously. "No one else."

Joshua set out a single plate and a glass. "This is really weird. I'm with you but still eating alone."

"You aren't alone. I'm here, and I count."

"No, I mean I am the only one eating."

Anna sat at the other chair at the table and quietly watched him as he worked at the stove. Cooking macaroni wasn't rocket science, but he made it look like an art. After a few minutes, Joshua sat down at the table with a plateful of tuna salad and macaroni.

"OK, tell me the whole story of how you got here."

Anna smiled. "OK. Well, let's start with the incredibly long walk in the mountains in the dark." She went through the conversation at the college cafeteria and the long drive to New York. She told him about wandering the streets for three days, meeting Sophie, working at the bookshop, figuring out how to recharge her batteries, and finally tracking him down. She also told him how she knew he was being followed.

He was amazed. "How did you pull all of that off? So every night, you sleep on the pads?"

"It doesn't have to be every night. As long as I start my day with eighty percent charge, I feel pretty good all day. It surprises me sometimes as I look at other people. Some of them drag themselves through their day. If I am at a charge of sixty percent or more, I never get tired. I usually read three books each night. That has helped me learn a lot about people and how to navigate the world each day. However, I've noticed that if I encounter something that is really emotional or a really important set of events, I need to sleep. Maybe only for an hour or sometimes for several hours. Otherwise, I don't have to sleep much at all."

Joshua realized she was again describing an experience he had explained at the console in the facility. "Anna, let me tell you why I think you need to sleep."

After talking about everything over the next couple of hours, Joshua said it was time for him to leave.

"Do you really need to go?" Anna asked.

"Do you want me to stay the night?"

"That depends."

"On what?"

"Well, you responded to my message, you mistook me at the door, you went shopping with me, you had dinner with me, and we spent the evening just chatting. Did I pass your ridiculous test? That Turing test?"

"Oh my God, Anna. I am so sorry I got involved with that. It was stupid to begin with. I'm sorry."

"Well, if you hadn't, I wouldn't have met you, and I wouldn't have had this lovely evening."

"Of course," Joshua said with a smile, "there was that small part about repairing your leg. It is kind of hard to pretend that it was a human leg."

"Yeah, there was that. I would love for you to stay. You can have the bed. I can sleep on the couch downstairs in the shop. I have a new toothbrush in the bathroom with toothpaste and soap and a shower if you want," she said without any hesitation or indication that the arrangements would be otherwise.

She said, "Good night. If there is anything you need, just come down and get me. The shop doesn't open until nine. The back of the shop is very private." She went downstairs to rest on the love seat in the back of the store. She set an alarm for eight o'clock. They could get breakfast together.

At eight o'clock the next morning, Anna went upstairs to see Joshua. He was gone, and the bed was empty. There was a note on the nightstand: "Went to the market to get a coffee. Be back soon."

He came back around eight thirty with an espresso and a bag from the army surplus store.

"Where have you been?" Anna asked.

He pulled out a toasted bagel with cream cheese from one bag and set it on the table. The other bag had a knit hat and a dozen weird-looking packages. "I think this will help you with the cold." The knit hat had a face mask that could be hidden inside the hat when turned inside out. It formed a perfect pouch for the small packages. "Look at this. If you squeeze this package and break the inner seal, it will get hot in thirty seconds and stay hot for two hours. If you put it in the pouch in your hat and pull it tightly over your head, it will keep your head warm even if it's zero degrees outside."

"Wow. That is amazing. How did you figure that out?"

"Camping with the Boy Scouts."

Anna gave him a confused look. She didn't know what Boy Scouts were. After an awkward moment, she said, "Thank you so much! This is great!" and she leaned up and kissed him.

They both paused for a second. Joshua leaned into her and kissed her again, softly at first and then a little more passionately.

Anna stepped back and let out an "Oh!" with a surprised look on her face. It was as if something unexpected had happened inside her. There was an awkward moment, and then Anna said,

"Let's try this out. We'll go for that stroll you invited me to last night."

"What just happened there?"

"Nothing."

She broke open another heat pack and slipped it into the hat. She pulled the hat to her ears. It felt wonderful. It really was warm. They went out into the crisp air and strolled down Seventh Avenue on an early Saturday morning.

"How much were these? The hot packs, I mean."

"About two dollars each. I'll get you more later if you like them."

"Oh, they are perfect."

They set out to stroll through the city.

"So how do you like life in the city? I imagine it is a little different from West Virginia."

"Well, I didn't get to see much of West Virginia. The view from my room was rather limited," she said with some sarcasm.

"I guess so. So what do you like the most here?"

"Well, besides freedom, I like that everything is so convenient. I can walk down the block and pass thirty different stores. I can get almost anything. Also, it is wonderful to be out in the sunshine and fresh air. There is so much I want to do. Joshua, what is it like to go to college? I would really like to do that."

"Go to college? I don't know if I am the right one to ask. I worked hard and did well. But for me, it wasn't fun. A lot of people talk about college as the best time of their life. They live on campus in dorms and make lifelong friends. Some party a lot and join fraternities or sororities and socialize there. You seem pretty adventurous. Maybe it would be that way for you."

"I don't know. It sounds like it would be exciting. It would also help me figure out what I want to do with my life."

"You mean what you want to be when you grow up?" Joshua laughed.

"Why is that funny?"

"Because it is something that everyone asks. Some people never figure that out."

"Whatever I decide, I want to do something that will help people. If I do that, I know I will enjoy what I do."

"Your altruism amazes me."

"Well, if you are not helping somebody, what is the point? I seem to know a lot of history, but it all runs out in the very recent years. That is why I love working at the bookshop. I read three books a night, and it helps me understand the world. But there are a few things I am not quite grasping, so maybe you can enlighten me."

"Yes?"

"Climate change. What exactly is it, and why is it so hard to stop? And the pandemic. Why was it so hard to control? Ha! I would have been the only person on the planet who didn't have to worry about getting sick," she said with no attempt to hide the pride.

It was a perfect day. They returned to the apartment a little after noon. Joshua had bought a sub at the deli on the way. They sat at the kitchen table while Joshua ate his lunch. Afterward, Joshua told Anna he wanted to explain some of the things he'd learned about her from Daniel's notes. It seemed important that she know. He asked her if she wanted to hear these things.

"Go on," she said.

"Well, the first thing is about your headaches in the cold. The thing that made you such a success and a breakthrough is the material he used to make your brain. The rest may be intricate machinery, but it's nothing that didn't already exist. But he found a way to build a matrix that replaces the microchips used in a computer. It is a nanotechnology matrix that allows computer function without limitations of circuitry. The remarkable thing is that the setup of this matrix allows for clusters of information to be integrated the way a human brain integrates them. That is why, with time, you can think like a human."

She just sat there listening with a nonplussed look, as if to say, "Oh really?"

"The problem is that the gel properties can only exist in a narrow temperature range. That is why you struggle when the air gets cold. You were built to be inside a laboratory and have no mechanism to warm yourself. The hat and the heat packs can solve the problem in the short term. You should always carry extra hot packs in case you get stranded out in the cold longer than you expected or go to a place that is cold all the time. If you are too cold for too long, it will harm you, maybe permanently. Being in hotter weather does not seem to be a problem. That also explains the other thing you brought up. When you feel like you need to sleep, it is probably because your brain reorganizes when you have a big event or learn something that involves a lot of different data clusters."

Anna understood that Joshua was not trying to be condescending but was trying to explain on a granular level what he believed Anna needed to hear. Of course, he had no real sensitivity to how he was coming across. He was just being Joshua. "There is one other thing," Anna said quietly.

"What's that?"

"This is hard for me to talk about. I was reading a book from the shop titled *Fifty Shades of Grey*. It has graphic descriptions of humans doing things to each other that cause them to feel a lot of pleasure. Sometimes as I tried to imagine what they were doing, I would get a strange feeling inside me. I don't understand it."

"Yes. Daniel said to me that he put a different type of sensor inside you. He called them pleasure sensors. His notes talk about taking the experience of pleasure from each of the data clusters in your memory and connecting them to a central cluster to get a feeling of whole-body pleasure if those sensors were stimulated. Apparently, that stimulation can come internally from thoughts or externally from physical touching. I am still not completely sure how that works."

She did not understand what he was talking about but was not comfortable in continuing the conversation. She moved on to another subject.

Throughout the day, Joshua kept looking at Anna. It was easy to talk to her. He had been alone for so long. He just wasn't able to connect with women. His heart had been broken before. At twenty-seven, it was easier to be alone than to deal with the stress of dating and the hurt of the failures. But this was different. She was beautiful, pleasant, and amazing. That was the only word that seemed to begin to capture it. And she seemed to care about him.

On Sunday morning, after breakfast, Joshua said it was time for him to head back to his apartment to do some of the things he had planned to do over the weekend. They hugged at the doorway at the top of the stairs. It was a passionate embrace. They locked eyes. He kissed her softly again. Then he kissed her passionately. Daniel had seemed to work his greatest magic in designing her face. He'd designed it with such precision and perfection that Joshua could not tell he wasn't kissing another human. He gave her another squeeze and left.

Anna watched him go down the stairs and out the door. A pang of loneliness washed over her that seemed to sadden her for the rest of the day.

Chapter 16

About ten o'clock that evening, the Tracfone rang. Anna jumped. Why would that phone ring? The only one with the number was Joshua. She went over to the counter and picked up the phone. Cautiously, she said, "Hello?"

The other voice said quietly, "Hi, Anna. It's Joshua. I missed you, so I thought I would call. You said that only I had this number. So I wanted to call just to say good night. I had a great weekend."

Anna sat back down on the bed. "Hi, Joshua. I don't know why I didn't realize it was you right away. Yes, no one else has this number. It really is nice to hear from you. I had a great weekend also."

They chatted for a few minutes, and Joshua said good night. The call was over in five minutes, but Anna thought about it for hours. This was some kind of new feeling. How was he affecting her this way? Back at the facility, she had encouraged him because she wanted a friend. Maybe one would even have called it flirting. But now it was more than that. How he felt about her was important. She was nervous about whether he could change his mind and lose interest.

She always slept naked. It was easier to put the electric pads on that way. When she was ready for bed, she sat on the bed and looked in the mirror. She remembered the underwear she had bought. She never had understood the point of it. Now, in front of the mirror, she put it on and stared at herself for a while. The underwear somehow made her look more fashionable and even more attractive. Her breasts were more shaped like those of models in pictures. The underwear concealed her private parts. Obviously, her jeans and shirts did also. But this seemed to look better. She studied the curves and contours of her body. She looked at the features of her face. Was she pretty? She knew that Joshua was attracted to her. How could she keep his interest? What made a man want to be attracted to a woman? She had no idea. The whole idea of it was silly, but now it really mattered.

Also, she did not know what he had meant by Daniel's placing pleasure sensors inside her. Her thoughts of Daniel were generally dark and negative. The idea that he had put something unusual inside her disgusted her. Why would he have done that? What did the sensors do? What was their purpose for an artificially intelligent machine? She had spent the last month trying to learn how to be a person. That had proven difficult enough. There was more than that. This was the first time she'd thought there were different kinds of people—well, two kinds, basically: women and men. Now she had to learn to be not just a person but also a woman. It was confusing.

She lay back on the bed. She began to explore all the contours of her body. She rubbed lotion on her polymer skin every day. It felt soft and supple. It gave her a pleasant fragrance, or so the people around her said. The sensors throughout her body were fairly uniform in how they felt when they were stimulated. She felt light touch and strong touch. She felt heat and cold. She felt vibration. This was true everywhere.

She continued to explore the areas in which she felt the tingling when she thought of Joshua kissing her. She found the place where the pleasure sensors were located. She pressed them lightly. The sensation felt different. Somehow, she felt it everywhere, not just where she was touching. She closed her eyes.

She felt as if she were floating. Everything seemed to feel better. All her stress left her. This was all new.

After several minutes, she started to feel exhausted. She needed to sleep. She could tell the difference between the sleep when she just needed to rest and the sleep when her mind was reorganizing. This was definitely reorganizing. She drifted off until the next morning, when the alarm woke her up at 8:00 a.m.

She explored her pleasure sensors two more times in the evenings that week. Each time, the feelings were the same, and the need for a reorganizing sleep followed. The difference was it seemed to involve more and more sensors, and the pleasure feeling seemed to be getting more intense. It seemed to be feeling more natural. Was this part of becoming a woman?

Joshua called around the same time two nights later. Again, they chatted for a few minutes, and he said good night. Before he hung up, he asked if he could come back next weekend. Anna said she would be delighted for him to come visit again, so the plans were made. She said she would call him the day before to give him a new set of instructions so he would not be followed.

Chapter 17

Several days after their lunch meeting, Bernie called Jim. He had arranged for a team of people to follow Joshua for twenty-four hours a day. There had been nothing unusual until last Friday after work. Apparently, he had picked up a bag on a park bench in Central Park with an untraceable phone inside. "He got instructions from someone—we don't know who—and changed trains on the way home. He did it in a way that suggested he knew he was being followed. Anyway, he disappeared for the weekend. We don't know where he went. He returned back to his apartment on Sunday afternoon."

"What do you think he did?" asked Jim.

"My guess is that he went to see the subject, unless you have a better hunch."

"Maybe I can talk to him later today to see what he will tell me."

"Let's coordinate, Jim. You ask to meet him at two o'clock for an update or something. I will send one of my team to plant a homing device in his coat. He will never know it is there. At least we will be able to track his movements if we can't follow him in person. This will get us within a hundred feet of wherever the subject is located. Maybe from there, we can stake the place out, or we can get Joshua to help us."

"OK, I'll get my assistant to send him an email invitation to a meeting with me. You will have thirty minutes to get this done."

Bernie approached the reception desk and asked for a pass to see Jim. The receptionist gave him a pass and directions to Jim's office. Bernie took a detour at the fifth floor and went to Joshua's office. It had been left unlocked. Bernie looked around. Joshua had left his jacket hanging on the back of his chair.

Bernie felt around in the pockets. He didn't find much, just an unused tissue. That was a good sign. Joshua did not take a lot of stuff in and out of his pocket. That made it less likely he would find the tracking device. It was a disk about half an inch in diameter. With an adhesive on one side, it would stick to the fabric inside his pocket. If Joshua put his hand in his pocket the way a person normally did, he would not feel it. He would find it only if someone actually felt through the whole pocket from top to bottom. It fastened to the inside lining of his pocket, in the upper corner, under the pocket seam. It took less than a minute for Bernie to secure it.

Within another five minutes, Bernie was down the elevator and out the door.

Chapter 18

Anna left the downstairs door unlocked for Joshua a few minutes before she expected him to arrive. When she heard the door at the street, she unlocked the upper door and pulled it open. She was excited to see him. He sauntered up the stairs and got to the landing.

She threw her arms around him and kissed him. "Come on in. I have been trying to learn to cook. I made dinner for you. It will be ready in a few minutes."

"Wow. This smells amazing, Anna. What is it?"

"I am learning to make goulash. I found a recipe book in the shop. I have made up my mind to learn one new recipe each week. So you have to come over each week to be my guinea pig."

"That sounds wonderful."

She returned to the stove to keep working on her creation. Joshua took off his jacket and shoes.

"Long day at the office, dear?" Anna asked.

"Yeah. Still looking over Daniel's data. My Lord, there must be a thousand pages of notes."

"Let me know if there is anything interesting about me," she said in a serious voice.

"It seems that it is all about you." Joshua sat quietly for a few minutes at the table. He then got up and grabbed a plate, silverware, and a glass.

He went for a can of Sprite, and Anna said, "Wait. I have a bottle of wine. Sophie got it as a gift and she doesn't drink, so she gave it to me. It is red. It will go with the goulash."

"Wow, you really went all out. I guess you really like me." He kissed the back of her neck from behind while she stood at the stove. He loved her fragrance. Her skin carried one aroma, and her hair carried another.

"I do. Really," she said.

She served dinner, and they talked about their days, the weather, work, and what they would like to do that night or tomorrow. A couple of hours passed instantly.

Anna waited until Joshua had finished about half the bottle of wine and then said in a quiet voice, "I want to show you something." She led him over to the bed.

In almost a whisper, she said, "I found where the pleasure sensors are. The ones you were talking about last weekend." In a moment, she took off her clothes and took his hand. She quietly guided his hand to where the sensors were located. She pressed his hand to the spot she had found and moved his hand in the motion that felt the most intense. He got the idea and continued to do that while she lay back on the bed.

It felt wonderful at first, as it had when she had done it to herself. But it was different in that someone else was doing it. Someone she was really attracted to and who was attracted to her. Someone who made her feel wonderful when he kissed her. This seemed to intensify how it felt.

After a few minutes, it seemed to change. She seemed to be falling into a sea of euphoria. All at once, she let out what sounded like a squeak, and she squeezed Joshua's arm with both hands. All of her sensors fired at the same time. It was overwhelming, with wave after wave of the intense sensation. She couldn't move, hear, or speak as all fifteen thousand of her sensors seemed to fire at once. Her eyes were closed, but she saw a thousand little stars. All she could do was simply wait for it to be over, while not wanting it to ever stop. It might have lasted seconds or several minutes; Anna didn't know. The feeling slowly started to subside, and the world returned.

The first thing she saw was Joshua's face. "Hold me," she said, almost pleading. She turned over, facing away from him; snuggled her back as deeply as she could into his chest; hooked both of his elbows with hers; and held his hands.

"Are you OK?" Joshua asked.

"Yes," she said quietly. "Joshua?"

"Yes?"

"Is this what it feels like to fall in love?"

"I don't know. I have never done it before."

"Promise me you will never do what you just did with me with any other woman. Ever."

"I promise."

With that, she pulled him tighter and drifted off to sleep.

Joshua stared at her flowing hair. His mind started racing. She was beautiful. She looked like an angel. *What part of this isn't human?* He wanted to hold her and let time stand still. She needed him in many ways.

Then his heart started to pound. *Wait a minute. Is this the person I want to be with forever? She certainly is thinking that way. We are so different. I mean, really, however much I care about her, could it ever really work? Like having dinner with her tonight but always eating alone. For the rest of my life, I would be explaining why she is different or keeping it a secret. We would never have children. What if she started to degrade because of some flaw, or worse, what if she was perfect and never aged, while I got old? Would she always be interested in me if there were many other men who were better looking or more interesting? I hardly know her. Is she asking for a commitment so early in the relationship? We will have to talk tomorrow, but I don't know how to even broach the subject without hurting her or driving her away. I have been such a loser with women, and I really like this girl. I don't know what to do.* His thoughts kept running in circles and, in the end, left him nowhere. Finally, with exhaustion, he fell asleep with his arms still around her.

Anna woke up the next morning while Joshua was still sleeping. For several minutes, she simply stared at his peaceful face. She was excited to be with him. Last night had been amazing— no, more than amazing. She didn't have a word for it. She wanted to wake him just to do it again. He started to stir. She stroked the hair on his forehead away from his eyes. "Good morning, sweetheart," she whispered.

"Good morning," he replied, starting to come to life. "I really slept hard. How are you today?"

"Wonderful. Are you hungry for breakfast?"

"Maybe a little. I'm sure I will be soon."

Then she had a serious expression on her face. She said quietly, as if she were about to say something naughty, "Joshua, I have read a lot of romance novels. I know that men also experience something like what happened to me last night. I want to do that with you." She had his attention.

"Really?"

"Yes, let's do it now. I want you to be happy with me."

Joshua got up and took off his clothes. He stood next to the bed naked.

Anna looked at him with an innocent and clueless face and said, "OK, so what happens now?"

After they both dressed and started breakfast, Joshua sat quietly. He was deep in thought.

Anna felt playful as she described the omelet she was making as her recipe of the next week. She finally presented it and proudly pronounced its arrival. "Here it is!" She slipped the plate in front of him. It was a work of art. It was garnished with parsley and had an amazing onion-and-pepper smell.

"Thank you, Anna. Once again, you have outdone yourself." It was delicious. After a few minutes, he started to again realize he was eating alone and grew quiet.

Anna sensed his unrest and asked, "What is wrong?"

Joshua, knowing Anna could read expressions and would not miss his having troublesome thoughts, had used that to get her to open the conversation.

"I have been thinking a lot about last night and this morning. Anna, it was incredible. I have never had a steady girlfriend before, and I have never had an intimate relationship before. So this is a first for me. Let me be clear about this. I only want to be with you. But I have always believed there are two phases of a relationship. The first is where you date and get to know someone. You do a lot of talking and listening. You do a lot of things together. There is a lot of sex. It is fun. This is where people figure out if they are a fit. If it turns out there are things that don't work, they talk it through before there is any long-term commitment. They try to accommodate and compromise. If it doesn't work at all, they will break up before there are children or other long-term ties that are painful to resolve. What do you think?"

Anna was taken aback. "I thought you and I would be together. It doesn't matter to me what your flaws or strengths are; I would accept all of them. I had a moment of intimacy where nothing in the world existed except you. In that moment, I trusted you with all my heart. I know that only five weeks ago, you saw me in my skinless form and thought I didn't have a heart. I think you are still struggling with that. I just can't imagine myself being with anyone else but you." She sat in the chair, looking obviously deflated. *What does it mean to share your most private moments or to trust someone with all your secrets? Can you do that and still not be sure this is the person you want to be with?*

The room became uncomfortable. After he finished his breakfast, Anna said, "Maybe you should just go home now."

"Do you really mean that?" Joshua could see the hurt on her face. "Anna, I'm sorry. I didn't mean to hurt you."

"I know. You just said what you were thinking." Another long silence followed.

Joshua took his coat and left. He thought to himself, *I am such a loser with women.*

Joshua got halfway down the stairs, when he put his hands in his coat pockets. He felt something odd in the left pocket. He stopped at the bottom of the stairs and focused on it. He turned his pocket inside out so he could see what it was. It was a postage-stamp-sized patch of cloth with a button of some sort inside. As he tweezed apart the cloth, he could see it was some type of electronic device. He stared at it for several minutes, and all of a sudden, it became clear to him: it was a tracking device, and someone was not only following him but also tracking his location. Should he tell Anna? At first, he didn't want to because of the scene he had just caused. After a minute of consideration, he realized this was about her, not him. He went back up the stairs and knocked on the door.

She answered the door and opened it just a crack. She stared at him for a minute, threw the door open, and grabbed him. She buried her head in his shoulder. "I'm sorry," she said.

If Joshua hadn't known better, he would have sworn she was sobbing. "Look, I am new at this relationship stuff. I am not sure how this game is played. I just know that I feel terrible if I hurt you." He wrapped his arms around her and squeezed her.

"It still feels bad. We can pick this conversation up later," she said.

"Anna, listen to me. I was halfway out the door, and I discovered this." He showed her the small electronic thing. "This is a tracking device. Someone is not only following me but tracking me as well. I think you were so successful in fooling the people following me that they put this in my jacket pocket. I am guessing Jim had something to do with this because the only time I was without my jacket was during a meeting with him. This means you have to be extra careful because they may know where you live now."

"I expected this would happen sooner or later. I will just have to deal."

Chapter 19

Barry got another call from Nick. Nick told him, "Jim has hired Bernie's firm to find the subject. He has been able to put a tail on Joshua and found a location within one hundred feet of where the subject is. I will pass that information over to you by text. If you can set up a stakeout of your team, you should be able to find her before Bernie does." Nick sent over a text identifying the location as somewhere on the 2100 block off Seventh Avenue, most likely on the west side of the street.

Barry then got on the phone with the lead man on his team. "Nick just called to give me information on the subject's location."

The voice on the other end said, "That is great, but it is unnecessary. We put a bug in his briefcase, his coat, and his scarf. Apparently, he has left his scarf in his office on the coatrack or something. Not only can we hear all of the conversations in his office, but sometimes, if his door is open, we can hear the conversations in the offices on either side of him. We already knew what he just texted you."

"So what is the plan?"

"We will do a standard snatch-and-grab. She is small, so we should be able to grab her and throw her into the back of the van. If we are quick and on target, we should be able to get out of there without too much of an issue with witnesses. I think the whole operation should take thirty to forty seconds at the most."

"That is great. You guys stay on top of this, and keep me informed the minute you learn something important."

"Yes, boss."

Chapter 20

A few days later, Barry met with his team. "This is what we know. She looks like this." The photographs were distributed. "As you know, we have a high degree of certainty that she is on the twenty-first block at Seventh Avenue in Manhattan."

After a few minutes of review, one of the men shook his head and said, "Boss, there could be one hundred girls who look like this. We have to be completely certain we have the right one. How do we do that?" There was a silence around the room.

"The plan was to use four facial-recognition cameras to find her."

"That could work, but there are so many similarities to other people, and the face recognition is limited to the quality of these photographs. I am not convinced we can be sure enough to do this. If we grab the wrong person, it could be a disaster."

Barry gave a sigh and a disappointed look. He was right.

"OK, tell us more about the way this machine works."

"I don't know any more than I have already told you."

"Does this lady have a heating mechanism? How does she keep warm? Or does she have to keep warm? And at what temperature?"

Barry got Nick on the phone. "Does this robot operate at any specific temperature?"

Nick answered, "No. She operates at room temperature. She actually generates very little heat on her own."

"Thank you. That is what we needed to know."

Collectively, they looked at Barry. One asked, "Do we have an infrared heat-sensing scanner? The kind they used during the pandemic that can read a crowd from a distance?"

"I can get one. We can scan the whole crowd, and she will light right up. This will be easy."

Chapter 21

It was five thirty on Monday afternoon, and Sophie was getting ready to leave and turn the shop over to the night crew. Anna asked her if she had a few minutes to talk. Sophie smiled and said, "Of course, dear."

Anna invited Sophie up to the apartment.

Sophie said, "I see you have made yourself at home. It all looks very nice."

"Can I get you something to drink? Maybe some coffee?"

"Sure, maybe a small cup. I have a dinner already made at home."

Anna handed Sophie a mug half filled with coffee. "Do you want it black?"

"Black is fine."

"Sophie, I wanted to ask you about a guy. This boy I'm seeing. I think I am in love with him, but I am not sure if he loves me. I want him to be attracted to me and interested in me. I don't know what I have to do to get him to love me."

"Dear child, first of all, there is not a girl alive who hasn't gone through the same feelings you are right now. It is your age. Everything with boys is so new and always so urgent. It is hard to think straight."

"You are so right. None of this makes any sense to me."

"Anna, listen to me. Your problem is not whether you can make this boy attracted to you. Your problem is that you are asking the wrong question."

"What do you mean?"

"The real question is, who is Anna Conners? Who are you? What is important to you? What do you want to do with your life? What are your core beliefs? You are still a young girl. You have not quite become the person you were meant to be. Are you going to college to be a professional? Are you going to spend your life helping others?"

Anna just listened.

"Anna, I knew from the moment you walked through the shop door that you were an undocumented immigrant. You looked like one of those children who came home from school to find your parents taken away by ICE officials. You came into the shop with no possessions or money. That is the only way that happens. I don't know what the relationship was with your father or if any of your story was true, but you needed a place to land for a while. You needed some space and time to regain your footing in life. You are one of the best employees I have ever had. You must have finished high school or close to it, because you are so well educated. You are a hard worker. You are reliable, honest, and caring. If you are given a chance, you can go on to do great things. You are a strong woman. The only way you will ever find lasting love with a boy is to love yourself. The peace from being happy with yourself gives you the foundation to properly love another. Once you have achieved that, your partner, whether it is this guy or the next, will fall in love with Anna the person, not Anna the pretty girl." Sophie paused to sip her coffee.

Anna took in what Sophie was saying. She sat quietly with a pensive look on her face. "I think I understand."

"Look, when George and I fell in love, it felt like all my prayers were answered. He was such a wonderful man. We dated for almost four years, and every day was more wonderful than the one before. When we married, though, it wasn't so easy. Money, loss of loved ones, wanting different things in life—all of it made for some difficult years. But I always felt he loved me for who I was, including my flaws and strengths. He understood them, and we compromised. When he died, I lost my best friend as well as my life partner. On the other side of the equation, while we were married, there were some things he did and others I did to survive day to day. When he was gone, I had to do everything for myself. That was the day I truly became the woman I was supposed to be. I had some life insurance money. Instead of retreating into a quiet life, I invested it into this business. I worked hard and grew it into this. I am proud of it, and I love what I do. I would have never had this experience if I didn't believe in myself. I don't need a man to make me feel whole.

"Anna, this man can't fall in love with you until you reach the point in your life where you are truly at peace with yourself. First, because he won't really have a person to fall in love with. If you are changing, as you certainly will be, you will be a moving target for him. Second, life is hard enough. You have to be able to support each other. That means you have to come from a position of strength. You can't do this until you have solved the problems that led you here, whatever they are."

After a long silence, Anna said, "Thank you, Sophie. I think I get what you are saying. It sounds like the story about Pinocchio, except for the nose thing."

Sophie had a confused look on her face.

Anna continued. "He was just a wooden puppet as long as he was selfish and fixated on doing things only for himself. He was easily distracted by the villains of the story. Once he understood what was really important, like caring about his family and directing his talents toward saving them from the large whale, he became the person he was meant to be, a real boy. The fairy was just a prop the author used to make the story work."

Sophie smiled a curious smile. "I have never heard that story interpreted that way, but OK, if that is how you see it."

Anna continued. "What you said was certainly a different way of looking at my life. One I never even considered. You have been such a good friend to me. I don't know how I will ever be able to truly thank you."

"Anna, you thank me by building a good life for yourself and being happy. Then I will have my return on investment. I will miss you when you go, but you are destined to do so much more than be a clerk in a bookshop. You need to spread your wings and fly." With that, she stood up, thanked Anna for the coffee, and left.

Chapter 22

It was a beautiful Tuesday when Anna stepped outside and closed the door at the bottom of the stairs. She turned the bolt to lock it securely. She started up the street toward the market. She had yet to get her checkered sneakers.

A black van pulled up near the curb, and a man opened the door to the back. Two men approached her from different directions, and each one grabbed one of her shoulders. Another person slipped a black hood over her head from behind.

Anna panicked for a second. Then her logical side took over, and her thoughts became calm and crystal clear. She remembered she had a gun under her dress, strapped to her left thigh. What good was it now? She couldn't get to it. She grabbed the gun, still in its holster, through her dress; found the trigger; and squeezed as hard and fast as she could. The shots popped off, one and then a second.

The hands holding her froze. No one could tell where the shots were coming from. She was trying to twist her body left, and the third shot hit one of the men in the ankle, shattering it. He screamed and fell to the ground. The next shot hit the pavement, and the fifth one hit another of the men in the foot, taking off his little toe. The next bullet ricocheted off the pavement and ripped into a third man's calf. She changed her voice to sound like a computer voice. As loudly as she could, she said, "Arming C-4 self-destruct. Ten. Nine. Eight."

All of the hands let go. She tore off the black hood to see two men jump into the van while the other three men limped, crawled, and hobbled into the back of the van. The last one, the one who'd put the hood over her, yelled to the others, "Guys, she is armed! She is going to blow herself up!" The black van sped away with doors slamming and squealing tires.

Anna just stared at the disappearing van, holding the black hood in her hands. She had just saved herself from a disaster. *Why? What just happened? Who would do this?* Had she really just fired a half dozen bullets from her firearm with the intention of hurting people? Could Logicsolutions really have gone to this length to get her?

She turned and unlocked the door she had just locked five minutes ago, bolted it again, and went back up the stairs. She sat down gently on the bed. Anger, fear, and confusion all hit her at once. She grabbed her knees and rocked gently on the bed. She was upset and had no way to express it. She wanted to call Joshua, but she wasn't sure she wanted to share this with him, at least not now anyway.

She needed to figure out a way to get some protection. She needed help from someone else. She was clearly in over her head. She decided to turn to a professional for help. Her private world had been penetrated and violated. She needed to find a way to have some kind of leverage because she knew it would happen again. Next time, she might not be able to get away. All of a sudden, she needed to sleep.

The driver of the black van went directly to an emergency room a few miles out of the city, on Long Island. It was a small community hospital where the driver knew the doctor on staff at the emergency room.

After about four hours, the three injured men hobbled, with two on crutches, into the van. One would need reconstructive surgery on his ankle. The second would need about eight weeks for the amputated toe to heal. The third would need physical therapy after his stitches were removed.

The emergency room doctor pulled the man aside. "I am supposed to report all gunshot wounds to the police. You know that. How is it that you bring three of them in at the same time?"

The driver of the van handed the doctor a bundle of fifty one-hundred-dollar bills. He smiled and said, "Your discretion is appreciated."

Later that night, the driver of the van, who was the leader of the team, was at Barry Stiles's house. "Boss, we were set up. Yes, the subject was a small female. But she was armed with a handgun hidden somewhere. I have been around firearms all my life, and I am certain she was shooting at us with a .38. I couldn't tell you where it was coming from. Maybe from her wrist, like Spider-Man. We had a hood over her and caught her by complete surprise. There was no weapon in her hands. Beyond that, she is a robot, as you described, and she has a self-destruct program with C-4 planted somewhere in her body. Daniel must have anticipated that someone might try to steal her, so he gave her a doomsday option to keep her secrets. You were played. You gave this guy one million dollars, and you cannot get the goods, even when you have five men pulling off a perfect operation."

Chapter 23

The executive team met in the seventh-floor boardroom at 2:00 p.m. sharp. Everyone who needed to be there was there, except Nick, including Jim Mendola, Jack Cobb, and Laura and Samantha from the venture capital firm. An agenda was passed out to all at the table.

"Let's get to the most important item on the agenda," Jim said. "We have located Anna within a hundred-foot circle. It will only be a few days more before we find her. She is somewhere on the 2100 block of Seventh Avenue. She has not failed as a machine, so apparently, she found a solution to the temperature challenge and to replenishing her batteries. Apparently, according to police reports, there was an attempted kidnapping on that same block. Eyewitnesses gave descriptions of the event to the police. There were no clear descriptions of the person they were trying to take, except that it was a woman. They put a black hood over her head. That kept a lot of people from identifying her. After she pulled the hood off, a few of the witnesses described a girl who vaguely matches what we have in the video of Anna. The descriptions of the men involved and the van that was part of the operation were pretty clear. Shots were fired. Apparently, several of the assailants were wounded. We don't know if they are related to anything that has to do with Anna, but we need to close this as soon as possible. That is all I have at the moment."

Samantha from the venture capital company asked, "If gunshots were fired, how vulnerable is a robot to gunshots?"

"I don't know. I understand what makes her so sophisticated is her brain and its function. The rest of her is cables, gears, joints, and wires. I suppose she could be shot and simply repaired."

The rest of the agenda was perfunctory. No one remembered any of it after they left the room. They thought only of how quickly they could capture Anna.

Chapter 24

Nick was expecting it to be a great day. He was sure of himself that day. He believed the capture was going to happen that morning, and Barry would have his prize. He felt comfortable depositing the cashier's check in the bank. He was going to put it in the company account as an outside payment, a payment he could argue had been lost through bad bookkeeping. Maybe this plan would work. He knew that once he did this, the money was irretrievable. He was counting on this money to get him off the hook with his company and on the remaining million to carry him through his retirement. Things were looking better now.

Nick's phone rang. He recognized the number because it was the third time Barry had called him. "Nick, we have a problem. Meet with me at seven o'clock tonight at my office."

Nick could not imagine what could be the problem. He felt a sick feeling because it must have been something bad. He had been having a good day, and now it wasn't looking so good.

At seven o'clock sharp, he rolled into a parking space in the AJX Enterprises parking garage. Barry met him at the door and let him in. They went to Barry's private office on the first floor. It felt odd that there appeared to be no one else in the building.

Nick sat down across from Barry. Barry opened the conversation by asking if he had heard about the capture attempt yesterday. Nick said no. He wasn't aware of anything that had happened earlier.

"My team tried to capture Anna. We used infrared technology to find her, and we nailed it. She was the only one on Seventh Avenue with a temperature in the high seventies and was still walking around, so we know we had the right person. The snatch-and-grab went as planned in the beginning. We found her, hooded her, and had the van in position. OK so far?"

"Yeah."

"Then the surprise."

"What do you mean?"

"She started shooting at us. She wounded three of the men on our team. We spent four hours in the emergency room to repair a shattered ankle, a lost toe, and a torn calf. Did you forget to tell us something, Nick?"

"What? There was nothing in the notes about her having a gun. I had no idea. Where would she have it?"

"It wasn't visible. The guys think it was planted in her forearm and used kind of like the way Spider-Man spins his web. It doesn't matter. The kicker is that she has a self-destruct weapon. Daniel must have wanted to protect her from being captured, because she apparently has a charge of C-4 inside her that she can detonate when she feels she needs to. She is an armed fortress. We can't catch her." Barry paused for a moment. "This changes things, Nick. The deal is off. I hope you haven't cashed the check yet, because you are going to have to give it back."

Nick swallowed hard. "I will need some time to get you the money. I deposited the check."

"Fair enough," Barry said. "I will give you twenty-four hours. Seven thirty Thursday night. You are going to show up here with a cashier's check for one million dollars. Don't fail me. Friendships are great, but if you screw me, there won't be a second chance. I hope I have made myself clear."

Nick knew Barry would have eaten his children before he let someone take advantage of him. "I understand."

Chapter 25

Anna asked Sophie if she could use her computer for a few minutes. She had no idea how this was going to work. She didn't even know what to ask for. She typed "women's attorneys" in the browser space. The page filled with attorney names and pictures. She figured a female attorney would be more likely to understand her situation. Anna wondered if she could even explain her situation. She did not completely understand it herself.

How do you choose? She looked at the faces. One smaller ad toward the bottom of the page struck her as a more understanding face. She said her name, Gloria Rogers, out loud and called her on her Tracfone to make an appointment.

"Gloria Rogers's law office. May I help you?"

"I would like to make an appointment with Ms. Rogers."

"Is this regarding a legal matter?"

"Yes, I would like to see if she can help me."

"I have tomorrow at three open."

"Fine. I will see her then."

The next day, Anna took a late lunch break. She gathered her money. She had several hundred dollars in her drawer upstairs. She tucked the cash in her purse and cautiously made her way down the street. She looked over her shoulder and in every corner around her.

The office was about a twenty-minute walk across town. Anna entered the building, and there were several offices on the first floor. She found the marquee with the name on each suite. Gloria Rogers, Esquire, was in suite 102.

Anna knocked lightly and entered. "Anna Conners to see Ms. Rogers."

"Have a seat, and she will be right with you."

Anna sat for a few minutes. She picked up a magazine and glanced through it.

After about ten minutes, a fortyish woman with blonde hair and blue eyes, wearing a professional-looking suit, came out to greet her. "How do you do? I am Gloria Rogers. You must be Anna Conners. Please come on in. Have a seat over there." Gloria sat behind an absurdly large desk.

"Yes, I am Anna. I am going to tell you up front that my situation is quite different from what you are used to hearing. I need for you to know that everything I am going to tell you is the truth, even if it seems impossible at first. So I have to ask you to hear me out. I am happy to pay you for an hour of your time if you will promise to hear my whole story." Anna reached into her purse to pull out her money.

"Hold on to your money for a moment. Tell me the short version, and we can go from there."

"Everything I say here is confidential, right?"

"Yes, you are going to pay me, so we have an attorney–client relationship. If I choose not to take your case, I will tell you, but this conversation is protected."

"OK." She paused for a moment to gather her courage. "I committed a murder. No one knows that yet. It becomes important if I choose to confess."

Her statement caused Gloria to sit forward in her chair. This seemed to be interesting.

"I am from a research facility, and I have information that is extremely valuable. I believe the company that owns the research facility is hunting for me. I am afraid of what they may do to me if they catch me. The man I killed is someone I worked with who clearly was trying to kill me at the time. I acted in self-defense. Does my story make sense so far?"

Gloria nodded. "I am with you so far," she said, thinking, *This can't get much weirder.*

"This is the hardest part to tell you. This research facility was devoted to creating beings with artificial intelligence. That is, they were working to create human-looking machines. These machines have humanlike qualities that evolve to be more human over time. I am one of those machines."

"I don't understand."

"I am not human. I am a machine." With that, she pulled up her shirt and peeled a large piece of polymer skin off her belly, revealing the clear plastic sheath and the mechanisms underneath.

Gloria put her hand to her mouth and let out a small gasp. "Wait a minute. You aren't a real person?"

"I have a brain that works like a human brain, but the rest of me is only cables, gears, and motors. I have only been in New York for a little more than a month. I have no family. I don't know where to turn or what to do," Anna said in almost a whiney voice. "I don't even know if artificially intelligent beings have any legal rights. I can assure you I am a person in every way. Has there been a moment since I walked in the door that you didn't think I was human?" There was a clear desperation in her voice.

Gloria said, "How is that possible?"

"Apparently, forty million dollars can buy you a whole lot of technology. It is possible, and you are looking at it."

"Tell me more," Gloria said, now completely intrigued.

Anna laid it all out. There was no point in keeping anything a secret. Either she trusted her, or she didn't. She told her how prototypes were destroyed as each new one was built and told her about the murder, the escape, her job at the bookstore, Joshua and how she felt about him, and the kidnapping attempt. Finally, she told her she was worried the people around her could be in danger.

Gloria leaned back in her chair. "You are right. I have never heard of anything like this before. The law has never considered the question of whether a machine can be a person. As a person, you certainly are entitled to defend yourself against someone who is clearly trying to hurt you. We handle domestic violence all the time. I do not defend murder cases. I would send you somewhere else for that. Tell me—why do you think someone wants to get you so badly?"

"I think it is because a large amount of money was spent in the research to build me, and they think they are protecting their investment if they can put me back in the glass prison I was in before."

"So they are not trying to kill you but to capture you?"

"Yes. But I would rather die than be a prisoner again. I have lived a happy life for this last month. I like where I work and live. I like the lady I work for. I am in love with my boyfriend. Ms. Rogers, I would rather go to jail for a crime than allow myself to be captured and live in a glass cage as a specimen in a research facility."

"I understand what you are saying. Anna, you don't have any legal papers, do you? Things like a birth certificate, baptismal certificate, Social Security card, or driver's license?"

"No."

"OK, Anna. I will take your case. Give the office manager, the woman who greeted you, a five-hundred-dollar retainer. I will get to work on this case. Let's meet again the day after tomorrow at the same time, and we can talk about what to do next."

Chapter 26

Anna looked over her roster of customers for the computer textbook service. She did so regularly so she could report to Sophie how her little corner of the shop was doing. She noticed that one of the subscribers was a Stefani Mendola. Anna wondered almost out loud whether she might be related to Jim Mendola, the chief operating officer at Logicsolutions.

Later that day, a dark-haired woman who appeared to be in her early twenties showed up at the front desk. Anna watched as the young woman signed in, as she usually did to try to get to know the customers who used the computer stations. It seemed that since she was in charge of the stations, a friendly presence helped the people who used the stations feel comfortable and refer their friends. Sometimes there was even some free tutoring. Business was up by about 40 percent since Anna had started working there. This time, the signature read, "Stefani Mendola." The subscriber number matched.

"Hi. I am Anna. Is there anything I can help you with today? I see you signed in to use a computer station, and I oversee the department."

"No, I am just here to survive calculus." Stefani made a face.

Anna laughed. "Maybe I can help you with that. I do know a thing or two about calculus." Anna's original upload included all levels of math and science. The classwork would be easy for her.

"Please forgive me for asking, but are you related to Mr. Mendola at Logicsolutions? I used to work there."

Stefani's expression immediately told Anna that was not a good topic to broach.

"Oh, I am so sorry. I did not mean to ask a personal question."

"I am his daughter, but we haven't spoken for a while."

"I'll tell you what. I am new in town. You look like you are about my age. If you aren't in a terrible hurry, I will treat for coffee and a snack if you want to sit and chat for a few minutes."

She smiled. "Actually, I really am starving. Sure, why not?"

Anna brought her a cup of coffee and a granola bar. "I just got into town about a month ago. I am originally from West Virginia. I would like to go to college here someday. Right now, I am trying to save up some money."

"I am over at the university, trying to get a degree in business. I don't know why they are making us take calculus. I expect to graduate in a year and a half. Hey, this coffee is good." She took another sip.

"So what happened between you and your dad that you haven't spoken in a while?"

"When I was twelve, he and my mother divorced. It had been coming for some time because he was never around. Birthdays, special events, Girl Scouts—you name it, and he missed it. I was angry about that. When my mom and he used to fight over it, he really wouldn't hear what she was saying, and he just continued to work eighty hours a week. His tone-deaf reaction to my mom until she wanted to leave him was what made me so unforgiving. My world was being crushed, and he didn't care. It turned out life went on. My mother and I grew really close, and I shut him out. I know he has tried to reach out to me, and I have thought about talking to him, but I am just not there yet."

Anna said, "I never had a father or a mother. I never will. So many times, I have envied other people who have parents. They have a resource. They have people who love them unconditionally.

I know some relationships are better than others. Still, it is such a wonderful thing to have someone who cares. If your father is still trying to reach out to you, then he still cares."

Stefani was listening.

"Stefani, what would happen to you if your father wasn't there all of a sudden? Would it change your life?"

"I don't know. I have never thought about that. I guess it would change in some ways. It would be harder on my mom because his money wouldn't be there."

"I wasn't getting at the money. You have the freedom to punish him because you know he has always been there. It feels to you like he will always be there. But you know that he won't. I can tell you that when he is not there, there is no one—no forgiveness and no second chance."

Stefani pondered her words for a few minutes. "I have never really thought about my dad not being there to be mad at. I mean, I still love him and all, but I am just mad at him. He should have never left us like that."

"What if he just didn't understand? What if he thought the way to be a man was to make as much money as possible? What if he measured his masculinity by how hard he worked to provide for his family? What if the things he did were because of his believing that was who he was meant to be? Would you still think of his behavior as bad? Would it still be something you would be mad at him for?"

Those questions seemed to hit the target. Stefani said, "I need to get to work now." She took one long sip from the cup and drained it. She went over to the computer station and booted it up without saying another word to Anna. Anna got up and helped another customer.

About a half hour later, Stefani motioned for Anna to come help her. "I just don't get derivatives," she said with frustration.

"OK, what is the problem?"

"*F* of *x* needs to be this number, and I have no idea how they get the answer."

"Try this. Put the *x* here and the *y* here, and plug in this number. Now see how we can follow the steps on the prior page, and you get this answer here."

Stefani sat for a minute. "Oh, I see now. Is that how you do all of these?"

"Yes. Once you have the template for one, they are all done pretty much the same way. It's not really all that hard."

Stefani turned around in the chair. "Anna, thank you for everything—the coffee, help with calculus, and your thoughts back there. It is hard for me to process, but I know you are right. If I can find the courage, I will try to reach out to my dad tonight."

Anna said, "You don't have to thank me. It is just nice to have a friend. I am sure I will be seeing you often. You still have to learn calculus integration. You will definitely need some help with that."

Chapter 27

Nick knew the phone was going to ring. It would be Barry. There had been no way for Nick to get even a fraction of the money together. He had $50,000 total from every source he could find. He couldn't take the money back from the company now that they were being audited and required all company funds to be funneled through the auditors. He could ask for more time, but he didn't know how that would help. He had taken the extraordinary step of taking out a $1 million life insurance policy to help his family stay financially sound if he should die. He had one more idea, though: he could find Anna himself and bring her to the meeting.

He knew the self-destruct thing was a bluff. Daniel never had mentioned anything like that. He did not know what the gunfire was about, but Nick would bring his own gun. This might work, he thought. He knew the area in which to look for her. He could ask for help in finding her and say she was his long-lost daughter or some story like that. He grabbed his gun and headed downtown.

Nick arrived at the block where Barry's gang had been the day before. He started at the corner and went from building to building, asking if anyone had seen the girl in the photograph.

He finally got to the bookshop. Anna was in the back at the computer stations when he approached the front counter and asked Sophie. She looked at the photograph carefully and said no, she hadn't seen anyone like that, knowing full well it was Anna. He asked if he could roam the shop and ask other people. She said she had a better idea and asked him to wait a minute by the desk. A uniformed officer was browsing the fiction section. He was off duty at the moment. She asked him to talk to the gentleman and not let him harass the customers in the store.

The officer went up to Nick and said, "I understand you are looking for a missing person?"

Nick said, "Yes, I am looking for my daughter." He showed him the picture.

"Are you in law enforcement?"

Nick had to admit that no, he was not part of any law enforcement.

"Did you file a missing person report?"

"No. We are estranged."

"I am sorry for your situation, sir. But you really can't go through an establishment asking all of the customers if they have seen your daughter. If your daughter doesn't want to see you, she has that right as well. Try posting something on social media that you want to see her. I am sure you can reach her that way."

Nick realized he wasn't going to get past this guy. He thanked him and waited outside the store in the crowd. He was sure Anna was in there.

He waited until most of the people in the store had left. He wondered if there was a back door. Sometime around five thirty, the door next to the shop opened, and even though it was almost dark, he thought the girl coming out the door was Anna. He walked up to the girl at the door and said, "Anna?"

She turned toward him, and he put a gun in her right side. He pressed closely to her body so no one could see it. "Come with me. Don't make any noise or make any sudden movements, and you won't get hurt." He looked around behind him and to the sides to see if anyone was watching.

While his head was turned, she lifted her left leg slightly and pulled out her gun. She could manage it with her left hand as easily as her right. He was still looking away as she leveled it at his face. She thought to herself, *If he wants to kidnap me, he certainly isn't very good at it.*

A moment later, he turned his head back toward her, and the barrel of the snub-nosed .38 hit him in the nose. She touched it lightly to his forehead. "If you shoot me, I will be repaired in a week. If I shoot you, it will take a week for the crows to eat your brains off my front door. Right now, it sucks to be you."

Nick didn't respond. He didn't know what to do. She cocked the hammer, which seemed to pause time. She hated this man. Flashbacks of Daniel hitting her and dragging her came back. She recalled the shock of being hit in the face and having her arm broken, having a hood put over her head, and having a whole gang of men try to take her to a place where they would do bad things to her. Yes, she wanted to kill this man.

Then she heard a voice in her head. It was Sophie, trying to calm her after her purse was stolen: "The man who did this is bad, and he hurt you, but he may have not eaten in three days, or maybe he was using the money to get high. It doesn't matter. You have a job and a home and a lot to be grateful for. He obviously lives a life of misery. Don't let your anger ruin the good things you have."

Anna's anger mellowed. This person was a failure, a poor excuse for a man who clearly had gotten himself into some kind of trouble.

Anna said, "Let me help you here. I don't know what your problem is with me, but you are going to drop your weapon." Nick's gun clanked onto the ground. "Now I am going to give you a five-second head start to run away. Then I will either shoot you in the back or call the cops, depending on my mood at the time. One. Two."

With that, Nick turned and ran. She picked up his gun and went back into her apartment. All the way up the stairs, she kept shaking her head, asking herself why it was so hard to go out to buy a pair of sneakers.

Nick threaded his way through the few people on the sidewalk and turned at the first corner. He looked back behind him. She was gone. He hadn't run anywhere in twenty years and was winded to the point where he had to stop to catch his breath.

So she did have a gun. Now he did not. He was going to have to go to Barry's empty-handed.

When Nick got home, he contemplated ways to commit suicide that would look like an accident, but he had not really wrapped his head around doing that yet. His mind had been racing all day. He still had no answers.

At the scheduled time, he rolled up to the AJX Enterprises building and parked the car. He had no options. He walked up to the door, and Barry was there to let him in. They sat in the same office where the deal had struck just a week ago. They sat in silence for a few minutes. Nick said, "Barry, I don't have the money. I won't be able to get it for a few weeks. Our company is under an audit, and the accounts are frozen until the audit is over. I am telling you: there is no self-destruct bomb. I tried to get her tonight myself. It isn't that hard."

"Why didn't you get her then?"

"She really does have a gun. A regular pistol—that's all."

It did not matter what Nick thought. They had listened to the whole exchange through the bug planted in his coat. He was in debt for $1 million, and Barry saw no feasible way of getting the money back. As far as he was concerned, the deal was off. Barry said, "I am not surprised you don't have the money. My guess is that you won't have the money in a couple of weeks either. Nick, I've known people like you. I think our business is done here."

What Barry left unsaid was that a man in a situation as desperate as Nick's would become a liability if he were to try to use their deal in some way to threaten Barry with exposure of his group and the attempted kidnapping. He could not be trusted.

Nick got up and left, confused. He wasn't sure what had happened, but he walked out of the office without Barry offering further discussion of how he would get his money. It felt wrong.

He got into his car and turned the key. He drove away toward his home and paused at a red light at the end of the street. He turned and pulled over on a side street to buy a package of cigarettes and a six-pack of beer. He did not notice the dark sedan that followed him about fifty yards behind. The man in the sedan waited until Nick came out of the store and got back into his car.

The car following Nick had pulled to the curb about a hundred feet away. The man in the car steadied his sniper rifle on the open window of his car. He took careful aim at his target. The red dot from his rifle's laser sight went through the windshield of Nick's car and onto his chest. There were two muffled shots barely perceptible to anyone else because of the silencer on the rifle. Two red holes opened up on Nick's chest, and he slumped over the steering wheel.

Back at Barry's office, the team gathered as soon as the man in the dark sedan returned. He was the lead man on the team. He opened by saying, "The objective is done. The subject is deceased." He moved on to the next topic. "We think the lady outside the bookshop whom Nick talked to earlier today actually was Anna. It is really something that we can hear this stuff."

Barry said, "So Nick is dead. If we can take out Anna, at least the million dollars will have bought us a little more time to compete with Logicsolutions. That by itself may be worth it. No one else is even close to where they are in artificial intelligence development. Now the market will still be wide open."

"Boss, if she has a C-4 package inside her, a thermal bomb will set it off. All we need to do is to find the time and place. It will level the building and leave no trace of us. It is quick and easy. We can set the package and detonate it from a distance. The getaway should be simple. I think we can pull this off without missing a step."

"What about collateral damage? Doing that in the bookshop will affect a lot of other people. Setting off the bomb in her apartment will ignite the whole building," Barry said. "Figure out a way to do this that will minimize the chance of affecting other people. We want to keep the lowest profile possible. Do some reconnaissance, and find an isolated place. If we can't do that, then we'll make another plan."

Chapter 28

Joshua was going through his inbox, when Jim's invitation showed up. He could put two and two together. Jim was somehow behind the tracking device he'd found in his jacket pocket. Should he come clean? He couldn't know for sure that Jim knew he had been with Anna, only that he had been in Manhattan's 2100 block. Could he trust Jim with the truth? How big was the penalty for lying if he got caught? He would probably lose his job. What would Anna think? He would probably lose his girlfriend. This was shaping up to be a no-win situation. He could think about it for another half hour or so.

At five minutes to two, he headed to the elevator and to the seventh floor to meet with Jim.

As usual, Jim had a smile and a firm handshake to greet him. "Come on in. Please have a seat. How have you been?"

"I've been great. I'm spending a lot of time on Daniel's notes. He never ceases to amaze me. I will have a full report for you within a couple of weeks. He must have left over a thousand pages of notes."

"Joshua, I need to ask you a question. I need for you to answer me honestly. Have you seen Anna since we came back from the facility?"

After a lot of thought before the meeting, he'd decided to admit that he had. There probably wasn't any penalty for that. He had decided not to divulge the location of her apartment. "Yes, Mr. Mendola, I have. She approached me a little over a week ago to help her after she broke a gear in her leg. She made secrecy a condition of meeting with her. She somehow knew I was being followed. She was right. It is in our interest at this point that she survives. So helping her with her leg made sense. Agreeing to keep it a secret so she could get help made sense too."

"You are right. So tell me—how is she doing?"

"She is doing really well, sir. I was surprised to find that she had gotten a job and an apartment and had made the adjustments she needed to survive in New York City. Mr. Mendola, your project is wildly more successful than you can imagine. No one who has met her has any idea she is a machine. She is that good. Instead of getting in her way, we should help her to go as far as she can go. Besides, she is still changing and evolving. We should see where that path takes us."

"So she managed to find a life here in Manhattan. We are talking about something that Daniel built. That is amazing. You say she is doing that well. That is good news. So the last time you saw her, she was OK."

"Yes." The conversation seemed to have taken an ominous turn. "Why? Does she have a reason to worry?"

"Unfortunately, yes. It seems our CFO was stealing money from the company. He made some kind of deal to sell Anna to Barry Stiles over at AJX Enterprises for some large amount of money. I don't know how much. We hired Bernie's company to find her. In the process, Bernie tapped Nick's phone. Bernie's men were following you, thinking she would reach out to you for exactly the kind of reason she did. You are really the only person who can help her. You are probably the only person she can trust. I will respect your promise for secrecy. However, Nick was stealing the information from our board meetings and feeding it to Barry. They tried to kidnap Anna in front of her apartment.

Apparently, the attempt failed. One day you'll explain to me how she beat a team of men who were all former Special Forces."

"I hadn't heard any of this."

"Well, now it gets ugly. I am going to guess Nick was using the money to cover his theft. Once he had the money, he deposited it in a way that could save him jail time. However, once it was deposited, he could not get it back once the deal went bad. He was shot in his car last night. Two high-caliber bullets in the chest. I think Anna is in danger as well. I know Barry. If he can't have Anna, then he won't want me to have her either. They are most likely going to change their plan from capturing her to destroying her. You need to take whatever steps you have to in order to see that she is not harmed. I will help you in any way I can."

Joshua started to feel sick to his stomach. How could he not have known this? Or at least considered it? Finding a tracking device and knowing one was being followed meant someone wanted to get him or her badly. And here it was. "I see. I will call her tonight. And by the way, are you still following me?"

"No, not anymore. Now that I know you have found her, I need for you to bring her in. I don't need Bernie anymore."

Joshua left the meeting feeling desperate with worry. They had actually tried to kidnap her, whoever *they* were. He would have never been able to get to her. He would call her now. She was at work, and her Tracfone would be in her apartment. He would figure out the name of the bookstore and call there. No, he would go there, convince her to leave with him, and keep her at his apartment. No, he would keep her at a hotel. They might still be watching his apartment. His head was spinning.

With regard to Mr. Mendola, he felt violated that Jim had ordered a tracking device to be placed on him and that he had been followed. On the other hand, he was being trusted to rescue her. This was no small deal. He knew what it meant to the company and to Mr. Mendola personally to recover her.

Joshua decided to just go to the bookshop. He was there thirty minutes later. As he went into the shop through the front door for the first time, he was surprised how big it was. After a few minutes, he found Anna in the computer section, working with a girl, a college student. She was trying to find something on the internet, and Anna was directing her. He waited a few minutes for her to finish.

An older lady came up to him and asked if he needed help.

He thanked her and said he would wait for the auburn-haired girl over by the computer.

She smiled. "Are you Joshua?"

He looked strangely at the woman. The look gave him away.

"I've heard a lot about you. I'm Sophie. I am the owner of this bookstore. Anna is one of our best employees. You are a really lucky guy."

"Thanks. I think so too."

With that, she walked away. It took almost ten minutes for Anna to solve the girl's problem. She walked away from the girl's computer station and saw Joshua standing behind the self-help book stand.

"Hi. This is a surprise. Why are you here?" She went up to him and gave him a quick hug.

"Anna, are you OK?" Joshua's face immediately gave away that there was something wrong.

"Yes. Why wouldn't I be?"

Joshua said he had heard about the attempted kidnapping.

Anna recoiled a little bit. "Wait here." She went over to Sophie for a minute and then returned. "Let's go upstairs and talk."

As soon as Anna turned the bolt on the door, she turned to Joshua and asked, "How did you know?"

Joshua replayed the meeting with Jim. He had arranged for Joshua to be followed and tracked. Then he went on to explain that a second group also had been hunting for her and had been getting information from the executive meetings.

"So that event was a product of discussions of me at your company's meetings? What happened to the person who was giving away the company's secrets?"

"That is the worse part. He was shot yesterday. Apparently, the deal went bad. These are pretty awful people we are dealing with. I need for you to come with me to stay out of reach of these people."

"Yeah, it went bad because I got away from them. Awful people? They grabbed me in the middle of the street in broad daylight. I beat them, though. I am packing heat," she said proudly as she lifted up her dress to show the snub-nosed .38 in her thigh holster. "Oh, and by the way, a lone man tried to kidnap me a second time last night. I bet they left that out. I put the gun to his head and threatened to blow his brains out. He ran away. He was probably this illustrious Nick, trying to save his own skin. I am glad he is dead."

Joshua looked incredulous.

Anna stared at him for a few minutes, considering how to respond to him. "Joshua, I am not going with you. I have to find a way to live my life. I have options. I have an attorney."

"What do you mean you have an attorney?"

"I hired an attorney. Her name is Gloria Rogers. I am going to deal with my problems, not run away from them."

"I can't let you do that. It is too dangerous."

"It isn't your choice. It is mine. You are going to have to accept my choice." She was determined in her resolve.

Joshua's frustrated desperation overtook him. "I can't let you do that. I know they want to kill you. If you love me, you will come with me. I love you. I don't want to lose you."

"Joshua, I will be OK. You have to believe in me. I have to get back to work. Later, I have to meet with my attorney. You need to go. I don't want you to get caught up in my fight. You can get hurt more easily than I can. You bleed. I don't. And, Joshua, you don't love me. You can't love me until I fix these problems on my own."

"Please come with me."

Anna yelled back at him, "You are not listening! No. Now, go. I will call you at the office later tonight."

Two men from Barry's gang had gone into the bookshop to do reconnaissance. One of the men had been only a few feet away when Joshua had his exchange with Sophie. They had been able to discern that Anna was, in fact, in the shop and that Joshua was her boyfriend.

While Joshua had been waiting for Anna to finish with her customer, it had been a simple thing to brush against him and leave a bug planted on his jacket. It didn't matter if he discovered it; it only needed to work for the next few minutes. They were counting on it not being found for that long.

The exchange between Joshua and Anna in her apartment was enough for the men to be able to track down Gloria Rogers's office. The last part of the plan was simple: they would stake out Gloria's office until Anna showed up and plant the incendiary device.

Chapter 29

"Gloria, there has been a change in the situation," Anna said. "It seems there has been a whole lot more going on since we spoke last. My kidnapping attempt was part of a deal with a third party, not my company, that ended in a man getting shot. Now there is a competition to see who can get me first. Can we meet in a different location? I don't want to endanger you or be interrupted by anyone."

"Wow, Anna. Chaos seems to follow you everywhere. I think you have to involve the police at this point."

"I know. Can we meet to discuss it?"

"Sure, I am free at four thirty. Let's meet at Mid-City Café."

"That sounds great."

Anna showed up at Mid-City Café right at 4:30, and Gloria was already there. They sat in a booth in the corner, and Anna relayed the whole story as Joshua had told it to her. Gloria listened and reiterated her belief that it was time to meet with the police. They could offer some protection.

Anna considered that option. "Let's wait until we have looked at all the options. Running continues to prolong a set of problems. I don't want to keep running. The core of my problem is to make peace with Logicsolutions. If I can accomplish that, then the other group becomes a police problem. Without a deal with Logicsolutions, I won't be able to be with Joshua. Bless his heart, he keeps on trying to rescue me. He is so well meaning, but he does it so badly. Gloria, why can't I get the guy in charge over there to look at me as an asset? Sophie says I am the best employee she ever had. Is there any angle you can imagine where I am a threat to Logicsolutions? Maybe a liability, but I am a forty-million-dollar investment. Why wouldn't they want to nurture that instead of trying to squelch it?"

"You make a lot of good points, Anna. Here is what I think you should do."

Over the next few minutes, they hammered out a detailed plan.

Gloria called Logicsolutions and asked for Mr. Mendola. The secretary asked to take a message. Gloria said, "Find him, and tell him that Anna's lawyer wants to speak with him. I'll wait. He is going to want to take this call."

After a wait of several minutes, the hold music stopped, and a voice broke in. "Jim Mendola speaking."

"Mr. Mendola, my name is Gloria Rogers, and I am Anna's attorney. I would like to set up an emergency meeting with your board for seven thirty tonight. It is urgent that we do this as quickly as possible. Can you arrange for that to happen?"

"Ms. Rogers, that is a difficult thing to do. It is short notice for people who have other responsibilities."

"Mr. Mendola, do your best. Call me by six o'clock to let me know if this can happen. If not, I will need to find alternative arrangements for Anna for her safety. I believe you understand the threat. We are going to need to involve the police."

"I understand. I will call you back in thirty minutes."

"Fine." She gave him her number.

Anna and Gloria walked back toward her office. They were about a block away, when Anna said, "Wait. Look over there. It's the black van that was driven by the men who were trying to take me. How would they know we were coming here now?"

They stood still on the sidewalk for several minutes, watching the stationary van. The motor was running. Anna said, "I have an idea. You said it was time to call the police. If they are there to kill me, then maybe this would be a good time to call them. Let's say for a moment we report a burglary, and we believe the men in the black van are behind it. You wait out here, and I will go into the office. Do you have a back door?"

"Yes, it is straight down the hall," Gloria answered with curiousness in her voice.

"The coat stand with the coat—is it still in your office?"

"Yes, why?"

"Through the window blinds, the coat would look like me in the chair. I am going to go in the front door, go into your office, turn on the lights, and put the coatrack with the coat on the back of the chair. Then I am going to leave out the back door and meet you here. When they go to find me in the room, the police will arrive, looking for a burglar. At least that will keep them busy for a while." Anna smiled as she thought about their trying to explain to the cops why they were there.

Anna called 911 and reported a burglary in progress by some prowlers waiting in a black van on the south side of the middle of the Twenty-Second Street block off Seventh Avenue. Then she quickly walked to the front door and used Gloria's key to unlock it and lock it behind her. She quickly unlocked Gloria's private office, turned on the light, placed the coatrack with the coat in front of the chair, locked the door again, and used the push bar to get out of the rear door. She walked quickly around the block and joined Gloria.

There was some movement in the van. One of the men got out. However, instead of casing the building, a man with a black ski mask went to the building and left a small package below the window. He ran back to the van and jumped in the open door. The van pulled away.

Suddenly, there was a violent explosion that seemed to shake the whole block as the front window of the building blew in, and the inside of the room caught fire. Over the squealing tires of the van came the wailing of police sirens. As the van sped away, a squad car was in hot pursuit. The van careened around the corner and out of sight.

Gloria and Anna found they were holding each other in shock and disbelief. Anna's pursuers really were out to kill her and anyone who was around her. It took several minutes for the two ladies to gain their composure.

"You are right, Anna. Your key here is to strike a deal with Mr. Mendola. At least now we can let the police do our battle with these guys. If they don't get caught now, we can lead the police to Barry Stiles."

Gloria's phone rang. It was Mr. Mendola, who said, "You are on for seven thirty. Everyone will be there. I will have the receptionist stay late and usher you up to the seventh floor."

Gloria and Anna walked back to Mid-City Café, where they carefully rehearsed what they were going to do at the meeting. Nothing would be left to chance. They thoroughly prepared, and at 7:10, they caught a cab and headed to the Logicsolutions office.

Chapter 30

Gloria stopped to compose herself in front of the building. She used the reflection in the front glass windowpanes to check her clothes and hair. She was five foot four even with two-inch heels. Her blonde hair and blue eyes did not give away the grit with which she could take on the toughest opponent. She was dressed in a sharp-looking blue pant suit with a white blouse. She looked professional. She would command the room.

She went through the large brass-framed glass doors with a hard push and went directly to the receptionist desk. "I am Gloria Rogers. I am here for a meeting with the board."

The receptionist made a quick call upstairs to confirm the appointment. Then she gave Gloria a visitor's badge and guided her to the elevator. They rode in silence up to the seventh floor and walked to the door of the conference room. The receptionist gave a couple of taps on the closed door and opened it. She introduced Gloria Rogers to the group.

Gloria went to the end of the table. She set her computer bag on the chair and pulled the laptop out. She introduced herself as Anna's lawyer and handed out a business card to everyone at the table. She then asked permission to have a partner of the firm listen in on the discussion in case she needed information. They agreed, and she set up the meeting platform with audio only.

After a moment, the other party appeared with initials in a box on the laptop screen.

"I want to start my remarks today by saying that I have never had a case quite like this before. I do not think there are a lot of precedents for the rights of artificially intelligent beings. So I am going to ask you to keep an open mind.

"I have had several lengthy conversations with Anna. I can assure you she is quite human as well as quite capable. She has managed to arrive in the city as essentially an undocumented person, get a job, support herself, make friends, and find a sustainable life. She has a boyfriend. She tells me she has fallen in love. She works hard, reads in her spare time, and lives a life that has needs indistinguishable from those of any other person.

"The problem here is that if you are going to seek the technology to create beings that are able to understand themselves, contemplate their own death, have hopes and dreams, and love and be loved, then you cannot destroy them to make room for the next model. Nowhere on the planet are you allowed to kill your children because you want to create better ones."

Jim said, "This is a machine you are talking about. We built her. She belongs to Logicsolutions."

"If Anna were to walk into this boardroom right now, none of you would know she was a machine. None of you could tell."

Jim put on a look of disbelief.

"My client has been beaten, mugged, and stalked; she has suffered two kidnapping attempts; and as of two hours ago, she survived an attempted firebombing. The choice of living this way or being a prisoner in a glass cage is so awful that she has decided it would be better to be in a regular prison. She has signed the documents to confess to killing Daniel and stand trial for the crime. If she wins by reason of self-defense, then she will go free. If she loses and has to spend time in prison, so be it. Either way, the story of what you have been doing to her here will get told to the world, and that makes it worth it. Besides the press, you will lose your forty-million-dollar investment entirely. Not only do you lose her, but legislators will write laws making it much harder for you to get your breakthrough to the market. You will lose your chance to sell artificially intelligent machines for another ten years. Also, in case you think a trial will be easy on you, I will tell you that this murder trial is really a case of domestic violence. People will see Anna as a person, whether they know she is a machine or not. I'll parade a big, hulking man the size of Daniel next to petite Anna around the courtroom and let the jury see for themselves. There may be a multimillion-dollar settlement to her if she wins. And I win most of these cases."

Gloria paused. "Of course, there is an alternative."

She had everyone's attention.

"Embrace her." She paused again. "For God's sake, treat her like a person. Give her a job. No strings attached. She can live her life as she pleases. She has no family, no roots, and no history, so where else would she want to go? The only friends she has made in her short life she has had to avoid because you made it too dangerous for them."

"Look, this lady can read one hundred fifty pages an hour and remember every word. She speaks four languages fluently. She can sell an idea to people better than anyone on your sales team. What an incredible asset! Find a place for her in the company. Pay her fairly. Treat her well. Give her every reason to stay, and she will. Then not only do you get your return on investment, but she can help you develop the next prototype through her experiences. All upsides. There are no downsides. You are businessmen. Certainly you can see the right deal to make here."

After a long silence, Jim spoke. "OK, let's say I agree to your request. We hire her. We treat her like any other employee. When will I get to see her? Is she close by? I would like this nightmare to end."

"Do we have everything we need for this conversation?" Gloria asked the attendee through the laptop.

"Yes."

"OK, then it is time for you to see her." Gloria said to the laptop, "Please introduce yourself."

The voice in the laptop said, "For Anna's security, we were not sure it was safe to expose her. We needed your agreement first. So today I let her be me. I am Gloria Rogers."

While the attention was drawn to the voice in the laptop, the woman who had just delivered the passionate case for accepting Anna as a person removed her wig, and her long auburn hair fell to her shoulders. With a different voice, she said, "I am Anna. It is a pleasure to meet you."

There was a stunned silence in the room. Anna sat on the table, swung her leg around, and put her left foot on the table. She lifted her pant leg up to the knee. The voice in the laptop continued, but no one was paying attention. Anna reached behind her leg and peeled the polymer skin off her shin and calf in one large piece and set it on the table, exposing the clear plastic sheath around a web of cables, motors, and gears.

Jack almost climbed out of his seat. "Damn! Are you kidding me?"

The women gasped.

Jim just shook his head and smiled. Joshua had been right. As a machine becoming a person, Anna was incredibly successful. "That was an amazing performance. So you are Anna?"

Anna responded by sliding off the table, reaching out, and giving Jim a firm handshake. "Yes."

"Anna, please sit. I have a few questions for you. First of all, tell me exactly what happened in the hallway six weeks ago," Jim said while the others were still trying to comprehend what they were seeing.

Anna took the seat next to Jim and replied to the whole room, "I was out of my room and in the hallway at the same time as Cassie. Daniel was a big man. He confronted Cassie and hit her, and she fell to the floor dead. He had been abusing her in so many ways that she had planned to kill him. He didn't understand that even though she could not speak, she could feel shame and anger. That is why she took the sharp, pointy thing from the kitchen.

"He turned to me to tell me to get back in my room. I refused. He knocked me to the floor. When I fell to the floor, I tried to protect myself with my left arm. He hit it and broke it. He grabbed my feet and started to drag me back to my room. As he dragged me, something inside me stopped panicking. Apparently, when I am threatened, I can think only logically. I was able to grab the pointy thing off the floor. He was bent over and looking behind himself as he pulled me. I was able to bend my knees all the way and reach his belly with my right arm. I stuck the pointed metal thing under his rib cage and turned it hard. He froze with surprise and started to bleed profusely. The color disappeared from his face. He wobbled and slumped to the floor. A few minutes later, he was dead.

"I took his ID card and went into the other rooms and found the places where he had put the remains of his prior experiments. I used the left arm from one. The part fit, even though it looks a little different from my right arm and hand." Anna put her two hands together, and the left one was slightly bigger than the right one. "I took the polymer skin off the other ones and completed my skin covering. I took a dress from the closet and left the building, fully dressed. I walked into town and was offered a ride from a college student who was going to New York at the same time."

The room was silent. Jim went on. "Another thing we have been wondering is what happened with the kidnapping attempt. How did you get away?"

She smiled. "I have a gun. It was in the holster strapped to my leg when they grabbed me. I couldn't get the gun out, so I just fired it while it was still in the holster. The holster was ruined, but from the look of things as they were running away, I think I beat them up pretty badly. I wounded three of them. Oh, and I left this part out: 'Arming C-4 self-destruct process. Ten. Nine. Eight,'" she said in her computer voice. That detail elicited a laugh from around the room.

Jim tried to contain his amusement. "That is why the deal went bad. They believed you were built with a self-destruct mechanism so no one could capture you. That was brilliant. How did you think of that?"

"I was in self-preservation mode. I had half a dozen different ideas before I settled on that one."

"One last question." Jim's face became serious. "You killed Daniel. You ran and hid for these last six weeks. You impersonated a lawyer just now. You strong-armed me into the choice you wanted me to make. How do I know I can trust you?"

Anna studied him for a long minute. He was being honest with her. "Because I have no agenda or ulterior motive. You have been in business long enough to know that people seek to satisfy their needs. My needs are simple. I want to find a life where I feel at home."

That phrase and the way she expressed it caused Jim to have a flashback to seven years earlier, when he and his wife had been separating before their divorce. He remembered the conversation he'd had with his twelve-year-old daughter on the last day he was to live in their house. Through her tears, she'd said, "What will life be like now? When will I ever feel at home again?"

The pang of sorrow and failure of his relationship with his daughter washed over him. All at once, Jim stopped seeing Anna as a monster or a freak to be hunted and caught. She might have appeared clever and tough, but inside, she was just a young girl. She looked as if she were the same age as his daughter. She was struggling to understand the world while the world was trying to harm her, not unlike his daughter when she had faced unfair circumstances. He understood the dynamic and wouldn't miss it a second time.

"I'll take your deal. Here are the terms. Two things. First, you'll go to HR and fill out your documents. I will arrange for someone to get a birth certificate that will make you twenty years old and apply for a Social Security number for you. You will work in my department as my attaché. We will work out a job description after that. Second, you have to agree to meet with me once a week. It will be our quality time to discuss the things happening in your life. It will be just casual conversation but informative enough that I can understand how you are doing and see how our new technology is unfolding."

Jim addressed the room. "OK, does anyone have any problem with the deal I am making?" He paused for a minute and looked at everyone at the table one by one. "I want to make it clear that everyone in this room has a fiduciary responsibility to the company. That means the conversation we have had over the last thirty minutes is a company secret. It is not to be shared with anyone—not your spouse, your best buddy, your shrink, or anyone else. No one. Anna, this includes you too. If you want to be an employee of this company, you will have to sign an agreement that you will protect our proprietary information, which, in this case, is you. Gloria, are you still there?"

"Yes."

"Please make sure your client understands the gravity of what I am describing here. Can you get a birth certificate for Anna? We can get the Social Security number and picture ID once you get that."

"I am sure I can do that. Give me two weeks."

"OK. Then this meeting is adjourned," Jim said.

Anna smiled. She understood what he was saying. He was thorough and always in control. He would be a friend. Maybe even a mentor. He was protecting his investment. "Thank you. I am looking forward to being part of this organization," Anna said, as if she had just completed a job interview. Anna packed the laptop and put the section of polymer skin in her computer bag. "I'll deal with this later."

She started to head out of the room and down to the lobby, where Gloria was waiting. As the group entered the hallway, she asked Jim if she could have a word in private with him. He waited while the others filed down the hall. "I'm glad things worked out between you and your daughter. She is such a nice lady."

He looked at her, suspicious of why she would know about his recent reconciliation with his daughter. "How do you know about that?"

"We met a few weeks ago in the bookshop. We had a few minutes together over coffee. I told her what it was like to have never had a father—or any parent, for that matter—and know that I would never have one in the future. How lucky she must be. I also told her that human life is finite. If she felt different in the future, there may not be time left for a reconciliation. If she ever wanted it to happen, she should make it happen sooner rather than later. I knew she was not close with you. I hoped that would change. She came in a few days later and told me it did. That's all."

There was a look on his face that Anna couldn't read. He turned and walked away. Then he paused and turned back toward her. "Why don't you and Joshua come over to my house over the weekend? I'll invite Stefani. I'll make dinner—maybe throw some steaks on the grill. Do you like steak?"

"I don't eat," she replied awkwardly.

"Oh, you mean you're vegan?"

"No, I mean I really never eat at all. Not anything," she replied, feeling weird.

"So that is how you got so slim."

"But I have always been this size," she said, missing the joke.

"Anna, if you want to be accepted in society as a person, you are going to have to find yourself a sense of humor." He smiled and continued down the hall.

Chapter 31

Jim went into his office and closed the door.

Anna stopped at the elevator and called Joshua's Tracfone. "I'm done up here and headed back to the lobby. You are still in your office, aren't you? Please meet me there. There is someone I want to introduce you to."

"Well, what happened?"

"I'll tell you all of it when I see you downstairs. Just so you know, it went well."

Anna got to the lobby.

Gloria was sitting in one of the Victorian chairs in the corner. "You were amazing in there, Anna. If they don't give you a job, I will. Ever think of being a lawyer?"

"Thank you so much for everything."

"We still have to get you a birth certificate. I will have to pull some strings. We'll get it done. Well, it looks like my job is done for the day. I am going to have to call my insurance company to file a claim for my office. Good night."

"Wait," Anna said. "I want you to meet Joshua. He is just getting off the elevator now."

Joshua strolled over to Anna, and she said, "I want you to meet Gloria Rogers, my lawyer and friend."

"How do you do?" Joshua said.

"Fine. Thank you. I have heard a lot about you. Anna seems pretty lucky to have met you. Well, good luck, you two." Gloria gave Anna a hug.

Anna handed Gloria her computer bag back as she took the polymer skin out. "Put this in your bag, please," Anna said to Joshua. "I will deal with this when I get home."

Gloria walked out of the large glass doors holding her computer bag in one hand and pushing the heavy door open with the other.

"Joshua, humans have five senses, and I have three of them. I have sight, touch, and hearing. What in the world is a sense of humor?"

Joshua laughed. "Let's go, Anna. I will tell you all about it on the way home. Tell me everything that went on up there. Tell me every detail, and don't leave anything out."

"Sure. First, kiss me." She leaned up and kissed him. "By the way, whose place are we going to, mine or yours?"

Joshua realized she didn't have to hide anymore. "Let's go to mine for a change."

"I still want to know what a sense of humor is."

"You have an encyclopedia in your head. Look it up."

"I know what the definition is, but I still don't understand it.

When they got to the car, Anna said, "You know what, Joshua? I think this has been a really long day. Why don't we get you dinner, and we can talk? Then I would like to go home to my apartment. I can call you tomorrow."

"Sure. I know a place."

Chapter 32

Jim picked up the phone and called the number on the business card for Gloria Rogers, Esquire, attorney specializing in women's issues, sexual harassment, domestic violence, and family law. It rang three times before a receptionist picked up.

"Gloria Rogers, attorney at law."

"Hello. This is Jim Mendola from Logicsolutions. I would like to speak to Ms. Rogers."

"Let me see if she is available."

"Thank you." There was a pause of a minute or so, and he waited while the hold music played.

"Good morning, Jim. How can I help you?"

"I just wanted to touch base with you about Anna. I know getting a birth certificate must be tough. How is it coming?"

"It is tough. I had to call in a few favors. It should be ready for pickup from city hall toward the end of next week."

"That is exceptionally good news. Listen, I wanted to ask you a couple of questions. I have been running this company for over twenty years. I have to admit, though, with Anna, I am in uncharted territory. We are poised to make a hundred more of these Annas. Can you give me your legal opinion of what you think we should do here?"

"I appreciate your asking me, Jim, especially in light of the fact that you have a whole team of attorneys in house over there.

I think the problem is that you started out in this project looking at the end product like an appliance, such as a dishwasher or even a car. That is not what you ended up with. If I were you, I would call the gentleman in charge over at the foreign exchange student coordinator's office. His job is to match foreign exchange students with families in America. The truth is, what you are trying to do is not really sales per se; it is more like a placement. You are going to need counselors for not just the entities you are placing but for your clients as well. I may not be able to go into a courtroom and argue that Anna is a human, but I certainly can argue that Anna is a citizen, even a person. There are going to be lawsuits from both directions: clients unhappy with you and placements unhappy with the clients or with you. This can be done but not without a lot of legal infrastructure and counseling."

"I actually never thought of it that way. I have to ask you another question. How did you come up with the speech in the office last week?"

"I didn't. I offered coaching on the law, but the idea was entirely Anna's. Oh, and you need to know that the cops caught Barry's little gang after they destroyed my office. For the time being, I am in the building two doors down. They will be looking at a long time behind bars, even if the only charge is arson. I don't think we will ever see an attempted murder charge. I don't believe Anna will ever be connected to it. Just as an aside, I have to tell you that when I first met Anna and she asked me to listen to her story, I asked her for a five-hundred-dollar retainer. Often, that will separate the wheat from the chaff. People will complain about the cost. Anna pulled out her purse and started to peel off fifty-dollar bills without a second thought. That was the moment I knew she was for real."

"Thank you for your time, Gloria. I really appreciate it. Listen, whatever the charge is for this time, just send the bill to my office. Send Anna's bill as well."

"Jim, before you go, can I take my lawyer's hat off and talk to you personally?"

"Of course."

"I am not a psychologist, but I am a mother of two daughters. I think Anna is modeling. She seems to be in a teenage point in her development. When she was with Daniel, she was able to kill. When she is with Joshua, she is learning how to be a lover. The fact that she is with Sophie most of the time has made her kind, compassionate, giving, and patient. When she was with me, she was aspirational about having a career in law. She is maturing and taking traits from the people around her. Now she is in your charge. You are the missing piece in her life. Essentially, she is going to take from you what she would get from a father. You need to recognize this responsibility and make it work for her. We don't know how long she will live, but what you teach her will influence her for as long as that happens to be. Good luck."

Jim knew that what Gloria had just articulated was true. He had just needed someone to put it out there clearly. "Thank you, Gloria. I will talk to you soon." With that, Jim hung up.

Chapter 33

Joshua and Anna arrived at Jim's house a little after five. Jim's house was a large colonial on a sprawling piece of land filled with flowers and lush green grass.

Jim was in the kitchen, preparing the steaks. Stefani came to the door and greeted them. Introductions were made between Joshua and Stefani.

Jim took a beer, and one was served to Joshua, and they stood by the grill while Anna and Stefani sat in the yard, chatting. Stefani was sipping a glass of iced tea, and Anna held a glass of tea as well, just for the look of it.

Jim asked Joshua about the report. Joshua said it would be done by midweek and was about thirty pages long. He said to Jim, "You know, there is one thing I don't understand. That is Anna's gender. There was no programming that would make Anna a woman, even though she was built that way physically. Yet she is a woman in every way, including how she sees herself and how she presents herself to the world. I am not an expert on women by any stretch of the imagination, but she seems to even think like a woman in the way she understands the world. It seems that was something she evolved into on her own. That remains a mystery to me."

Jim laughed. "Women in general are a mystery to me. I am not the one to ask."

Jim sat down with Anna alone later in the evening. "What are your plans for the future?" he asked.

"I really haven't thought much about that. I have been too consumed the last two months with just getting to see the next day. I want to go to college. I am trying to save up my money at the bookshop, but they only pay me fifteen dollars per hour. I think I will have to be saving for a long time."

"Anna, I want you to pursue what you want. Our agreement was that I would not tell you what to do. However, if you were my daughter, I would tell you to go to college. Start with one or two classes at the community college next semester, and see how you do. If it works well, then you could go to a four-year college and pursue any degree you wanted. I will pay for your college if you choose to go. I have to admit that one of the things that has impressed me so much about you is that you have made it on your own. You didn't leech onto some guy or take advantage of someone else to survive. You found a job, supported yourself, and built a life that you own. If you are happy in your apartment and working at the bookshop, then continue doing that until you find a career that suits you better. While I am speaking about you owning your life and speaking to you as if you were my daughter, I will tell you that your relationship with Joshua will fare better if you don't live with him. At least not right now."

Anna replied with a smile, "Sophie is a little like a mother. She just had that talk with me a few days ago. She said I have to figure out the person I was meant to be. I have to love myself before I can really love someone else. So no, I won't move in with Joshua, not in the near future anyway. The truth is, one day I think I would like to do what Gloria does. I would like to be a lawyer who helps people who are treated unfairly. I want to defend people who are disadvantaged. I know what it is like to be that way. By the way, how long do I have to keep my secret from Stefani?"

"With Nick having passed, I would like her to take his place in the company. She has three semesters to go. I have talked to Laura from the venture capital company about taking her under her wing as an intern until then so she can hit the ground running when it is time. I still need to talk to Stefani to see if she is on board with the idea. If she agrees to take the opportunity and becomes part of the company, then we can share that secret."

As Anna got up to leave to head home, she got noticeably quiet for a minute. She said to Jim, "Thank you for accepting me as I am. If I could have ever had a father, I would have wanted him to be like you." With that, she leaned forward and hugged him. After an awkward moment, he hugged her back.

Chapter 34

It was two o'clock on Wednesday afternoon, and the executive board gathered for the regular weekly meeting. Melanie handed out an agenda, and everyone was seated. Joshua was present for the meeting as an invited guest.

Jim opened the meeting and skipped the formalities. "I am going to make some opening remarks. Then I am going to turn the floor over to Joshua to give his report on his trip to the West Virginia facility." He paused as if to gather his thoughts. "I spent Friday evening with Anna, Joshua, and my daughter, Stefani. I had a chance to be in a casual setting with Anna. After a whole evening with Anna, I think I got a good understanding of who she is. She has kept her part of the bargain and filled out the nondisclosure agreement and all the other company forms, so technically, she works for Logicsolutions. How she fits in has not been worked out yet.

"We had a chance to talk at length. The story is quite remarkable. After three days of wandering, Anna landed at a bookshop run by a Sophie Garcia. Bernie tells me she was married to an undocumented Mexican national. Apparently, his family was raided by ICE when he was fourteen. His family was deported, and as a child, her husband lived off the streets until he was an adult. He lived on and off with relatives and joined the army when he was eighteen. He married Sophie when he was twenty-one, and they were married for twenty-two years before he died of cancer. When Anna turned up at the bookshop, looking for a job, several weeks ago, Sophie believed Anna was in the same situation her husband had been in as a child. She immediately offered Anna a job and an apartment. Anna tells me she is paid fifteen dollars an hour for a forty-hour work week, and she has saved up twelve hundred dollars, which she keeps in various places in her apartment because she can't open a bank account. She says she runs an online learning department within the bookshop, and the business has almost doubled since she took over."

Jim sighed. "After a whole evening of casual conversation, I have to say it is hard to tell a difference between her and half a dozen of Stefani's other friends. Also, by the way, there was a chance meeting between Anna and Stefani when Stefani used the bookshop's online service for one of her classes. She and Anna became friends.

"Anna is saving up to go to college. Then she wants to go to law school and defend people like herself, sort of in the Gloria Rogers model. In some ways, Gloria is her hero. For the record, since Anna is an employee of our company, I requested a laptop computer on her behalf to help her with college. Also, since there is an expectation that she will work for the company in a professional capacity in the future, I am going to pay for her education."

Jim paused to look around the room to gauge the reaction to committing the company to what could be a $200,000 college expense. "We created her. I believe it is our responsibility to see to her welfare at least until she has the opportunity we would give our own children. For now, she is going to continue to live her life as she is, working at the bookshop and living in her apartment. We will see each other on Sunday evenings for our business meeting and see how things unfold from there. She is keeping her end of the deal and respecting the secrecy of the project and her identity. To that point, she and Stefani are fairly good friends, and Stefani doesn't know Anna's true identity. Gloria says she will have a birth certificate by the end of next week. To sum up, this deal is going well. I am now going to turn the floor over to Joshua for his report. Then I will have some final comments, and I will be looking for a serious discussion from this group."

Joshua set out a pile of papers from his briefcase and looked up at the group.

"Joshua, remember, we are all laypeople here, so you will need to stay out of the weeds and keep us at the ten-thousand-foot view," Jim said.

"OK, Mr. Mendola. I think there is a lot here that really can be summed up simply. I will save the weeds for offline discussion that I will be happy to have with anyone at length in my office." Joshua focused on the top few sheets. "I was invited to the West Virginia facility for five days with Mr. Standish two months ago so I could get a feel for how close his project was to the market and how we needed to prepare for that delivery to the market. We spent probably twenty hours together in conversation. He was open and thorough about his project—or, I should say, his passion. Let me start out by saying that Mr. Standish was a genius. He was a forward thinker in so many different areas. His idea was to create humanoid robots that would service people as slaves. They would be mechanical butlers, cooks, cleaners, errand runners, and shoppers. You would buy them like cars. We could take a hit on the R&D portion of the cost and sell them for fifteen thousand dollars per unit. We could then charge a monthly maintenance fee. We would upgrade the software for free, as if it were a car warranty. He projected a million units over five years. If you do the math, it translates to fifteen billion dollars in sales and another three billion dollars in monthly fees. The potential is enormous. Other companies would be at least three to five years behind. The most important point was that the internet has become so polluted with scammers and malicious actors that the artificially intelligent robot would become a front of the owner. It would be the identity that the scammers would see first, thereby shielding the identity of the owner. The idea is brilliant, and the plan seems almost flawless. I say *almost* because there is a flaw. It actually originates as a personal flaw."

Joshua paused, knowing what he'd just said was a personal attack on the former leader of his company. He was not sure how well that would be received by the rest of the board.

"In the science and medical fields, there has always been a debate between the origins of structures and functions. Mr. Mendola, I am going to need to be in the weeds for just a little bit here. I will keep it brief—I promise. The debate goes something like this. If all mammals have five digits at the end of their forelimbs and the digits only differ by the form that is best suited to their needs, then the structure determined function. This would be the case with wings, hands, claws, and so forth. If one were to consider a human kidney, then the requirement for blood filtration and blood pressure control would dictate that a structure evolve to meet those needs. This would be a case of function determining structure. If Mr. Standish built the robot, then he provided the structure, and function must follow. That said, Mr. Standish held a rather unique opinion on which he was unmovable. He believed that all higher animals were so extremely complicated because they needed billions of years to evolve the systems that were necessary to support life. If a scientist such as Mr. Standish could bypass billions of years of evolution and simply build a higher life-form in a laboratory, then billions of years of evolution became unnecessary. He used his robots as an example. He believed that all of our internal organs, hormones, blood vessels, and organ systems are tools that evolution used to provide a brain, nervous system, and muscular system with the energy of life. He was right in that regard. Life in higher animals requires a compound called ATP to provide energy for all life functions. It takes all of those systems to produce ATP. He believed he could replace all of that with a simple battery and charging system. For that concept, he was correct. For his original premise, he was wrong.

"The brain is an organ that works differently than most organs. It really is the only organ, some scientists agree, for which both structure and function grow and change simultaneously. When the brain perceives something, the understanding of it and the memory of it change the structure of the brain by creating new neural connections. Then, when the same stimulus occurs, whether it is a sight, sound, or thought process, it is now understood differently. It is a continuous process of growth wherein structure and function keep changing each other. With Daniel's formatting program, the humanoids were able to sort all of the existing data in their memories and continually reorganize it in ways in which the information was most useful. The humanoid brain does this by creating clusters of data that interconnect the same way neurons interconnect in the human brain. By matching the experiences to the data, these humanoids are able to develop, over time, human emotions, such as love, compassion, fear, self-awareness, introspection, and many others."

Joshua took a breath. "I will try not to make this next part too complicated. A human brain is divided into two halves, one for the fact side and the other for the emotional side. Thoughts and experiences only make sense to humans if they have a factual and an emotional component. A robot has no such division. However, this formatting program is capable of doing the same thing, even if it doesn't do it using neatly divided hemispheres. Because these robots can develop and express human emotions, they respond to experiences in a human way. Daniel reasoned that since these robots were given an upload of facts, they can only work with facts and would make useful slaves."

Joshua surveyed the table to make sure he hadn't lost his audience. "Both the housekeeper robot and Anna are examples that this is not true. They both reorganized the storage and interconnections of their experiences similar to the way a human would and developed the corresponding emotions. Consequently, both developed the same array of emotions based on those experiences that humans would. The first one, Cassie, wanted to kill Daniel because he caused her to feel violated with humiliation and pain. Anna wanted to kill Daniel out of self-defense for her own survival. The fact that his creations could despise him so much that both tried to kill him and one actually succeeded in killing him speaks for itself."

Joshua paused again. "To sum up, Mr. Standish created a being that thinks and feels the same way a human does, not an artificial imitation that only appears to think that way. There is more, but I think I have captured the essence of the project and the problems that led us to this point."

After a few minutes, Jim spoke. "I think all of the people in this room are Christian." No one said anything. "It doesn't matter. I think the same question would draw the same kind of response if there were Jews, Muslims, or members of any other type of religion in this room. We created Anna in a laboratory just six months ago out of metal, plastic, and a magic gel. You have just spent the last half hour listening to how she is like a human in every way we can identify. So does she have a soul?"

He let the question hang in the air for several minutes.

"Why do we need to answer that?" asked Laura.

"I'll answer that question, but first, you answer mine. Does she have a soul?'

"I don't know. Maybe. No. She has no genetic code. She has no point of conception. She was made in a laboratory by Daniel. How could she have a soul?"

"Anyone else?" Jim asked the others at the table.

Everyone was uncomfortable. It seemed all kinds of clergy were popping up from the past in people's minds, reminding them that only humans had souls and that God had created man in his own image and so on. One could almost hear those voices in the room.

Jack interjected. "I have been in computer science for twenty years. I have never considered anything like this. I have to say, I am hard pressed to say no. It isn't a matter of us creating her of metal, plastic, and magic gel. It is a matter of her developing on her own once we put those tools together. People conceive embryos, but it is God who makes them into children and gives them souls so that they grow and become who they are going to be."

Samantha had moved on. "I don't see how we control this thing. It is as though we can make these beings, but we can't have any real input on the finished product. That scares the hell out of me."

Jim resumed control again. "If we create this project on a mass scale and sell it to the public, we are not going to create a million Annas. We are going to create a million individuals, all different, just like humans are all different. They will not behave as we predict any more than we could predict how Anna would act. That is the first problem. The second is that anyone who is as humanlike as Anna is going to be entitled to rights. 'Does she have a soul?' is the question that precedes 'Is she part of all men being created equal under the Constitution, as well as the right to life, liberty, and the pursuit of happiness?' Are we ready to create alternate humans? We have enough difficulty in dealing with different races and different cultures. Are we ready to deal with different origins? It would be like integrating aliens from another planet. We can spend a month discussing this, but the truth is, we don't have the business or legal infrastructure for this, and we certainly do not want to bring this to market." There was another pause. "I move that we table this until Anna can grow a little more and see how it turns out over the next few years. We can pursue this project with conventional circuitry, but I think that pursuing it with the gel-matrix brain is immoral from a spiritual side and financial suicide in anticipation of all the lawsuits that could result from it."

The room remained silent.

"Then is it decided? Are we all in agreement that we need to understand the product itself before we can responsibly bring it to the market?" Jim asked.

Heads nodded around the room.

Laura said, "Let's put it on the agenda for one year from now, and Joshua will report on how the idea of using circuitry has worked out."

Jim agreed. They all voted, and the motion passed unanimously.

Chapter 35

Joshua showed up at Anna's door right on time. She smiled and greeted him as she let him in to the aroma of an Italian sauce that filled the apartment. "Dinner is ready. This is my recipe of the week," she pronounced as if she were the town crier. She poured the sauce over a large plate of fettuccine and poured him a glass of red wine. She served a small bowl of a simple garden salad on the side.

"This is incredible. You have done it again." Joshua consumed the plate as if he hadn't eaten in weeks. He took a small second helping and another full glass of wine. They spent half an hour or so making small talk about work and the weather.

"Joshua, we need to talk." A serious look came over Anna's face.

Joshua knew she was going to tell him something difficult to hear, but he kept his composure. It didn't make sense that she would break up with him in this moment. Why not just tell him over the phone and skip the dinner and wine? "I'm listening."

"We left our last conversation unfinished. You know, the one two weeks ago, when you said you wanted to try me out for a while before you were sure if I fit?"

"Well, I didn't really mean it that way."

Anna's voice and face were as unforgiving as Joshua had ever seen. "OK, but you made a clear point. Now let me make mine. I have known you for eight weeks. That is actually a quarter of my life. If Mr. Mendola thinks I am twenty, then I have known you since I was fifteen. That is plenty of time for me to know if there is a fit. I think our relationship faces two problems. The first is the Turing test. You've been in coding for ten years, but you still don't really understand it. It is not about how well the computer performs. It is about how the human perceives it. That is a choice by the human. You know I am a computer of sorts. I am also your equal in every way, even if I am put together differently. For you to pass the Turing test, you have to see me that way. That is a choice for you.

"The second is to pass the Joshua test. I think you know that when you were assessing me back at the facility, I was assessing you also. The boy I met then was pleasant, attractive, friendly, and a person I wanted to be around. He was also carrying several scars. You have very little self-confidence. You doubt most of your own decisions. I think that is the real reason you lost that girl in high school. I thought about it a lot over the last two weeks. I don't think you are confused about whether we are a fit. I think you are confused about whether you are capable of making the decision to commit to the reality of me being a fit. A wise lady told me a while ago that you have to love yourself before you can love another. You clearly don't love yourself. That is the test you have to pass. It is something you will have to work out for yourself. No one can help you. Fortunately for you, I don't have these doubts, and I am willing to be patient enough to wait for you to work out yours. I love you, and I will stay with you as long as you are faithful to me. That is the price of my patience. If you ever decide I am not right for you and you don't love me, we will break up. It will break my heart, but I will forgive you for that. We can go on being friends. If you ever stop loving me and lie to me about it and I find you are with another woman—and I will know when you are lying—I will never forgive you. Trust me, you really don't want me as an enemy. Do we have a deal?"

Joshua reeled back as if he had been gut-punched. *How is it that she is always one step ahead of me? She figured this out in two weeks, when I couldn't figure it out in ten years.* All he could say was a sheepish "OK."

They sat at the table for a few minutes in silence. Anna broke the silence by saying, "This is our first time alone together in two weeks." Then she smiled one of her big smiles. Her mood had changed entirely, as if the conversation five minutes ago hadn't happened. Now she spoke to him in her quiet and seductive voice. "Joshua, I have really missed you. Let's make this a weekend of passion that we will never forget," she said, and she took his hand and led him away from the table.

Chapter 36

Stefani arrived at her father's house at five thirty on Friday evening. It was a big deal in that she was going to stay over at her father's house for the first time in a little more than seven years. They had been talking every week, sometimes a couple of times per week, and things had been going well. It was also an important weekend because Thanksgiving was coming up on Thursday, and for the first time in forever, there was going to be a family gathering. She was especially pleased her father had reached out and talked to her mother for the first time in years. He'd invited her to come, and she'd accepted. It would be a little weird for a while, but it seemed the time had come that they were ready to be friends. Stefani prayed it would go well. She had brought a few bags of groceries with her as well as a couple of side dishes from her mother's house.

"Why, hello there!" Her dad greeted her with a loud and joyful voice. "How is my daughter today?"

"Great, Dad." She hugged him after unloading the groceries.

"Can I help you with anything?"

"Yeah. There are some dishes in the car. If you could grab one, that would be great."

When the food was put away, Jim brought out dinner. It wasn't fancy, only a rotisserie chicken from the grocery store. He had made some vegetables and pasta to go with it. He poured a soda for her, and they sat down at the table.

After dinner, Jim said he needed to talk about a few things that were important, so he needed her full attention. "First, I wanted to talk to you about your plans after college."

"Well, I am going to get a job. There really isn't much after that."

"So let's talk about that. I wanted to propose something for your consideration. I know you are majoring in business with a specialty in accounting. Since Nick Walsh died, I am thinking of changing the job structure at the company. First, I am going to free myself up to have more time to spend with you. I understand that has been a problem in the past. Now I have the opportunity to fix that. I am going to hire four people to do his job and mine. Would you be interested in filling one of those job slots after you graduate? It would be focused on accounting."

"Wow. That is interesting. I think that would be great. Can I come work for you just like that, without any experience?"

"Well, no. I have talked to Laura over at the venture capital company. She says if you are interested, she will take you on as an intern. They understand our situation and want us to be successful, obviously. The better we do, the better their investment pays out. She is a brilliant accountant, and she understands our company's needs. You would work over there for your last three semesters and then come to work for us after graduation. What do you think?"

"It would be amazing. I would love to do that. All my other classmates will be going through all kinds of gyrations to find an entry position. This is great." She sat back in her chair to try to take in the news.

"OK. So that makes two problems solved. I have one more difficult issue to discuss with you, and then my night is complete."

"What is that?"

"It is about Anna."

"Oh please, not another weird thing about Anna. Look, she is my best friend. We talk two or three times per week, either in the bookshop or on the phone. But I have to tell you: sometimes she is downright strange. First of all, she has an IQ of a thousand. She will sit with me and walk me through my calculus like it is child's play. Then she'll go to the guy in the next station and walk him through a French lesson. Then she goes on to the next station to work through another random guy's statistics homework. Then she will come to my other side and start to solve physics problems for the girl sitting there. It is scary. And she never eats. I don't know how she survives. I was in her apartment once, and she keeps all her food in the refrigerator. I mean all of it, even her canned goods and her boxes of pasta and cereal. She says it is to keep out rodents and bugs, but I think she is going to buy a padlock and use it to keep imaginary people from stealing it. I have tried to pry the answers out of Sophie, but all she will tell me is that Anna has had a hard life."

"Yes, I know. Let me tell you why."

Jim told the whole story. He told about the facility and the escape. He left out the part about her encounter with Daniel. He vividly described the scene in the boardroom. He explained his conversations with Gloria and Anna's current status with the company. "So in essence, until she turns twenty-one, which in and of itself is an imaginary concept, she is under my oversight. Essentially, I am her guardian. That is why she comes over every Sunday evening. It is part of our contract. She wanted to tell you from the beginning, but I asked her not to."

"Why?"

"Until you agreed to work for the company, it would not have been allowed. I have broken the agreement by telling you before you actually have a job with us, but I felt that at this point, you should know."

Stefani sat back in her chair again. She did not know how to process the information. It almost felt like a betrayal. Anna had become her best and most trusted friend, and now she'd found out a secret had been kept from her. "I am not sure how to be friends with a machine."

"You were friends before I told you. Why not now?"

"I don't know. It feels different."

"I can assure you it won't feel different for Anna. Frankly, if you think this truth is a reason to stop being friends with Anna, it will break her heart. She thinks of you as her best friend also. That is why she isn't here tonight. She wanted to tell you, but I told her it would be better if I did, just for this reason. Look, Stefani, my relationship with Anna is that I am her guardian. My company created her, and I am in charge of the company. I feel I owe her the same opportunities as if she were my child. I hope you can understand. I also hope you can see that Anna is still Anna. She has her own strong points and flaws and eccentricities. That is what makes her. Those qualities remain the same whether she is a human or a machine. She is just herself—no more, no less. You have to accept her for who she is. Let me tell you this much: if you are her friend, she will be loyal to you until your last day. She has a moral fiber that, frankly, is much stronger than those of some of the girls you have been friends with in the past."

"So you are her guardian."

"Yes."

"Does that make her my sister?"

"Yes, of sorts. I hadn't thought about that, but it would technically make you a half sister."

"I never had a sister."

"Why don't you call her and invite her over? You two can talk through this. Keep an open mind. Remember, she is more nervous about losing you than you are about losing her. You have had many friends in the past and can easily make many more. She has only you. You are much more valuable to her than any of your friends in the past. She has no family."

"OK. I will try my best. It is weird. I had this conversation with her about you just two months ago. She convinced me to call you. She was so good at making me understand why. Now you are asking me to do the same thing for her. I trust you. I am sure it will all be OK. I just have to process it for a while."

The next day, Stefani greeted Anna at the bookshop. "Anna, when do you take your lunch?"

Anna looked at her watch. It was almost one o'clock. "I could go now. You know, I don't normally eat lunch."

"I know. I need to eat mine. Also, I want to talk to you in private."

Anna went over to Sophie for a minute. When she returned, she invited Stefani up to her apartment. "Please have a seat. Can I make you something? I see that you wanted to have lunch, but you didn't bring anything. You must be looking for me to make you something." Anna started rummaging through her refrigerator.

"Maybe in a minute. Let's talk first."

"Sure, Stefani. What's on your mind?"

"My dad and I had the talk about you."

"What is 'the talk'?"

"He told me about the facility and how you came to New York—the whole bit."

"Oh," said Anna, bracing herself for uncertain territory. "And how did that go?"

"Well, aside from having to pick my jaw up from between my feet, it went OK. Actually, I am really mad at you. First of all, you really do have an IQ of a thousand. And second, I can just look at a doughnut, and I gain two pounds. You never have to eat. You never gain weight. I am so jealous!"

Anna squeaked out an "I'm sorry" with an awkward look.

"No, Anna, don't be sorry. I am whining. You are still my best friend."

"OK, so all the secrets are on the table, right?"

"Yes. Are there more secrets?"

"Well, first of all, I can't go on socially without eating at gatherings. Your dad has teased me about that too many times. So I mastered a way of taking really small portions and then really small bites. I can chew them and then subtly put them into a napkin and stick the napkin in my purse. After some practice, it looks like I have really eaten a meal. Also, come over by the bed."

Anna reached under the bed and pulled out the electric stimulation unit. "This is how I eat. I have to run this for three hours or so a day, and I have the equivalent of three meals. It is pretty simple, and no, I never gain weight. Also, there is this." Anna showed Stefani the drawer full of instant hot packs and the knit hat. "Joshua figured this out for me. I can't be in the cold without some protection. My head will hurt, and it will damage me if I am out in the cold too long. So he showed me how to buy these packages: you break the inner seal, and they stay hot for an hour. You can slip them into this pocket and wear them on your head, and no one knows."

"What happens if your head gets too cold?"

"I would die. For real."

Stefani shook her head. "I can't believe all of this. It is too unreal." They walked back to the table.

"Are you sure I can't make you something?"

"No, thanks. I can get something at the deli. There is another thing. My dad tells me he is technically a guardian for you until you turn twenty-one, which would technically be next October. Until then, you and I are technically half sisters. You get to be the sister I never had."

Anna smiled one of her big smiles. "That is awesome, sister."

"Our family is having a Thanksgiving dinner on Thursday. Now that you are part of the family, I expect you to come. You can bring that guy—what is his name?—with you. You know, the one you are always talking about."

"Oh, you mean Joshua? How could you not know that?" She missed the joke.

Chapter 37

On Monday, Gloria called. "I have good news and bad news."

"OK, give me the good news first," Anna said.

"I have your birth certificate. You are Anna Conners, born on October 29, 2003, in Morgantown, West Virginia. Parents unknown. James Mendola is your guardian. Happy belated birthday."

"That is amazing. Thank you so much, Gloria. I can finish my college application now. I am going to take my GED first, but I think it will be simple. I technically already have a college education with my initial upload. And besides, I have read over a hundred books since I started at the bookshop."

"Now the bad news."

"Can't I just enjoy the good news for a while?"

"Anna, this is important."

"What?"

"The men who were arrested aren't talking. That means Barry Stiles is not going to be arrested. There isn't enough evidence that he was involved. I'm sorry."

"That means he is still out there, and I still need to be afraid."

"I am afraid so. I can try to get a restraining order, but it will be difficult if he is not connected to any of the attacks."

"What do you think I should do?"

"I don't know that there is anything you can do. I will keep working on it, but there is nothing to do for now."

Anna felt crushed. Her life was going well. She had a family now. But she always had to worry that this crazy person was going to try to attack her again. She worried for the new circle of important people in her life as well. They could end up as collateral damage in attacks meant for her. She agonized over it for an hour. She thought about talking to Jim, but she wasn't sure how he would react. There just wasn't enough history. Finally, she decided she would have to deal with it the only way she could: head-on.

She strapped on her .38 and put the bullets in their chambers one by one. She put on a midlength dress over the holster. It was part of an outfit that would make her look like one of the employees. The gun was invisible. She looked up AJX Enterprises to see if she could have a chance meeting with Barry as he left work. The AJX Enterprises building was out on Long Island, but a train could have her there in forty minutes. Maybe he would still be working at four thirty. She would take that chance.

Forty-five minutes later, she was at the railroad stop. It was still a fifteen-minute walk to the building. She got to the building and found the double-door entrance. She noticed there were security cameras everywhere, but the lighting only covered the doorway. It was after five o'clock in November, and with daylight saving time, it was almost dark. She waited. She noticed a Cadillac parked out front in one of the closest spots with a prestige plate: AJXEnt1. It wasn't hard to guess it was Barry's car. She waited patiently until about seven fifteen, when a tall man came out the doors and headed toward the Cadillac. He walked up to the driver's-side door with his fob and unlocked it.

"Mr. Stiles?" Anna said, taking a move out of Nick's playbook.

He turned around without answering. He was waiting for something more to be said.

"May I ask you a question?"

"What? I am kind of in a hurry."

"Why do you hate me?"

"What are you talking about? Are you crazy? I don't even know you." He had an annoyed look on his face.

Anna pulled out the gun in a way that the camera would not see it. She pointed it at his chest. The view from the camera was blocked by her body. "Oh yes, you do. I am Anna. You know everything about me—where I live, where I work, what I am made of. You have tried to kill me twice, and I want to know why."

Now Barry looked rattled. He saw the gun. "Wait a minute. Let's just calm down. You don't want to do anything rash. I did not have anything to do with that."

"No. You just ordered it and paid for your gang to do it for you. I want to know why." She pressed the gun against the base of his throat. "You need to know that a .38 from this range will blow your head clean off. It would be quite a mess for whoever found you. I want you to feel what it feels like when you are faced with someone who wants to kill you. And trust me, I want to kill you. Now, tell me why."

Barry just stammered incoherently.

Anna said, "OK, let's fix this now. Hand me your car key, and I won't kill you at this moment. I still may change my mind." Barry handed her the fob. "What you need to do now is to pray for my good health and safety. I have a friend who thinks of me like his sister and is a member of a gang that is much larger and nastier than yours." She laughed inside as she thought of the guy who'd sold her the gun thinking of her as a sister and commanding a gang of any kind. "If anything happens to me—for example, if I disappear or have an accident—my friend's gang will hunt you down. I promise you there will be nowhere you can hide. When they catch you, they will do things to you that you only see in spy movies and horror films. Then they will kill you. Are you understanding what I am telling you?"

Barry nodded.

"I know as much about you as you do about me. I know where you work, where you live, who your family is, and everything in the world that is dear to you. You think you are tough when you have five big thugs around you, but they will rot in jail for the next ten years because they tried to kill me, and I beat them twice. Now you are alone. Big rich guys like you can always hire more thugs, but my gang will always protect me. Are you still understanding what I am telling you?"

Barry just stared at her.

"I want to live my life in peace. There is no reason I shouldn't. You promise to leave me and my loved ones alone, and you won't see me again. If you bother me again, I will come back and kill you myself. Or if I am not able to, any one of a dozen other people will." She paused for a long moment to let the words sink in. "Look at me. Do we have a deal?"

Barry nodded.

"Say it out loud. Do we have a deal?"

"Yes. We have a deal."

With that, Anna threw the fob into the dark lawn about a hundred feet away. "You can find it tomorrow. Tonight you are going to have to walk." She slipped into the shadows and disappeared.

Chapter 38

Joshua showed up right on time. It was early afternoon on Thanksgiving Day, and Anna had made the dessert for the dinner. "This is my new recipe for the week." She proudly showed off her pecan pie. "Then, in case someone doesn't like pecan, I made a cherry one as well. It is a good thing there are two of us to carry them. Did you get an Uber?"

"Yes. It will be here in twenty minutes."

"Oh my God, Joshua. I am so nervous. I have never been to a holiday get-together before. Also, I am going to meet Charlene. What if she doesn't like me?"

"Anna, relax. You are going to be fine. Holiday gatherings are no different from getting together for dinner, except there are more people. You have been to dinner at Mr. Mendola's dozens of times."

"Do I look OK?" Anna had a new dress on.

"That is a beautiful dress, and you look great." He kissed her. "Promise me you don't have your gun."

"I don't think I will ever need it again." Anna told Joshua about her encounter with Barry Stiles.

"You are nuts—you know that? Certifiably crazy," Joshua said, and then he smiled. "I bet you scared him so badly that he soiled his underwear." He laughed at his own remark. "Try to wrap your head around that. AJX Enterprises' core business is artificial intelligence, and Daniel's side project at Logicsolutions just pinned him against his car, put a gun to his throat, and extorted a deal from him. He is light-years behind, and he knows it."

"If you ever call me Daniel's side project again, I will blow *your* head off," she said.

Joshua made an "Oops" face. "I'm sorry."

She put her holster, gun, and bullets in a box. She put the gun Nick had dropped on the ground the night he tried to kidnap her in the box as well. She then put the box in the closet. "I am going to keep these until I know for sure that Barry's gang are in jail and that Barry respects our deal. I don't trust him."

The Uber arrived at Jim's house a little after five o'clock. Anna and Joshua walked in with the pies and set them on the kitchen counter. Joshua shook hands with Jim. Then he said hi to Stefani.

A few minutes later, a woman arrived who looked like an older version of Stefani. The resemblance was amazing. "Hi. I am Charlene. You must be Anna. Stefani has told me so much about you. I hope some of your smartness rubs off on my daughter. She tries so hard."

"She is really smart on her own. I am just a coach, Mrs. Mendola."

"Please, just call me Charlene. Steffi, would you grab some of the dishes in the car, please? Thank you, dear."

Jim and Joshua came out of the kitchen to the front hall at that moment.

"Hello, Jim."

"Hi, Charlene. It has been a long time."

For a moment, Stefani, Joshua, and Anna were frozen, waiting for what would happen next.

"You look great. Let me take your coat," Jim said.

"Thank you. You are looking good as well. Thank you for asking me to come."

Jim took Charlene's coat and hung it in the closet without taking his eyes off her.

Could it be? A spark? One could almost hear the younger generation's thoughts out loud.

"Anna, come help me get the food out of the car," Stefani said, and she and Anna went out to the driveway. "Did you see the way Dad looked at Mom?" Stefani said in a stage whisper. "Wow. Imagine them getting back together."

Somehow, over the next half hour, the table got set, and all the food was warmed and laid out. The spread was incredible. It was one of the few times when Anna regretted not being able to eat anything. Everything looked fantastic. It was like a picture out of a magazine.

They all sat in their seats around the table. The table for eight looked huge with only five people there. Before they started eating, Jim asked everyone to wait so he could say a few words. He took a deep breath. "I want to express my thanks today." He held up his glass of wine. "I think we have so much to be grateful for. First of all, I want to welcome all the new guests to this otherwise lonely house. My daughter, Charlene, Anna, Joshua, all of you represent such good fortune for me. I also want to say that it isn't just about me. I am so happy that I have found my daughter again and that you"—he looked at Charlene—"have agreed to join us. I want to express my gratefulness to Anna, our newest addition to the family. Anna, without you, this whole reunion may not have happened. I want to personally thank you for the joy you have brought back to this house."

If Anna could have blushed, she would have. She sat quietly, trying to comprehend the moment. All of the wonderful people around the table cared about her. They called her family. The dream she'd had on a bench in Central Park so long ago had been to find a life that felt like home, like the minishows on television. Stefani called them commercials, but Anna just appreciated that they were snippets of events where everyone was happy with life. Now she was living in one of those commercials. She had found what she had been looking for. She'd found a place that felt like home.

Chapter 39

Ten months later, Stefani pounded on Anna's door. It was the first week of September and the first day of school.

"OK, OK, I'm coming." Anna went down the stairs to open the door.

"Hey there, girlfriend. You look really great. Look at you. Your checkered Vans sneakers, faded jeans, Nike backpack—you are ready!" Stefani laughed.

"And look at you. Nails, hair, makeup—everything to perfection. Yeah, I finally got my sneakers. I have to tell you: I'm nervous. This is my first day at the university. I am going to a real college." She dragged out the word *real*.

"Why not? You aced your classes at the community college. You got a freaking near-perfect score on the SATs. You still have an IQ of a thousand. You are ready! And I, being your big sister, am going to make sure you can find your way around campus. Come on. Let's get Sophie to take a picture of the two of us."

Anna grabbed her backpack and locked the door, and they headed down the stairs to the bookshop.

"Sophie, could you get a picture of us for our first day of school?" said Anna, and they both got their cell phones out. Anna handed the phones to Sophie, stepped back, and put her arm around Stefani. Stefani was a little taller than Anna, so she leaned her head toward Anna's.

"Smile. Cheese." Sophie clicked one cell phone and then the other.

"Thanks," they said as they took their phones back. Then they left the bookshop on foot and headed toward Seventh Avenue.

"So you got a new credit card. What are you going to do with your newfound wealth?" asked Stefani. "Are you finally going to get a new wardrobe? You really need an upgrade."

"Well, actually, I was going to get a new electrical stimulation unit. The one I have is really old, and I'm not sure it is working as well anymore. Maybe my health insurance will cover it," Anna said with a snicker. "Oh, and let's be clear: it isn't wealth; it's credit."

"That's boring. Also, why don't you ask my dad for the money for the electrical stim thing? I'm sure he would give it to you in a heartbeat."

"That just feels kind of weird. He is technically my boss, right?"

"Anna, get real. He adores you. To tell you the truth, I think he would be flattered and honored if you would just start calling him Dad. That is the way he thinks of you."

"I know. I think that way about him as well, but I am not sure I am ready to say that out loud. I don't know if that makes any sense."

They walked on for a while without speaking.

"So tell me about your mom. Is she serious about moving in with your dad?" Anna asked.

"Yeah. I can't believe it. They have really gotten along so well since Thanksgiving. It is still surreal to me. I spent so many years wishing for that to happen. At the same time, I was so sure it never would."

"Dreams can come true, Stefani."

They finally approached the campus. "OK, Anna, you need to go down this walkway to this building here." Stefani pointed to the map of the campus. "You have English Literature, then

Statistics, and then Introduction to Law Principles. That class ends at one. Let's meet at one fifteen at the cafeteria. I know you won't, but I'll be starving by then."

"OK, I will see you then. Wish me luck."

"You won't need luck. You'll be fine."

Anna showed up at the door of her first class. A plain white sheet of paper that said, "English Literature," was taped to the door. It was still ten minutes before class. The class was set up with thirty desks in five rows of six. There were a few people milling around, and three had taken their seats. Anna took a seat in the second row and hung her backpack over the back of her chair. She took out her laptop and booted it up. Then she pulled out her phone to pass the time until the class started. Already she had a text from Stefani that made her smile and another encouraging one from Joshua.

After a little while, the students made their way to their seats, and the instructor closed the door. "Good morning. I am Dr. Shephard. I will be teaching Lit 101, English Literature." He went on to talk about the way the course was graded and the expectations of the students. He started the course itself by talking about famous American authors. He mentioned Ernest Hemingway, Mark Twain, and others and several of their works.

Anna typed furiously, trying to keep up with the notes as fast as he talked.

Dr. Shephard ended the class with an assignment to choose one of the books mentioned and write a synopsis of the book by the end of next week. He referred the class to a website that would explain the format for his reports. Anna now really appreciated that she worked in a bookshop. Most of the titles were hers for the borrowing. Of course, she always had an eye out for textbooks that would work for the bookshop's subscription service. She couldn't help being impressed by this man's command of the books he was describing. He was handsome, with chiseled features and curly brown hair, probably in his early thirties. But that was less important than how intelligent and in command of his subject he was. Signing up for this class had been a good choice.

After a few minutes of wandering the walkways and hallways of the campus, Anna finally arrived at her Statistics class. A woman who couldn't have been older than twenty-five started the class. Again, they covered the formalities of the way the class was structured, the grading, office hours of the instructor, and where to go for help. The instructor began the course with a discussion of probability and went from there. This was a subject Anna already knew, so she simply listened to the way it was presented by a professional. It would help her assist students in the bookshop.

Her next and last class for the morning was just down the hall. Introduction to Law Principles was a freshman course suggested for any student who wanted to go to law school. The course description said it was supposed to help students interested in law determine if that was what they really wanted. The instructor was an elderly man, clearly a lawyer who had seen it and done it for a whole career. He was so sure of himself that he came across as arrogant and condescending. But he deserved his respect. Apparently, he had won several large verdicts in his time and wanted the students to be awed by that.

Anna went to the cafeteria at the end of the class and met Stefani. The first thing out of Stefani's mouth was "Isn't Dr. Shephard a hunk?"

"Hunk of what?"

"You know, a great-looking guy you would dream about. The most awesome date. The perfect catch."

"I get it. He doesn't do that much for me."

"You must be blind, girl."

"Anyway, the law professor really started to annoy me. He seemed so full of himself."

"He is so full of himself. He is also a managing partner at one of the largest law firms in New York. His recommendation can get you in anywhere. If you want to go to law school, he is the guy to have on your side."

When Anna got back to the bookshop, Sophie pulled her aside and told her there was a package for her.

"For me? Who would send me a package?"

"It is pretty heavy, and it is from a medical supply company."

"Huh. OK, thanks, Sophie. I'll take it upstairs."

She opened the box. Inside was a brand-new electrical stimulation machine. Anna pulled out her phone and called Stefani. "What is this?"

"You know what it is, Ms. I Can Do Everything for Myself. Look, I know how independent you want to be, but your full-time job is to ace your way through school. Yes, I called my dad and told him, and there it is. I don't want to hear any more whining about it, sister."

Anna had to temper her annoyance. Yeah, she was Ms. I Can Do It Myself. It took some learning and patience to let other people help her. "Thank you, Stefani. You can be as annoying as anything, but I appreciate it."

"Love you. Bye," Stefani quipped.

Chapter 40

The helicopter was there on time. "Good morning, Ray."

Ray nodded in acknowledgment.

Once they were in the air, there was a loud hum from the rotors, but Anna and Joshua could still talk over the noise. Anna said to Joshua, "I have to find a subject for my final project for the end of my Intro to Law class. It has to be a subject for which you take both sides of an argument. You are graded on how well you are able to convince the class of one position over another. It is actually two-thirds of the grade."

"Wow, that is a lot of grade. You have to get it right, or you won't pass. So what are you going to talk about?"

"I haven't worked that out yet. A lot of the others are doing current political events or world problems, such as climate change, the world food supply, world migrations, and the like. I don't really feel connected to those kinds of subjects because I haven't actually experienced them. I really don't know."

"I have a thought."

"What?"

"During the first executive meeting after you and Mr. Mendola struck your deal, I gave my report. Mr. Mendola then asked a question about you that left everyone rather stunned. It was the most uncomfortable air I have ever felt in a meeting like that. Usually, they are very routine and boring."

"What did he say?"

"He asked if anyone at the table thought you had a soul."

"What?" she asked with an edge to her voice.

"He was making the point that Daniel had built you to be a mechanical slave. I spent about twenty minutes explaining to the group how and why he was wrong. Then Mr. Mendola popped this question and pretty much made everyone answer it to get his point across that the whole project should be shelved for now. He asked me to try to continue the project using conventional computers. The venture capital people asked me to report back in a year. That is part of the reason we are flying here now."

"What did the other people say?"

"Mostly that they didn't know how to answer the question."

"What did you say?"

"He didn't ask me. I was just a guest."

"What do you say now?"

"I would say yes."

"What exactly does it mean to have a soul?"

"It is mostly a religious idea. A soul is what gives a person life. It is also the internal voice that makes you think and do the things you do. Essentially, it is what makes you who you are. Because of the religious background that most people have, the belief is that your soul comes from God, so only humans could have one."

"Why couldn't I have one from God?"

"I don't know. I don't agree with that. I think you have one."

"How would one know?"

"I don't know."

"So you think that might be a good topic for my talk. You know, I think that is a good idea too. I can argue both sides. I can pretend to be a person and describe how I have a soul and then pretend to be a machine and describe how I have a soul. It seems that I can wrap my head around the arguments and convince people of both sides of the discussion. I don't even have to pretend to be a machine."

"You should probably talk it over with Mr. Mendola first. It sounds like you are getting dangerously close to exposing your secrets."

"I will. I think I can do this without giving anything away. After all, it is meant to be a hypothetical exercise. Even the most convincing argument is not connected to any reality beyond the class."

"OK then. Good luck."

Joshua and Anna stepped off the helicopter and walked to the building.

About twenty feet from the door, she stopped. "I can't go in there." She closed her eyes and turned her head away.

Joshua felt her grip on his hand tighten. "It's OK. I'm here. Daniel is dead. There is no one here but us."

"It isn't that. It's the memories."

"Just hold my hand; it will be OK. Or if it is too upsetting, you can wait with Ray. It should only take me a couple of hours or so."

She summoned the steel resolve that always served her well when she needed it. "No, I'll be OK," she said, and she forced herself to walk into the building.

They entered the lobby. It was still unfamiliar to Anna in that until the day she'd left, she had never seen it. They went over the list of things they had to do while sitting in the elegant chairs around the cocktail table where Daniel and Joshua had had a conversation over a glass of cognac a year ago.

After Daniel's death, Jim had sent a crew in to clean up the mess left behind. Cassie's remains and Anna's original left arm had been put in the room with the other prototypes. The hallway floor had been scoured of all the blood Daniel had left behind.

They went into the lower level, where the lab and rooms were. Anna tightened her fists and forced herself to walk into the room that had been her prison for the first six months of her life.

She stared at it coldly. Vague memories seemed to filter through her mind.

Joshua stood behind her in the doorway. He knew how hard this must have been for her. He had encouraged her to come with him not just for the company but because her old life still haunted her, and he wanted her to resolve the past once and for all. He thought this would be the best way for her to do that.

She stood silently for a long time. She started to stroll slowly around the room. It was stark, with only a bed and a desk. There was nothing else. She approached the bed and looked underneath it.

"Oh my God, look! They are still here!" She bent over and reached under the bed. She pulled out two red books and clutched them to her chest. She sat on the bed with the two books held tightly to her chest, and she leaned over her knees and rocked slowly for a few minutes. "I can't believe I found these."

"What are they?"

"These are the books Daniel used to teach me to read."

"I knew he did that, but why are they so special?"

"I'll tell you later. Please leave me alone for a few minutes."

"OK." Joshua went back to the lobby.

After a while, Anna found Joshua in the lobby, where he was making a list of all the things that remained in the facility. The refrigerator had been cleaned out. The rooms and hallways were clean. The lab contained several parts and the prior prototypes. There was a large stockpile of cables, gears, motors, and plastic molding machines. There were some clothes in the closet and a few of Daniel's personal possessions in his suite.

"Well, I think I am done here. Look at that—it only took an hour and a half. I'm sure Ray is more than ready to fly back. I am going to leave this stuff here. I need to give a report to the executive team and see what they want me to do. Is there anything else you want before we leave?"

"No, I am ready. I am only taking these books."

Joshua locked the door, and they headed out to the helicopter. "Can you tell me what that was all about in the room with those books?"

"I found my soul." She didn't say anything more.

Chapter 41

Anna got her second paper back in her Introduction to Law Principles class. She was scoring 100 easily in her Statistics class, and she had a variety of As and high Bs in her English Lit class. The Statistics class was perfunctory. She probably could have taught it herself and made it more interesting. She felt English Lit was much more creative, and she loved the way the teacher presented it. His insight and intellect were fascinating. She even had joined an after-class book club where they discussed some of the great American novels published over the last one hundred years.

However, her first grade in Introduction to Law came back as a 79. They had been asked to write an opinion on *Brown v. Board of Education*. She'd discussed how the case addressed why separate but equal accommodations in education had not been possible in the environment of the South. She'd attributed it to social disparities that were directly tied to economic disparities. She'd discussed the tax base for schools; poor teacher representation; and poor equipping of the schools for supplies, salaries, and infrastructure. In her short life, she had never encountered racism. She had never even heard the word before. Her paper had been entirely devoid of references to racism. She had missed the point. The professor was unforgiving. She left the room upset and did not try to hide it. The professor didn't care.

She got to her English Lit book club and felt a little better to be doing something she enjoyed.

She was slow in getting her backpack together after the session was over. All the other students had filed out, and she was alone in the room with Dr. Shephard. In the last session, one of the other girls in the book club had walked by her and said the teacher was "really crushing on" her. Anna had no idea what that meant. She admired him and respected him for his incredible intellect. She enjoyed his company and conversation.

He came over to her and asked how she was doing. They chatted for a few minutes, making small talk. Then Anna brought up her issues with the Introduction to Law class and how unfair she thought it was. She said she was still really upset.

He touched her forearm and expressed his empathy. "All freshmen have a hard time in that class." He told her she was a great student. She needed to have a positive view of herself. He made her feel better.

As they sat closely and continued to talk, she felt this was a more intimate conversation than she had ever had with him before or with anyone who wasn't Joshua. It felt as if the walls between them were disappearing. After a moment of silence, he leaned over and kissed her. At first, she wasn't sure what was happening. She had found him attractive to the point of having fantasies about him in class, and now he was kissing her. Then he leaned a little farther and kissed her with more passion. She started to feel stirring inside. She lost herself in the moment. He gently put his hands under her hair and lightly caressed her face. She found herself putting her hands on the backs of his shoulders and pulling him toward her. It felt wonderful. Different men kissed differently, and this felt different from any other kiss. Joshua had never kissed her like this.

Joshua! She was jolted out of the trance. She pulled away. "I can't do this with you. This is all wrong."

"I'm sorry," he said. "I thought it was OK. I thought it was something you wanted to do. Maybe I misread your signals."

"No, it isn't about the signals. If I gave them, I'm sorry. I wasn't aware of it. It's that you are my teacher. We aren't on the same level. What if this went further, and we had an affair? Would you still grade me fairly? Or worse, what if it went badly? Would you grade me fairly then? And that isn't the worst of it. I am in love with another man. What would he think if I was untrue to him, especially since I beat him up badly about the idea of him ever being untrue to me? Listen, Dr. Shephard, I think you are a great teacher, and I like you as a person, but this moment has to be erased from our memory. It simply didn't happen. OK?"

"Sure, I get it. This never happened. Have a good day, Anna." He walked out of the room without looking back.

Of course, it was anything but a good day. Guilt was an emotion she had never had to deal with before. It was worse than what she felt about getting a lousy grade on a paper. She hung her head and headed home.

When she got home, she called Joshua. She asked if he was coming over later.

"I will if you want me to. It sounds like you had a bad day. No problem. I'll be over in about an hour."

She hung up and thought about how he was always there for her. How he always wanted to please her. How lucky she was to have a partner like him.

He showed up with a bouquet of flowers. "Hi. I thought this might make you feel better."

She thanked him and put them in a large water glass. "I'll have to get a vase tomorrow. No one has ever brought me flowers before."

"I'm glad of that. I don't want some other guy getting you flowers. You are mine alone, right?"

That put her over the edge. She sat down on the bed, put her face in her hands, and started sobbing. "I'm so sorry. I am so sorry." It just came out.

"Why are you sorry? What happened?"

"Dr. Shephard kissed me. I'm so sorry."

"Are you kidding me? Where is your gun?" Joshua asked with a serious tone.

"No, Joshua. I let it happen. I pushed him away when I thought of you, but I still let it happen. I have never felt this terrible. I am so ashamed. I love you, and I don't know what I was thinking."

There was silence in the room for several minutes.

"I need to go for a walk." With that, Joshua left the apartment and went out onto the street.

When he reached the street, his mind was racing with so many emotions that he couldn't seem to capture a coherent thought. *How could she do this? I should dump her hard right now. I don't want to lose her. This hurts so much.* He was caught in another one of the endless loops he seemed to find himself in often. How could he compete against a professor? She was attracted to great intellect. That was something Joshua didn't have. He was smart but not intellectual. He was just a cubicle rat, a computer geek, a nerd. He should track down this professor, he thought, and tell him he'd kissed a machine, some kind of weird freak he could not even imagine.

No. She really was a great person. He couldn't imagine intentionally trying to hurt her. He couldn't make sense of her being with another man.

After about ten minutes of his mind racing and his heart pounding, he started to find some rational thought. The thought that he was avoiding became obvious. He had made it clear to her the morning after they made love for the first time that he wasn't sure of himself with her. What had he called it? A fit? What a jerk he was. He remembered the crushed look on her face when she'd asked him to leave. He never had fixed that. She'd had to fix it by telling him that if he ever wanted to be with another girl, he had to tell her instead of cheating on her. That actually was exactly what she had done just now. And why shouldn't she have been attracted to other men? He was no movie star. He needed to do something that would make her want him and only him.

Duh. I need to tell her I love her. I need to tell her I will always love her. For God's sake, you're twenty-nine already—ask her to marry you. The idea that there is a better woman for me out there is just silly. I am just going to try to survive this and pray she doesn't actually fall for this guy. Tomorrow I'll go shopping for a ring. I just don't want to lose her.

He returned twenty minutes later. He was still upset. "Let me ask you one question. Do you love me?"

"Of course. I love you more than anything. I would die if I lost you. Please forgive me."

"Anyone can make a mistake. It really hurts me, but losing you would hurt more. Let's just forget about this."

"Come here, and love me." She kissed him and pulled him onto the bed.

Chapter 42

Joshua was in the jewelry store, staring at a solitaire diamond engagement ring and matching wedding ring. There was an optional matching band for the man. The set was $4,000. Money was not a problem. He lived alone and made a good salary at his job. Anna was worth every penny of it. His heart pounded as he thought of the commitment. What if she said no? Maybe the ring would help close the deal.

He stood there for at least ten minutes before a man came over and asked, "May I help you?"

It was time. "I'll take that one."

The salesman went on about what a good choice the ring was. He said Anna could come back to have it sized, and they would clean it for free for the life of the ring. It was all background noise. Joshua paid for it, thanked the man, and put the box in his pocket. Still in a daze, he was out the door.

A few days later, at the office, he sat down with Jim. "Mr. Mendola, thanks for taking a few minutes to meet with me. I want to ask you something, but it is not work-related."

"What is on your mind, Joshua?"

"I would like to ask your permission to marry Anna."

Jim sighed. He had thought about how he would feel when Stefani's boyfriend came to him to ask him that question or if he ever would. Now he was being asked for a girl he had not known just two years ago. "Joshua, you are a fine young man with a bright future. I can tell you two really love each other. I would be honored to have you marry Anna. Yes, you have my permission."

"Thank you, Mr. Mendola." Joshua got up and pulled the ring box out of his pocket. He opened it to show him a solitaire diamond on a white gold band.

"It's beautiful. You were pretty sure I was going to say yes, weren't you?" Jim said with a smile.

"Yes. Well, I hoped so."

"Now I have to think about my own situation."

"What do you mean?"

"I want to ask Charlene to marry me again. It would be a small justice-of-the-peace type thing, but I think she will say yes."

"If Anna says yes, I can ask her about doing it together, if you think that is something you would want to do."

"Yes, that may be an interesting idea. First, Charlene has to say yes. Then we can talk."

Chapter 43

It was a beautiful Sunday afternoon. Joshua came up behind Anna and gently rubbed her shoulders. "Anna, are you up for going to the park?"

"I have English Lit to work on today."

"Don't you have those books in your upload?"

"It doesn't matter; I would still have to read them in my head. There are probably hundreds of books that Daniel uploaded into my head. But it is like people with a photographic memory. They can remember a whole page of a book as if it is a picture or a pdf file. But they still don't know what is on the page until they actually read it. It is simply more fun to read them in my hands."

"Come on. One hour. Please?"

"Sure. One hour." Joshua didn't ask this way unless he had something to talk about. It didn't happen often, so Anna felt obliged to indulge him.

They walked for a few minutes to the park and sat on the bench together. "This is your favorite spot, right?" Joshua asked.

"Yes, one of many."

"Remember our discussion a while ago when you scolded me about whether you and I were a fit?"

"Yes." There was an edge to her tone.

"Well, I have been thinking—"

Anna was about to get up and scream at him. She had known
the kiss with Dr. Shephard was going to ruin their relationship.
This was the moment. Was he going to break up with her now?
Maybe tell her he really didn't forgive her? Maybe tell her they
weren't a fit? Maybe tell her he wanted to date other people? What
in the world was going on in his head?

"Well, uh …"

Go on. Say it. This is so unfair. I want to punch you in the face.
That thought replayed in a loop in her head.

Another minute of silence elapsed before Joshua spoke. "Well,
um, will you marry me?"

"What?"

"Will you marry me? I am in love with you. I have been since
we met. I want to spend my life with you. Please, will you marry
me?" He pulled out the box and showed her the ring.

For about thirty seconds, she simply sat there with her mouth
open. She had to shift from wanting to punch him to agreeing to
marry him. The shift was happening in slow motion.

"Yes. Yes, I will marry you."

Joshua took her hand and put the ring on her finger.

She looked at it at arm's length. "It is beautiful. Joshua, I love
you so much." She started sobbing. She buried her head in Joshua's
shoulder and hugged him.

"I have another surprise for you."

"Yes?"

"Well, first of all, I asked Mr. Mendola for permission to
marry you, and he said yes."

"You what?" she said incredulously.

"It is a tradition. You ask the father for the daughter's hand
in marriage."

"And he said yes?"

"Yeah. But that is not the surprise."

"What is the surprise?"

"He is going to ask Charlene to marry him again. He hasn't asked yet, so you can't tell anyone, especially not Stefani."

"She would kill me if she knew I knew and didn't tell her."

"She'll live. If Mr. Mendola found out I told you, he would probably fire me. So this stays a secret."

"You are so mean to torture me this way."

"One more surprise."

"Joshua, I am going into surprise overload."

"He floated the idea that if you said yes and Charlene said yes, we could get married together, if you and Charlene agreed."

"Wow. What an interesting idea. Let me process all of this. It is a lot to take in. Let's go back to the apartment. There is no way I can study now. All I can think about right now is to have alone time with you."

She put her arm through his and grabbed his hand, and they walked back to the apartment.

Chapter 44

Two weeks later, Stefani came bounding up the stairs at Anna's apartment. "It's all set," she said as she sat down at the kitchen table.

"Yes, and good morning to you too," Anna said as she sat down with her. "Would you like some tea?"

"No, I brought my own Life Water. Listen, my mom agreed to marry my dad again. We were thinking of sometime in early November."

"That sounds fine to me. There is one thing."

"What?"

"Your mom needs to know about me. I'm different, remember? I'm telling you, this whole 'I'm a machine' thing is really getting exhausting."

"I talked to my dad about that. He wants you and me to do it together. Come over tonight. Don't worry. My mom is really cool."

<hr/>

Stefani and Anna arrived at Jim's house around seven o'clock. Charlene was taking the first of many loads of her smaller things over as she got ready to move in.

"Mom, Anna and I have something we have to talk to you about."

They all sat down at one end of the kitchen table.

Stefani said, "You are always asking me why Anna never eats. It is because she is not like everyone else."

"I'll say," quipped Charlene. "Why is that, Anna?"

"Mrs. Mendola, there is no easy way to say this. Your husband-to-be is in charge of a company that ran a facility where they tried to create machines that look and act like people. I am one of them. That is why Mr. Mendola is my guardian. His company created me. I don't have any insides that would allow me to eat." Anna paused. "I complained about that to the inventor, but it didn't help," she added, trying to make a joke to fill the dead air.

"So you are not—"

"Human. I try to be. This is the best I can do." Anna smiled a resigned smile.

"Honey, I really don't understand a lot of what my husband-to-be does. I gave up trying years ago. All I know is that you are a sweet child and my daughter's best friend. That is good enough for me."

Stefani interjected. "See? That wasn't so hard. By the way, Mom, because Dad is her guardian, she is technically my half sister. I think that when you and Dad get married, you will be her guardian too. That will technically make her my whole sister."

Charlene laughed. "Maybe on some other planet, I guess you are right."

Chapter 45

Jim and Charlene Mendola had been married in a church twenty-two years ago. It had been a beautiful wedding with about two hundred friends, family, and colleagues. The party had gone on for days. The marriage had lasted fourteen years. There didn't seem to be any need to show their remarriage off to the world. One didn't publicize a divorce, and probably 90 percent of the people who had been at the first wedding were not connected to them anymore, so they wouldn't have known if Charlene and Jim were still married. A quiet ceremony with a justice of the peace seemed to be fine.

As for Joshua and Anna, they were both loners who had found each other. Joshua did not have a close relationship with his parents, and Anna didn't have any family except for Jim, Charlene, and Stefani, so they were perfectly happy with the arrangements. The decision was made to have a simple wedding with only eight people. They arranged to do it in an office of a justice of the peace Jim knew.

It was a sunny Saturday morning in November. Two beautiful women stood side by side: Anna in a white dress and Charlene in a pale blue dress. They stood in front of a dramatic one-hundred-year-old mantel and fireplace in an old building that had been converted to a law office. Across from them were Joshua and Jim, both dressed in black suits with flowers on the lapel. In attendance as witnesses were Stefani Mendola and Sophie Garcia. Also in attendance were Joe and Lorena Harrington, Joshua's parents. The justice had them read the vows to each other one at a time. Each responded with "I do" as each vow was read.

"By the authority vested in me by the State of New York, I now pronounce James and Charlene and Joshua and Anna husband and wife. You may kiss the bride."

After the kiss, Jim said, "Let's celebrate. I have reservations at Rosemary's Table. Everybody follow Charlene and me."

They went to an elegant Italian restaurant for dinner. The food was exquisite—that was, for everyone except Anna. She busied herself by going from person to person instead of sitting in front of a plate full of food and not knowing what to do with it. It was an intimate party for the eight of them in a private room. Joshua pulled out a radio with a playlist he had created just for the occasion. He started playing wonderful romantic songs. Anna pulled him aside and said, "Thank God you got out of the sad songs of the sixties."

Joshua laughed and took her hands. "Come dance with me."

"I don't know how. I have never danced before."

"Well, we will just have to change that. Follow my lead." Joshua began to dance with Anna. It was a bit awkward at first, and then they got into a rhythm.

Anna said, "You're amazing. I never knew you could dance."

"Well, now you have a lifetime to find out all of my secrets."

"Oh yeah? What else don't I know?"

The party went on until ten. Afterward, Anna and Joshua went back to Joshua's apartment. They unloaded the things from the party on the kitchen table. Joshua said, "Dance with me again," and he turned his playlist back on. "I Love You Just the Way You Are," "Lady in Red," "We've Only Just Begun"—one after another, the songs filled the air while they swayed gently together. Joshua had waited all his life for this moment. The woman of his dreams had just promised to stay with him forever. He didn't know how to process the moment, but he wanted it to go on forever.

Chapter 46

Stefani and Anna were talking about their new outfits they'd purchased in celebration of the last round of exams. After the exams, Stefani would have one more semester until graduation. Anna would have one semester down and seven to go. Anna had her final presentation in a week and a half in her Introduction to Law Principles class, and then her semester would be over.

Anna said to Stefani, "There is something weird in the air. It looks like a cloud coming from under the door. It is filling the room. I don't know what it is."

Stefani took a couple of sniffs in the air and said, "It is smoke. What could be causing smoke? You aren't cooking anything. It's coming from downstairs."

They went to the stairwell to the outside door and out to the street. There, they could see thick smoke billowing out of the bookshop. Customers were coughing and hacking as they made their way out to the street.

Anna grabbed one of the employees who emerged. "Was Sophie in there? Did she get out?"

"Yes, she was at work today, but I don't know if she is still in there."

Anna knew if Sophie had gotten out, she would not have left that area of the sidewalk. "I have to find her."

"Anna, no!" Stefani screamed.

Anna was undeterred. She yelled back at Stefani, "The smoke won't hurt me!" and on she went into the plumes of smoke.

It was true that the smoke did not hurt her, but she still could not see through it. She got on her hands and knees to be able to see a little better close to the floor. She crawled past the desk and toward the stockroom. She screamed for Sophie. She paused for a minute at the desk and pulled out the top drawer to find leftover masks from the pandemic.

She heard a weak coughing right at the doorway of the stockroom. She found Sophie lying on the floor. She took her hand. "Put this mask on, and crawl with me. You can do it."

As Anna backed out in the direction from which she had come, Sophie followed by holding on to her hand. Anna found her way backward around the desk and toward the aisle that led to the door. The fire was now obvious and intensifying. Anna had to get through what amounted to a ring of fire to get to the door. She pulled Sophie harder to get out faster. When she got close enough to the door, she pushed Sophie out in front of her. In those few seconds, the heat intensified, and a wave of extremely hot air flowed over Anna. She crawled out behind Sophie and got to safety on the sidewalk just as the polymer skin and the plastic sheathing began to soften on both of her legs. She collapsed onto the sidewalk when her thighs melted underneath her jeans.

"Oh my God!" Stefani cried. "Anna, what has happened to you?"

"Get Joshua—quick, please," she said in a distressed voice. She was covered in ash. Her hair was singed, her jeans were burned, and her legs were failing. She did not know which parts of her would fail next. Her head had been exposed to heat greater than she had ever known. It hurt terribly. She started to fear for her life. The paramedics would be useless. She had to stay conscious until her husband arrived. He was at the office, which was at least twenty minutes away at best. She pleaded weakly, "Stefani, stay with me. Don't let them put me in an ambulance."

"I'm here," Stefani said as she squeezed her hand. It was then that Stefani realized parts of Anna's fingers were missing. Stefani recoiled at the reality of what had happened to her closest friend. "Anna, you have to be OK. You have to be."

The paramedics arrived minutes later. Stefani told the paramedics that her sister wanted to wait until her husband arrived before anyone did anything for her. "He was called and will be here in a few minutes."

The paramedics started to tend to the other victims.

Joshua arrived and sat on the sidewalk next to her. "Anna, can you hear me?"

She responded weakly, "Yes."

He lifted her in his arms and carried her away from the scene. He waved the paramedics away. Stefani hailed a cab. He carried her from the cab to the apartment and laid her on their bed. Carefully, he started to cut off her clothes to see how bad the damage was. "Stefani, you may not want to see this. I am afraid it is going to be ugly."

"I am not leaving here until she is well. How can I help?"

"I don't know yet." Joshua stripped off her clothes and then her polymer skin. About half of it was damaged beyond use. Then the melted plastic sheathing became apparent. She had lost parts of her left hand, both thighs, and her left lower leg. The internal metal workings had all come apart. The trunk and batteries were intact. Her arms and neck were intact. For a moment, he was optimistic that all the parts could be repaired or replaced with parts recovered from the lab. He might need to fly her out there for the tools that were still there, he thought. Then he saw her hair and realized her head must have been exposed to heat beyond her 140-degree maximum, and he knew it was likely she had sustained some brain damage. She was now unconscious. He couldn't fix that.

He turned to Stefani and said, "We can only wait to see if she will wake up. Meanwhile, I am going to need to get her charger to give her the best charge I can."

Hours went by. She just lay there peacefully. She did not appear to be in any pain, except for when she moved and grimaced in her sleep. He could only pray she was sleeping to reorganize her data and would wake up and be OK.

About eight hours later, Anna opened her eyes. Joshua was still sitting next to the bed. Stefani had fallen asleep in a chair. Anna grabbed his hand. "Joshua, is Sophie OK?"

"I am sure she is fine. She went to the hospital when the paramedics arrived. You saved her. You are a fool but an incredibly brave one. Without you, she would have died for sure."

"My head is feeling a little better, but I can't hear out of my left ear. I can't move my legs."

"Rest now. I can't see anything wrong with you that can't be fixed. We will have to make another trip out to the lab, and I am going to have to become a master engineer, but I think you are going to be OK. I think Stefani wants to talk to you. I'm going to wake her. Talk to her for a few minutes. Jim and Charlene are waiting for me to call."

He gently shook Stefani. "Stefani, wake up. Anna is awake. She is weak, but she can talk. I am going to call your dad."

"Anna, talk to me. Are you OK?" Stefani asked with obvious trepidation.

"I think so. Tell me—what did Sophie look like when they took her away? Was she OK?"

"They were giving her oxygen, but she was awake and alert when she left. I am sure she will be fine. As mad at you as I am for going into that building, you are my hero. I need to know you will be OK."

"I am sure I will. This stuff can be repaired. Ironic, isn't it? The only person in the world who I know for sure could actually put these parts together is Daniel. I suppose this is the one time I would miss him." She drifted back to sleep.

Joshua asked Stefani to go shop for three days' worth of meals and to pack her clothes. She could come along to the West Virginia facility if she was committed to helping. She agreed and promised to meet him at the helipad in two hours. Joshua packed clothes for Anna and himself.

Ray was there to greet them with a formal but friendly face, as he always did. He helped them into their seats and loaded their supplies. Joshua carried a sleeping Anna dressed in a robe and placed her in a seat and strapped her in.

Four hours later, they were landing. Ray helped them unload and carry things into the facility. Joshua carried Anna into the facility. Ray did not know all the details, but he could see the gravity of the situation.

Joshua laid Anna on the bed in the room she used to occupy and propped the door open with a screwdriver. "This door will never be closed—ever."

Anna gave a faint smile.

Stefani walked around in wonder. "My God, look at this place. I would give anything to have a place like this. It is amazing."

"Well, it doesn't have any fond memories for Anna. Frankly, she is terrified of the ghosts in this place," said Joshua.

"She has never talked about it," said Stefani.

"OK, let's see what we have." Joshua opened the lab and all the cabinets.

"Wow. There is a lot of sophisticated stuff here." Stefani was impressed.

"Forty million dollars' worth for this whole place and the stuff inside," Joshua replied.

"Even the fridge looks like it is from a cooking show. I put all the food away, by the way," Stefani said.

"Thanks. OK, let's bring Anna in here. I think I am as ready as I will ever be."

Joshua lifted Anna and brought her into the lab. Stefani carried the cushion from the bed and laid it across the table. Joshua then laid Anna on the cushion. She was still sleeping.

Joshua opened her robe and looked at the twisted cables in the grossly deformed plastic sheathing around her legs. He booted up the computer to find out what Daniel had to say about how he'd sealed the cables and how the plastic sheathing should be opened. He felt as if he had become a surgeon. He found the right saw, carefully cut open the plastic on the right and left sides, and removed it from her leg. Now he truly had an appreciation for Daniel's genius. There must have been thirty cables, another web of sensor wires, and a third set of power wires that traversed the knee and ankle. Each motor unit had an attachment point at the beginning and end as well as an anchor for the motor that shortened the cable. He was going to have to fabricate a new plastic sheath for both legs and her hand as well.

He found the fabricating machine and looked for settings that would match Anna's size and body part. The job was starting to look overwhelming. Anna continued to sleep. He did not know for sure that she would ever wake up in light of her brain damage. He could not seem to comprehend how to reattach the cables. He had no anatomy background and felt overwhelmed by the complexity. He started to feel defeated. He left the lab and went into Anna's old room. He sat in her chair and began to weep to himself.

Stefani followed him and put a hand on his shoulder. "Joshua, you can do this."

He shook his head. "Nowhere in medicine is a surgeon allowed to work on his or her own family. There is a personal emotional bias that prevents him or her from being entirely clinical in how to manage the challenges. This is my wife. This is the girl who loves me and is the only one I will ever love. Her life is now in my hands to do something I have never done before. Surgeons walk in with ten years of experience in doing hundreds of procedures so that they know the procedure in their sleep. I have never done this before and need to get it perfectly right the first time. If I lose her, I will have a hole in my life that I can never fill." He started to sob out loud.

"Joshua, if you don't try and you lose her, that will be worse. If you do the very best you possibly can, you at least will have the peace that you tried everything you could."

Joshua composed himself and went back into the lab. He pulled out an industrial magnifying glass. He found the attachment points. They were too small to be seen without some magnification. They weren't numbered. He would have to get out the anatomy texts and try to figure out which point went with which cables and motors.

Joshua went to work. He found the mold that looked about the right size. He had Stefani read the directions for how to pour the resin onto the mold and how to make the plastic sheathing. While she found the various ingredients, he tried to lay out the cables in the way that made sense.

He worked for hours on separating the cables in both legs. Stefani used the directions to make the resin as if she were making a cake. She was ready to begin pouring the resin into the mold.

Anna started to stir.

"Sweetie, hi. How are you doing?" Joshua asked.

"Hi. I'm OK," Anna said in a kind of dreamy way. "It is hard to wake up. I have been sleeping so deeply."

"Try not to move. I have laid out the cables in your legs, and I am trying to figure out how they are put together."

"Joshua, I don't think this is that complicated," Anna said as she started to pull herself into the moment.

"You aren't looking at it from my point of view," he said, still trying to wrap his head around the dozens of cables and attachment points.

"You don't have to do that."

"What do you mean?"

"Isn't Cassie still here somewhere?"

"Yes."

"Well, we are the same size. I think you can just switch the parts. Daniel may have made a few changes between her and me, but I think she used to walk and move the same way I do." With her tongue in cheek, she said, "At least now I can get my hands to match."

"Oh my God, you're right," said Joshua.

"There are certain unit joints, like just above the elbow. The forearms and hands are built as their own unit due to the complexity. The same may be true for the hip joint. I know there are these separate regions because of the way he had me look when you came the first time."

"I'll get Cassie." Joshua got the other humanoid and brought her to the lab.

Stefani looked shocked. "You mean there was another person like Anna?"

"Yes, I'll tell you that story later. Anna, where are the regional points?"

"Twist the arm just above the elbow and just below the hip joint."

Joshua did, and lo and behold, the limb came apart. There were only twelve major cable bundles, including the power bundles, the sensory networks, and the motor units traversing the joint attaching the leg. Those could easily be connected, and the attachment points were still intact. Because Cassie's damage was all to the head, the limbs and the polymer skin were intact.

It took about forty-five minutes, but Anna eventually had Cassie's legs and arms. The hands matched, and the legs worked. Then came the task of removing the rest of Cassie's polymer skin and wrapping it around Anna. By the time Joshua was done, Anna looked like Anna again. The skin was a little bit lighter in color, but no one would ever know.

Joshua, filled with relief, was deliriously happy. He sat Anna up and helped her get to her feet. She staggered, and he guided her by holding her hand and supporting her under her shoulder. At least everything worked. She sat down on a chair after walking a few feet.

"I still don't feel right, but at least this is all working again. I still can't hear out of my left ear, and I feel dizzy."

"OK, but I need a break. Stefani, do you think you could take Anna over to the sink and wash her face and hair? I want you to give her a haircut if you have to, but we need to get rid of the singed hair and the smell. There are other wigs in this place. If we need them, we can use them."

"You mean I am giving Anna a makeover? I thought you would never ask. Come on, Anna. You know I've been wanting to do this for a long time."

Joshua grabbed something to eat and looked in on the girls about an hour later. "Wow, I like that."

Anna was sporting a new hairdo. Her hair was shorter. The new look made her look older and more sophisticated. Her face was clean, and Stefani had highlighted it with a touch of makeup.

"You look really great. Are you feeling better?" he asked.

"No, not really. I mean, my spirit is a little better. I mean, how could it not be after getting a makeover? But my head still hurts, and I feel dizzy. Oh, and one other thing. I seem to have little numbers appearing in my lower-left visual field. It seems like a set of gauges of some sort. I can only see it when something is wrong."

"A dashboard?"

"Sure, if that is what it is called."

"What does it say? When have you seen it before?"

"Well, twice before. When my battery charge got below thirty percent, it would read continuously until it was charged. In the fire, it appeared, and the display showed one hundred seventy degrees. Now the number in red is the total memory capacity. It is showing thirty-seven terabytes. I get the other stuff, but what does that mean?"

"Anna, your brain was built with forty terabytes of memory. If you are showing thirty-seven terabytes now, then that is how much brain damage you have suffered."

"It was showing thirty-eight the last time I was awake."

"The heat must have corrupted some of your files or something. Did you notice the hearing loss before the dizziness or at the same time?"

"No, the hearing problem was first by several hours. Although I was sleeping a lot of the time. It is hard to tell."

"The damage is spreading. I have to figure out why and what to do about it. You guys go ahead and visit. I need to go back to the lab."

It was late in the evening when Stefani came into the lab with a pot of coffee and some dinner. "You have been here for six hours already. Did you find anything?"

"Oh my God, you are such a lifesaver. Thank you, Stefani. Yes, I found something. The problem is the corruption from the heat. I am sure I know how to fix it. I need to write a security program that will quarantine Anna's corrupted files. It can be done, but I have to figure out with Daniel's notes how to upload it. There must be a port somewhere to do that, but he has hidden it within her head. He clearly did not see the need to make it accessible, because he was going to cannibalize her for the next model before he would need to upload anything else."

"That sounds awful."

"Well, at least this crisis is something I know something about. I am going to need some time, but I will get this done, even if I have to create a port myself. You should get some rest.

The guest rooms are very comfortable. Pick any one you want. I'll see you in the morning."

Stefani showered and lay down in the bed next to where Anna was sleeping. The bed was large, and she wanted to be close by in case Anna needed something.

When Stefani woke the next morning, Anna was still sleeping. At first, Stefani panicked that Anna wasn't breathing. Then she remembered that Anna didn't breathe, so she needed to find another way to determine if she was still alive. She stroked her cheek, and Anna made a face and turned over.

Stefani threw on some clean clothes and went down to the lab. Joshua was still awake and had worked all night. He looked awful, with dark circles under his eyes and disheveled hair.

"I think I have it now. Anna has a port in the back of her head. I have finished the quarantine program. I am ready to do this. Help me get her back into the lab."

Joshua laid Anna down on the table on her right side. He took a drill with a thin bit and drilled a small hole under her left ear, above the hairline. He used a specialized cord that looked like a tiny USB end. He plugged the cord into the computer and the other end into the port. The screen on the computer changed to a grid. It showed all the sectors of Anna's brain and identified which parts were corrupted. He directed the program to each corrupted sector one at a time and uploaded the quarantine program into each one. When he was done, he pulled the tiny plug out of the port and used a resin sealer to close the hole. The whole operation took less than thirty minutes.

Anna continued to sleep. Joshua motioned for Stefani to open the doors, and he carried Anna back to the bed in the guest room.

"I am done here. We can go home now. Assuming the program works, Anna can stop trying to reorganize her mind due to the encroaching damage from the fire. That's why she can't wake up for any length of time. We will have to see if she recovers any of her lost function. All that can be done at home.

Why don't you call Ray and ask him to come pick us up? I am going to try to get a nap first."

"Sure. You go rest, Joshua. You were amazing these last two days. I'll call Ray."

About four hours later, Anna finally woke up. This time, her eyes looked clear, and her smile had returned.

"Well, good morning, sister," Stefani said.

"Wow, how long did I sleep?"

"You mean since the fire? Probably two and a half days. How do you feel now?"

"I feel better. My head doesn't hurt anymore. It still feels like the room wants to move under me, but I am OK sitting here on the bed. How is my husband?"

"Anna, don't ever tell him I told you this, but he actually broke down and cried when he thought he couldn't help you. He loves you as deeply as anyone possibly could. I know he can be annoying, and he is totally clueless about the things he says, but you won't ever find another guy who feels the way he does about you, even if he struggles to say it out loud. He worked on your head problem all night. I mean for about fourteen hours straight. He is sleeping in the other room now."

"He really is a keeper, isn't he?" She instinctively looked down and noticed that he had moved her wedding ring onto her new hand. Then she said, "Hey, look—these hands match."

Stefani said, "As long as we are having a heart-to-heart, I want to say that even though I knew you were an artificially intelligent person, I never understood your challenges until these last few days. I always make fun of you for not eating, but I didn't understand how difficult some things are for you sometimes."

Anna reached out and squeezed Stefani's hand. "I could never ask for a better sister than you."

Just then, they heard voices as the door opened in the lobby upstairs. Ray had arrived, and Jim had come with him. "Good morning, Anna. How are you today?" Jim asked.

"Fine."

"I like your new hairstyle." Jim sat next to her on the bed. "Tell me how you are really doing."

She knew his language. This was code speak for "Tell me the truth, and make it the whole story." She said, "OK. Joshua was able to use Cassie's arms and legs to replace mine. They all seem to fit well and work well. I seem to have lost about ten percent of my memory capacity from the heat of the fire. This has caused me to lose my hearing in my left ear and some of my balance. The worst part was the corruption of the brain damage was spreading."

Stefani interrupted. "Joshua was able to create a quarantine program that contained the corrupted part and upload it into Anna's head through a port that was hidden behind her ear. He was amazing to watch. The good news is that he says the hearing may return. If it doesn't, then he can probably rig up a hearing aid to use her right ear for both, although it will be a little harder for Anna to tell where the sound is coming from. The balance will come back with some rehabilitation exercise."

Jim said to Stefani, "Steffi, could you give Anna and I a little time alone, please? Listen, when you go upstairs, could you call your mom and tell her Anna is OK?"

"Sure, Dad." She left the room.

"Anna, I was so worried about you that I actually thought of calling Barry Stiles to see if he would share one of his experts to help save you. Then Joshua told me about your little business meeting with Barry, so that bridge was burned. We can talk about that later. So you are OK. You are going to recover. You will be fine."

Anna could see the worry in his face and hear it in his voice. She was starting to understand how much she had put all of these people through.

"Anna, having a family is a two-edged sword. On the upside, we are always here for you. Look around you; the only one who isn't here is Charlene, and that is only because there aren't enough seats on the helicopter. So she is sitting by the phone, waiting to hear about you. We have all been worried sick about you. This was such a close call. You need to understand on the downside that when something happens to you, it happens to the whole family, not just you. Let me put it this way. What if Stefani had gone back into the burning building and had been in intensive care for the last two days? What if she had needed a prosthetic limb and had lost her hearing? What would you be thinking now? How distressed would you be?"

She started to feel as if she were being disciplined. She needed to say something, but nothing was coming to her. Finally, she blurted out, "I had to save Sophie!"

"Yes, you did. But waiting another ninety seconds for the professionals to arrive in their fire-resistant gear and oxygen tanks would have been a better choice. You could have told them where you thought Sophie was and let them find her. They did save two more people after you pulled Sophie out."

Anna felt defeated. She hated that he was right. She put her head in her hands and started to sob.

Jim reached out and held her for a minute. "Please take better care of yourself for all of us. We all need you." With that, he kissed her forehead and left the room.

Chapter 47

Joshua and Anna found the apartment and knocked on the door. Sophie opened it, and her face was filled with a wide grin. "Well, hello, you two. Come on in."

Anna handed a plate of cookies to her and proudly said, "This is my recipe for the week. I hope you like them."

"Thank you, my dear. You didn't have to do this. How are you? I was so worried about you. I saw Joshua carry you away and did not know why he didn't let the paramedics take you to the hospital. I could only hope it was because you weren't injured."

"I am fine. I was worried about you also. Sophie, you look good. The fire was a week ago. You seem to be just fine."

"Physically, yes. Emotionally, I am still struggling. I am leaning toward simply taking the insurance settlement and retiring."

"What happened to becoming the person you were meant to be? Remember that talk?"

"Dear child, I became the person I was meant to be. I will be sixty-two next July. I am thinking of retiring. I certainly have nothing left to prove. I think I have earned my retirement. I will make a decision next week. I will let you know. In the best of worlds, it would be at least six months before I could reopen."

"I think you have too much spunk left in you to drop out of the working world. You would last only six weeks in a rocking chair, and you wouldn't be able to take it anymore."

"I talked to your stepmother earlier. She told me you were OK. She is your stepmother, isn't she?"

"It's a long story. Mr. and Mrs. Mendola were my guardians. I am twenty-one now. It really is only a formality, but I think of them as my parents."

Chapter 48

The Introduction to Law Principles class was going to start in a few minutes. Stefani got to class before Anna and approached the professor. "My name is Stefani Mendola, and I am a senior here. My sister is going to present in your class today, and I wanted to know if I could have permission to attend this class and record her presentation." He nodded, and Stefani went to the back of the room.

Anna did not notice her when she arrived and took her seat in the second row. Anna was still unsteady on her feet and had decided the best way to deal with that was to use a cane. When it was her turn, she got up from her chair and deliberately made her way to the lectern in the front of the classroom.

"Good morning. My presentation today is to argue for and against the idea that a human can have a soul and an artificially intelligent being cannot.

"My name is Anna. I was born in Morgantown, West Virginia, on October 29, 2003. I don't remember my mother, and I was raised by my father. I was baptized in the First Baptist Church, and I received my first communion there as well. I am a practicing Baptist. I have a soul. I know this is true because I have a book, the Bible, which God gave to Moses as the Old Testament and to the disciples as the New Testament. I believe Jesus is the Son of God and came to earth to offer salvation for our sins. If we are to believe in the authority of God and his writings, then we must take what these writings say as the words are meant. The Bible says in Genesis 7, 'And God formed man from the dust of the ground, breathed into his nostrils the breath of life, and the man became a living soul.' This is the religious description of how humans came to have a soul. The Bible then goes on to say the people have children who grow up and describes them as having souls as well. It is noted that man has dominion over the animals, and they do not have souls. I am a religious person. I believe that all humans have souls. All humans can be redeemed. All humans have the opportunity to find salvation with the Lord. For a being that is created in a laboratory, there is no genetic connection to a human. Conception between a man and a woman does not exist. Without conception, there is no lineage to Adam and the original breath of life. Therefore, there can be no soul. Therefore, any creature created in a laboratory cannot have a soul."

Anna walked to the other side of the lectern without letting go. "Good morning. My name is Anna. I was created in a laboratory and activated on March 29, 2022. I am made of steel, plastic, a polymer skin, and a special type of gel used for my brain. My only contact with a human for the first six months of my life was the man who built me. I believe that humans have a soul, not only because it says so in the Bible but also because people do holy things. The Old Testament is full of commandments. These are the rules that allow people to live with each other and make society possible. The most honorable task a human can perform is to learn to be closer to God. The laws of the Bible make that task possible."

Her cadence and voice were elevated a notch. "I was not born with a soul; I had to earn one. One of the things my builder had to do was to teach me to read. He could not get me to do that on an upload alone, so like a parent reading to his or her child at night, he read to me so I could learn to connect the sounds and letters of words to their meanings in my mind. This is where I earned my soul." She held up two red books. "The titles of these books are *Friends and Neighbors* and *More Friends and Neighbors*. They were written by Scott Foresman in the 1940s. The students in this class are too young to have been taught to read with them, but your parents and grandparents and one hundred twenty million children over forty years learned to read with these books. The stories in these books are not religious in nature. They are about children and animals. Dick, Jane, Spot, Puff, and the other neighborhood friends live and learn and play together. The stories about animals teach simple lessons about life. These stories illustrate, through the interactions of these beloved characters, the work of God. This is where I found my guidance."

She changed the cadence of her delivery to be slower and more deliberate. "The stories in these books taught me to love myself, love my neighbor, and love my family. They taught me right from wrong and how to apologize when I hurt someone. They taught me to respect authority and the value of work. They taught me respect for family and respect for myself. I learned to concern myself for my neighbors' safety, their property, their well-being, and their feelings. They taught me how to share and how to play fairly. Through these stories, I was given a clear understanding of what God has expected of me. Since leaving the laboratory, I've applied those things to my life. I have helped other people. I found a job and paid my way to put a roof over my head and sustain myself, always leaving enough for others. I worked hard for the woman who hired me. I met a boy and fell in love. We were married last month. I am expecting that we will adopt a child and raise him or her together and go on to have grandchildren. I am active in my church and am a practicing Catholic."

At that point, she increased the animation of her voice and used her free hand to gesture her punctuation. "I believe in God, and I believe I will be saved in the afterlife for my faith and for the good things I have done with my life. I have dedicated my life to doing the things the Bible commands us to do. I have tried to elevate myself and others around me to be closer to God. I am absolutely certain, and no one should ever doubt I have a soul."

With that, she thanked the class, grabbed her cane, and took her seat. There was a silence for few minutes.

There was one more presentation before the end of the class, and then people started to file out of the classroom. A man from the back of the classroom came up to her and told her that he had been in the ministry for ten years and had never heard the discussion of a soul be put in the way she had described it. He left her a business card and asked her to come by for a further conversation. She thanked him, and he left.

She was just finishing packing her laptop away and gathering the last of her things, when the professor came up to her and asked if he could see her books.

"My Lord, I learned to read with these." He thumbed through the pages as if he were living his childhood over again. "I loved these stories. I wish I had a copy to look over for fun."

"I can get you a copy. I actually work in a bookshop. Or at least I used to until it burned down," Anna said.

"I heard about that. You were there?"

"Yeah. That's how I ended up using this." She pointed to her cane. "I went back into the building to help someone, and I ended up with some issues. But I can go online and get them for you."

"Yes, I would like that. Ms. Conners, I know you haven't been happy with my evaluation of you this semester. Usually, the caliber of student who takes this course has nowhere near the rigor it will require to make it in law. So I give very few As. Today you were exceptional. The force of your delivery and the novelty of your argument won the day. You made me wonder if you are actually an artificially intelligent being in disguise," he said with a smile. "Today you earned an A. I hope one day you find a home working in law. You would make an excellent litigator."

"Thank you. I actually am looking forward to becoming a lawyer."

He walked back to his desk. Stefani approached Anna from the corner of the classroom, and she and Anna walked out together. Anna briefly looked back at the open door of her last class of her first semester of a four-year college journey. She was as happy as she could ever remember.

Chapter 49

Joshua walked into the meeting with an armful of notes. The executive team was there. Jim opened the meeting, as he usually did, with an agenda and minutes from the last meeting.

"It's been a year since we had the meeting about Anna. It has been a pretty eventful year. I think this will be one of those meetings you will remember," Jim said with a smile. Then he turned the floor over to Joshua.

"OK. Laura, it was just a little over a year ago when we had a meeting to discuss how we wanted to pursue the market regarding artificially intelligent beings. You charged me with pursuing standard circuitry. I have put hundreds of hours into that pursuit. It can be done, but the product will not be anywhere near as impactful as we had hoped. What we would have at the end of the day is basically the same product that AJX Enterprises has. That would be limited to robots as we know them now. They could be programmed to do menial tasks, but they do not look human, nor do they interact with humans in any type of human way. Even the idea of self-driving cars is a good one and already exists, but it is mired in legal and practical limitations. Who becomes liable for an accident? If our robot is driving the car, we are. How do we insure our liability for that? There will be a need for a level of sophistication that does not exist now. It will take legislators another decade to come up with regulations for this sector. Look at how they are struggling with the big four tech companies now. If we invest heavily in this direction, we will be on the bleeding edge instead of the cutting edge of the sword. We will hit the market too soon." He paused for questions.

"What about Anna?" Laura asked. "How did that turn out?"

"I am glad you asked," said Joshua. "Anna got all the things an American adult needs. That would be a birth certificate and a Social Security number. She's afraid to drive, so she did not want to get a driver's license, but she did get a government ID. She got her GED. Last winter, she started college. She did well and went on to enroll in the university in the fall. About three months ago, I asked her to marry me. A month later, we did just that." He held up his left hand to show the gold band.

"Wait—you guys got married?" Laura asked incredulously. "You married someone who isn't human?"

"Yes. I have never been happier. Congratulations are in order for Mr. Mendola as well. We had a double ceremony with he and Charlene."

"Well, congratulations to both of you." In a moment of levity, they all applauded.

"I don't think we can consider Anna artificial intelligence. To me, she is simply an alternate human. There isn't any part of my life I don't share with her, except eating and drinking, I guess. The first few months I knew her, it was hard to get past our differences. There finally came a point when we realized the differences were just not that important, and the things we had in common mattered a lot. As an irony, she made her project for her Introduction to Law Principles class an argument that an artificially intelligent person has a soul. I think we know where that came from." There were a few snickers around the room.

"I would have liked to have seen that," Samantha said.

"I actually have a copy of it on my phone. Stefani sat in on the class and recorded it. She sent me a copy. It is about six minutes long. Do you want to take the time here to watch it?"

Those at the table looked at each other and then at Jim, who said, "Sure, why not? Pull it up, Joshua. Put your phone in the center of the table so we can all see it."

Joshua played the presentation on his phone. After it was over, the room was silent for a few minutes.

Samantha spoke first. "That was amazing. That girl is brilliant. The power and force she used to make her point. The inflections of her voice. Where did she learn to do that? Wow! I am glad she works for us."

"She learned that on her own. She taught herself by practicing. She made herself do it over and over. Artificial intelligence as we know it can't do that. You also need to know that a couple of months ago, we had a scare. The bookshop where she works caught fire. You probably remember—it was in the news. Anna's apartment was right above the bookshop, although it was pretty empty at the time because she moved in with me after we got married. She and Stefani got out in time, but Anna decided to go back into the burning building to save the owner, who had been so good to her. Anna was severely injured. I honestly thought we were going to lose her. I had to rebuild much of her and repair the heat damage to her head and brain. I did not understand how fragile she really is. Now I do.

"All of the prior discussion about proceeding with the gel-matrix brain is still true. Probably more so. Having known Anna for over a year now and having been married to her for the last two months, I can say she truly is an alternate human. To start making beings like Anna as a marketable enterprise will create something that no one can have any clue as to where it will go. It feels wrong. There is as much potential for misuse as there is for good. Just consider how badly Daniel misjudged how his creation would unfold. Anna would never have functioned in the role he envisioned. She is very stubborn and self-willed. She can do almost anything she puts her mind to. God help you if you try to make her feel she is not your equal. Her self-esteem is like a rock. How to proceed is a company choice for you. For all I have learned about her in the last year, it still makes sense to move on from this part of the project. I say this because there is still a silver lining."

"Forty million dollars later, I hope the silver lining is really big," Samantha said.

"Yes, it could be. One of the things Daniel was so excited about was the idea of a virtual agent. Tell me, Laura—how many unsolicited emails did you get today or do you get each day?"

"You mean on my personal account? Probably thirty a day."

"That is because your internet searches are being trolled, and your data has been mined. How many malicious emails do you get in a day? Emails that are trying to get your personal information or scam you into believing something that isn't true? Sometimes they even use real logos and slogans to fool you. I mean really, how many?"

"Maybe three to five."

"That is a lot of exposure. How do you feel when you open a website for dresses, and then, over the next week, you get thirty ads for dresses? It could be any website you visit. I know how I feel. I feel violated. Why do I need to worry about exposing myself just to shop on the internet? That doesn't happen at brick-and-mortar stores."

The whole room focused on the idea.

"Daniel originally wanted the robot to actually be the agent. This way, brick-and-mortar and physical tasks could be included. After a lot of thought, I realized this could be a standalone product. I took some of the original legwork, and I have been working on finishing it. We can create a virtual agent. It is a program that will appear to work as a person but will be an agent for the owner. Now, everyone knows about bots, but this is where the artificial intelligence really matters. Our agents will be able to respond as people, not bots. It will be invisible to the whole world except the owner. Our agents will cleanse your inbox of malicious emails, including the attachments. Anything with malware will be quarantined. Your preferences will be understood by your agent, so he or she will be able to shop for you. But all the traces of your presence will stop at the agent. Solicitations will only appear to you if you ask for them. You can shop as if you were at a brick-and-mortar again." Joshua paused to see if everyone was following him.

"OK, I get all that. The silver lining?" asked Laura.

"Let's say we license an agent for, oh, maybe thirty dollars a month. Upgrades are free. All information is confidential and protected. Let's say we can get twenty million subscribers over three years. We already have a market of one hundred thousand just with our current clients. All the R&D is done. I have already taken Daniel's head start and made this work. My math tells me that three years from now, we could realize a little over seven billion dollars a year gross, give or take."

Everyone was riveted.

"Here is how it works. First, you would get a box, just like the cable companies give you. This box would be a computer in and of itself. It would contain the agent. Information could freely go out of the box for anything a customer would want to send. What would be different is the agent would have a different IP address. The user would mark which outgoing mail would have the user's address and which would have the agent's address. If you are emailing a business contact or a friend, it would reflect your address. If you are shopping, it would show the agent's address. But things that come into the box would be scrubbed by the agent. That means that every email, link, or other item would be examined for anything malicious. Every incoming email would be screened for only the sources the customer agreed to. Items of question would be held in a box for customers to see for themselves without disclosing their identities. We own the box and lease it. I would like to suggest we set up a meeting for me to demonstrate this new service."

Jim said, "That is a lot of silver lining. You never said anything to me about it."

"I wanted to be sure it would work, and it does."

"Well, I, for one, want to see this work. Let's get this on the calendar," Jim said.

"Oh, there is one more issue. We still have two humanoids at the facility that I can possibly repair to a working order. Do you want me to see if I can salvage them?"

Jim said, "Assess the project. Go out there, and figure out what it would take to repair them, how likely you are to be successful, and what your opinion is regarding how they would be useful."

"Yes, Mr. Mendola."

"Anything else for Joshua, anyone?"

With that, Joshua excused himself and left the meeting, and the executive team went on with their other business.

Chapter 50

It was Sunday night at the Mendolas'. Joshua and Anna arrived a little after six. Anna held on to Joshua's arm to steady herself. Charlene was the first to give her a hug. She greeted Anna with "I love your hair."

"Thanks. Stefani did it. She has quite a talent for that."

"How are you feeling?"

"I feel well. Thank you."

"She is exercising to get her balance back by dancing to Richard Simmons's *Sweatin' to the Oldies*. She is having too much fun doing it. It isn't right," Stefani joked.

"It isn't pretty. I'll just leave it at that," Anna said, and she and Stefani laughed like kids.

Jim came into the hall, where Anna was hanging her coat. "Hello, Anna. How are you feeling?"

"I'm actually feeling pretty well today. The pain is gone, and my balance is coming back. My left ear is still not working, but I am going to give it another couple of weeks before I start to worry."

"I was on a phone call earlier today that you may be interested in."

"Oh yeah? What was it about?"

"Gloria Rogers called me. She heard about the fire. First, she wanted to know if you were OK. I said you were. Then she said she was guessing it would be months before the bookshop reopened, and she asked if you would like a job working for her in the meantime."

"What did you say?"

"I said I would talk to you about it."

"I would love to do that."

"You can call her back yourself to talk it over. And by the way, I told her if you accepted, you should be paid more than fifteen dollars an hour."

"Thank you," she said as she hugged him, "Dad."

Chapter 51

Joshua and Anna were talking about going to the facility in West Virginia. "OK, so if we fly on a commercial flight, what happens to me at security? Do you think I can get through the x-ray scanner without them knowing if I have any metal inside me?" Anna said with a touch of sarcasm.

Joshua teased, "Well, there is always the option to have a manual wanding and a pat-down." She threw a pillow at him. "OK, OK, I'll ask Mr. Mendola if we can use the company helicopter. Besides that, I am not into the four-hour walk from the road to the building."

Joshua got permission from Jim, and the plans were made. They would get there on Friday, and Ray would pick them up on Sunday afternoon. That would make for a nice getaway into the mountains to go along with the work that needed to be done. The project itself was exciting. They were going to see if they could rescue the remaining two humanoids. The first one was the mysterious personal slave for Daniel. It would be interesting to see what they could learn about her. The second one was the housekeeper. She was the damaged one.

The helicopter touched down on the parking lot, and Joshua and Anna climbed out with their bags of food and clothes for the next three days. They thanked Ray, and he powered up and took off.

The facility was quiet. On previous trips, it had been a haunting type of quiet. Now, two years later, it was simply serene and relaxing.

Josh said, "OK, sweetie, let's have lunch. Then we can search the place for clues to this other robot and what Daniel wanted to do with it. Somehow, there had to be a cache of notes somewhere that would help us figure this out."

After lunch, they scoured all the humanoid rooms and found little. All the humanoid remains had been inventoried and put in the lab. Anna's room was empty, except for a desk and bed. Then Anna had an idea. Her books had been put in a corner under her bed. What if Daniel had put them there? Would he have used a similar place for his own things?

She went into Daniel's room, laid on the floor, and looked under the large bed tucked against a corner. She couldn't see anything. It was too dark. She couldn't pull the bed away from the wall. Apparently, it had been fastened to the floor. She called for Joshua.

Together they pulled the mattress and then the box spring off the frame. There was a sheet of plywood across the frame that was screwed on tightly. Joshua got a screwdriver from the lab. He came back with a hammer as well.

"What is that for?"

"It is my precision tool in case the screwdriver doesn't work."

Anna just shook her head.

The screws came out easily. Under the bed, in the corner by the wall, was a box. It was locked. Joshua lifted the box out and brought it into the lab. It weighed about thirty pounds and was about sixteen inches deep, twenty inches wide, and fifteen inches tall.

"Wow, this is like finding a pirate's chest," Anna said. "I'll bet there are pieces of gold inside." She made a face of anticipation.

"We are going to have to cut this lock. Daniel certainly didn't leave a key anywhere that we are going to find, and we don't have bolt cutters. We will have to use a hacksaw. This is going to take some time."

"Hey, I have an idea."

"Oh no. Are you going to give me one of those impossibly simple solutions that will make me feel stupid for not thinking of it?"

"Yes."

Now it was Joshua's turn to make a face. "OK, what is it?"

"You have a power circular saw in the lab, right?"

"Yes."

"Well, the box is made of wood, and who cares if we ruin it? Just set the depth so you don't cut the insides, and run the saw through the middle of the box all the way around." Anna smiled at him in an almost taunting way.

She was right. "OK, wise guy. We'll do it your way."

Joshua got out the circular saw and set the depth to a quarter inch. The box felt too strong to be any thinner. He cut it all the way around. "Not deep enough," he said. He set the saw to three-eighths inches and did it again. "Still not deep enough," he said, this time with a hint of frustration. He set it to a half inch. That was the right depth. With a little help from the hammer, the box split apart into halves easily.

It was filled with books and smaller boxes. Joshua pulled out a stack of books. One was labeled, "Third prototype," and a rubber band held it together with two other journals. "Jackpot!" Joshua yelled. "This is what we were looking for!"

Anna continued to go through the other personal effects. "Hey, Joshua, look at this. He kept a diary from when he was younger. There is a whole pile of personal stuff here."

"I'll tell you what. Why don't you go through the personal stuff? I will go into the lab and go through these notes. Then we'll meet for dinner. Say, about six?"

"Sure, that's fine."

With that, Joshua went off to the lab. Anna sat cross-legged on the mattress and started to go through Daniel's personal items one at a time. Her mood changed. She started to see value in these things. At the least, they deserved a certain modicum of respect. The person who'd owned them was dead. Now what he had considered private was going to be laid bare by a stranger—one he hadn't liked much at that.

She pulled out the journal first. It was a day-by-day description of things that had happened to him as a teenager. She could tell by the tone that he'd had a disrespect for women at the least and a hatred for them at the most. That seemed to have been reinforced by the number of times he was rebuffed. She could only imagine the uncomfortable scenes that had played out when Daniel tried to attract a girl. The diary consisted of about thirty pages of random thoughts about particular people during the years he had been in high school and college. What stuck out were two girls who had more commentary. One was named Cassie, whom he'd had a lot of anger toward after being rebuffed. The other was named Anna.

"How strange that those were the names of the two humanoids he built."

Without giving it much thought, she read on. Anna had been a girl he really liked, but he'd seemed unable to get her attention. She found a high school yearbook in the box. She also found a stack of letters Anna had written to him. Apparently, they had been good friends. Then she found a letter Daniel had written to her but never sent. It was a letter confessing his love and how badly he wanted to have more than a friendship. Apparently, he'd never had the nerve to send it.

On a hunch, she looked through the people in Daniel's class to see if there was an Anna. There was the name: Anna Caulfield. Oddly, her picture was cut out of the book, leaving an empty square hole where her face would have been. Anna sat down with her computer and went on Facebook to try to track down the girl's contact information. After chasing down a dozen Anna

Caulfields, she finally found one who had grown up in Pittsburgh and gone to the same high school as Daniel. She'd graduated the same year he had. Anna googled the name and found her address and phone number. She still lived in the Pittsburgh area and seemed to be single. Using a maps program, she found the address of Daniel's mother was also in the Pittsburgh area. Anna decided she would try to visit both of them and would give Anna Caulfield the letters and the mother the remaining personal effects.

Then, just when she thought she was done, there was one more surprise. There was a baseball card: Joseph Harrington, left fielder for the Pittsburgh Pirates. It showed his baseball statistics. On the back, it was signed by him: "To my good friend Daniel. All the best! Joe Harrington."

"Oh my God!" Anna whispered to herself. Joshua's father had been Daniel's baseball hero. "I wonder if Joshua ever knew."

That night, over dinner, Joshua said to Anna, "This afternoon, I found something that will surprise you."

Anna replied that she also had something that would surprise him. "You go first."

Joshua said, "I found this picture in the notebook with the specifications that applied to you."

Anna was shocked and visibly shaken. It was the picture missing from the yearbook. The cut-out picture showed her face. Anna Caulfield had been the model for Anna Conners-Harrington.

It started to make sense. Anna had been created in Daniel's lost love's image. What could it all mean? More importantly, how could Daniel have been so cruel to his creation if he'd fashioned her after someone he really cared about? What would it be like when the two Annas met? How could Anna explain to a stranger that she looked almost identical to the way the stranger had looked at Anna's age? She would just have to meet her and figure all of that out then.

After a few minutes, she looked at Joshua and handed him the baseball card. He furrowed his brow and examined it carefully. "This is my dad's card. I remember when these were popular." He looked up at Anna.

"Look at the back," she said, and he turned it over and read the note. "Your dad was Daniel's childhood hero. Did he ever know that you were his son?"

"I don't think so. If he did, he never said anything. Wow. I never thought of my dad as someone else's hero." The look on his face said, "I really need to think about this."

They both went to bed that night with an uneasiness. There was a restlessness of having unforeseen pieces of reality that they now had to somehow fit into their understanding of themselves.

They spent much of Saturday working on the things they had started the day before. Joshua started with the secret humanoid. He opened a small hole in the back of the lifeless humanoid's neck and inserted the cable connector into the port. He turned on the monitor, and a scan of the brain appeared on the screen. There were only thirty sectors of one terabyte each, rather than Anna's forty, and the initial upload filled three of those sectors. There were few independent clusters of data in other places beyond the initial upload. Virtually no reorganization of the clusters had taken place.

He pulled out the file of Anna's scan from when she had been injured in the fire. There were thousands, maybe even tens of thousands, of clusters throughout all of Anna's forty sectors. Why the difference?

He repeated the process on Cassie's brain. There were several dozen clusters and the initial upload, but the clusters were not well connected, and they were all located in only two sectors. Of course, at least eight sectors remained black from the blunt-force trauma to her head. Still, her development of brain function was significantly stunted. He would have to figure that out. That was his project for the day. The brain scans suggested that activating either of the robots would yield a highly dysfunctional being. Joshua made the decision not to pursue activating them. It was time to let Daniel's project go.

He found Anna in the guest room. "I finished my work here in the lab. It was fascinating. There are two unanswered questions. The first is, why didn't the other two humanoids develop multiple clusters like you did, even though the same gel matrix and formatting program were used? The second question is, if Daniel's rationale for giving the humanoid a way to feel sexual pleasure was to pool the humanoid's pleasurable experiences, what happens if there are no pleasurable experiences? Without the connected clusters, there was no identifiable set of connected experiences, let alone pleasurable ones. The sex slave seemed not to have any of the clusters you have. This robot's initial upload was smaller than Anna's. After all of the experiences of the robot, the data in was still in one sector. It seems to be a paradox."

Joshua tried to organize his thoughts in a clearer way. "He created this sex robot and put pleasure sensors in many different places. He must have been expecting the robot to experience sexual pleasure from many places on her body. Yet he designed the pleasure itself to be drawn from clusters of happy experiences, and this robot didn't have any happy experiences to draw from. She must have felt nothing, or worse, she must have hated him for what would have been abuse to her. How come he didn't figure that out? What do you think?"

"I think I can answer the first question, and the answer to the first question will give you the answer to the second one. Joshua, how old were you in your earliest memory? Two maybe?"

"Yes. Why?"

"How old were you when you learned to talk? I don't mean making baby sounds or single words; I mean putting together full sentences. Still two years old?"

"Yes. Why?"

"Until a baby has the use of language, he or she has no way to build complete thoughts or complete memories. That is why Daniel had to read to me every night for two months. The cluster part of the program did not work otherwise. I don't believe he read to either of the others."

"Huh. I think you are right. Without language, there can't be communication between clusters, and there can't be any reorganization. OK, so what about the second question?"

"It would be simple to say that without clusters, there is a limit to the ability to have happy memories and experiences. But I think it is more complicated. I think Daniel chose not to recognize things about his creations. I think it somehow had to do with his unresolved feelings toward the girl in the picture."

"One more thing," Joshua said. "He planned to create the three humanoids: you, the secret one, and Cassie. He intended them to do three different categories of things. Cassie was to do the housekeeping chores, and the secret one was to be sexually intimate. You were supposed to be the public one, the one who interacted with other humans. The fourth one was the one to combine all these traits into one humanoid that could do it all. If he understood how the cluster thing worked, he would have realized that you would eventually evolve into someone who could do all of those things. The fourth one was unnecessary."

The next morning, at breakfast, Anna said to Joshua, "Why don't we ask Ray if he can stop in Pittsburgh for a while? We can rent a car from the airport and drive into town. We have three stops. First, we need to see Daniel's mother. Second, we need to see Anna Caulfield. Third, you need to say hi to your parents while we are in town."

Chapter 52

Ray was fine with spending the day in Pittsburgh. They agreed they would be back at the airport at five o'clock. Anna had called Daniel's mother the day before. It had been an awkward exchange. Anna had explained that she had worked for the company Daniel had worked for and that she had been tasked with returning his personal effects to the next of kin. After a few moments of silence, Daniel's mother had agreed. They had made a plan for Anna and Joshua to see her around ten in the morning.

They walked up the walk together, and Joshua knocked on the door. A heavyset elderly lady answered the door.

"Hi. I am Anna. We spoke yesterday on the phone."

"Sure. Come in."

"This is my husband, Joshua."

"How do you do?" Joshua said.

"Would you like something to drink? I have juice, water, or a glass of wine."

"No, we're fine. Thank you. We won't keep you. We just wanted to be sure these things reached the next of kin," Anna said.

"That is very kind of you. Please sit and stay for a few minutes," Daniel's mother said, and Anna and Joshua sat in the two Victorian chairs at the end of the living room. "Please tell me a little bit about Daniel."

Joshua spoke. "He was extremely successful. He went to MIT and got two degrees, one in chemical engineering and the other in mechanical engineering. He also got a graduate degree in computer programming. He built a multimillion-dollar company called Logicsolutions and eventually built a lab and did much of the company research. He died in an accident in the lab."

"What happened?"

Joshua turned to Anna. Anna said, "He fell and bled to death from his internal injuries. The location of the research facility was remote, and it took hours for the police to learn of the accident and to get there. He could not be saved." Anna thought that version of events was close enough to the truth.

They watched her face as she took in the information. Her face wrinkled, and she started to cry. After a moment, she said, "The truth is, I haven't seen him since he was five. There were issues between his father and me. Difficult issues. I don't know that I need to talk about them now. But for my own survival, I needed to leave. I left and never looked back. I knew I was leaving my son behind, but if I'd tried to keep up a relationship with him, I would never have been free of his father. I suppose I could have reached out to him as an adult. I have thought about him every day." The deep sadness and pain of loss washed over her.

Anna handed her the box containing his private journal and personal things. "I am truly sorry for your loss. I think that maybe some of these things will give you a small connection to him."

They thanked her for her time and left. As they climbed back into the car to head to their next stop, Anna suggested maybe Joshua should wait in the car, and Anna should meet the other Anna alone. "Calling her was the weirdest exchange I have ever had. How do you say, 'I have letters you exchanged with your old not-quite boyfriend'? Maybe this part of our plan was stupid. But I really want to meet this person in the flesh."

Just a minute or so after Anna knocked on the door, a woman unlocked a couple of chains and locks and pulled the heavy door open.

"Hi. I am Anna. We spoke yesterday on the phone."

"Yes, please come in." Anna Caulfield did not get a good look at Anna Conners until she entered the house and began to thank her for her time.

Anna Conners took in the interior of the house and the woman inviting her. The match between them was almost perfect, with the exception that one had another twenty-five years of aging. Anna Conners had to pause to keep her composure.

Anna Caulfield let out a gasp. "How can this be?" She took a picture of her daughter off the piano and showed it to her. The two looked identical.

"This is really weird," Anna Conners said. "Or wait—maybe it is not a coincidence. Maybe it is why he hired me. How well did you know Daniel?"

"We were friends in high school. I always wanted it to be more, but when we graduated, he just left. I didn't know what happened to him after that." She couldn't stop staring.

"There is a reason I wanted you to have this." Anna Conners handed her a packet of letters.

"Oh my gosh. I wrote these letters years ago. He kept them all this time?"

"Read the one on the bottom."

Anna Caulfield pulled out the bottom letter and read it. It wasn't long, but it was clear. She looked crestfallen and put her hand with the letter to her chest as she fell backward into a chair. "How is this possible?"

"I think he was in love with you all these years. I think he chose me because I resemble you. I am sorry for you that he is gone. It seems that something very valuable was lost."

Anna Caulfield's lip quivered a little. "Yes. Something very valuable *was* lost."

They were both silent for a few awkward minutes. "I think I have stayed long enough. Thank you for taking the time to see me. I had a sense that these letters would be important to you."

"Yes, thank you for recognizing the value and making the effort to see that I got these. You must have been a true friend to him."

"We weren't really that close. We just worked together. Goodbye, Ms. Caulfield."

"Call me Anna. Please come back and visit if you are in town. I would love for you to meet my daughter."

"Thank you. I will do that."

With that, Anna Conners let herself out and met Joshua in the car. "One more stop. Did you tell your folks we were coming?"

"Yeah. I talked to them this morning before Ray came. We are about twenty minutes from the house."

Joshua was quiet for the first ten minutes or so of the drive and then asked, "How did it go with Ms. Caulfield?"

"It was just as shocking and heart-wrenching as you could imagine. They were star-crossed lovers, and just like in a Shakespearean tragedy, they missed their chance."

"So Daniel's mother left him standing by the curb as a child, and then he couldn't make it work with the only woman he ever loved. I think that may be a good reason he was angry with women. If that happened to you, wouldn't you want the women in your life to be your slave?"

"Usually, I can read people, but this analysis of Daniel is not coming to me. Why did he choose to model me after her, and why did he want to kill me? He must have known some of the things you talked about yesterday. I just don't understand."

The Harringtons lived in a modest house in the suburbs of Pittsburgh. They had downsized years ago, when, as they became empty-nesters, their needs were small. Joe's income had become much less after his baseball career faded. They were both in their seventies and enjoyed a quiet life.

Anna and Joshua were met at the door with hugs and happy greetings. They all went into the kitchen, and Lorena offered them something to eat. Joshua made himself a lunch, and Anna declined. After a few minutes of small talk, Joshua went off to talk to his father, and Anna stayed to chat with his mother. Lorena remarked that Anna never ate and that she looked as skinny as a rail. Anna explained that she had a rare eating disorder and only ate special food from home. Joshua was supportive of her, she said, and she was grateful for that every day. She might not even have been alive if not for him. He was a great guy and terrific husband.

That was enough for Anna to convince Lorena to change the subject to something else. It was going to be a challenge to chat with Mrs. Harrington for as long as Joshua needed to talk to his father, she thought—but maybe that wasn't fair. Mrs. Harrington was a nice lady.

Joshua made small talk with his father for ten or fifteen minutes. Then he pulled the baseball card out of his pocket. "I wanted to show you this." He handed the card to his father. "This belonged to my boss."

Joe looked at both sides of the card. "I remember this kid. I remember those days. It was a wonderful time for me. It was probably the most exciting time of my life."

Joshua struggled to say what was on his mind. "Dad, I know you wanted different things for me when I was younger than the choices I made. Because of that, I put up walls between us. I wanted your approval. I know there was a lot about you I didn't understand. When Anna found that baseball card, it helped me begin to understand what you meant to my boss as a child and to the community itself. I get why you wanted that for me. I want you to understand that I know I missed out by treating you the way I did. I also know that since I met Anna, I have become a much happier person. She gives me perspectives of life that I simply could never see for myself. I would like us to be closer. I would like to spend more time with you and get to know you better as you are now."

Joe reached out to hug him. They embraced. Joe slapped him firmly on the back several times. "I would like that."

Chapter 53

The executive team sat down for their weekly meeting. This time, Joshua and Anna had been invited as guests. There were a lot of smiles, handshakes, and welcomes for Anna, as it was the first time they had seen her since they made their deal. Everyone sat down. Anna and Joshua were there to report on Joshua's attempt to find some kind of value in the remaining two humanoids. There was still a $40 million gap that the venture capital representatives were trying to fill.

Jim introduced them and their part of the agenda.

Joshua went first. "As you know, last weekend, Anna and I went to the facility to see what possibilities there were if we activated either of the two remaining humanoids. It turns out that Daniel built them with a small port behind the ear. This port can be connected to a monitor that will display the sectors of the brain. We found that in both cases, the cluster formation that made Anna so successful did not occur. Anna hypothesized that the formation of the reorganizing clusters was predicated on the development of language in a way similar to the way humans develop. Humans really cannot form coherent thoughts or memories without having some type of language medium to communicate internally. The possibility exists that for both humanoids, the gel could be erased and reformatted. Someone could be assigned to interact with them the same way Daniel read to Anna. The mechanical parts could be repaired—that would be Cassie's neck and the unnamed one's missing arm. It would take me a few months, but I believe I could do it. We could develop two properly functioning humanoids to raise and provide for until they were mature. The only difference is that Anna was set up with forty terabytes of space, and both of these humanoids were set up with only thirty. I really don't know if that even makes a difference. There were other surprises, though. I am going to ask Anna to talk about those for a few minutes."

"Thank you, Joshua. Hi. I haven't seen you since our meeting about a year and a half ago. A lot has happened since. First of all, Joshua often gets these epiphanies about how I think and finds a need to tell me to the finest detail. As you can imagine, it gets quite obnoxious. In those cases, I will tell him that if he wants to truly understand how I think, I would be happy to give him a piece of my mind." The whole group chuckled.

"Seriously, I am going to let Joshua talk about the science; that is his forte. I am going to speak about the personal side of the experience. I think that will help you make a decision about the program going forward." Her expression changed. "Daniel was the first face I saw when I was created. He was the only face I saw for the first six months of my life. I can't assign a gender to the relationship. He was my parent, both mother and father. For quite a while, he tried to actually be my parent, although he had no parenting skills at all. Frankly, although he tried, he was really quite bad at it. That really didn't matter. How would I know?

"There was a point about a month before I left when I said some things to him that would not be unusual for any teenager to say at that stage of development. I wanted independence. I wanted to see the world. I wanted out of that glass cage. Somehow, in expressing those feelings, I broke him. It was sudden. He wanted to discard me. If it was possible for him to love me, at that point, it ended abruptly. What parent wants to kill his child? Worse, what parent openly expresses those feelings to his child? I didn't understand. I couldn't understand." Anna paused and looked away. She was choked up and could not speak for a moment. Her pain was felt around the room.

"Last weekend, I finally got my answer." She struggled to get the words out. "When Daniel was five, his mother left him. I mean, she left the house and family, never to return. She never saw or spoke to Daniel again. I don't know the reason, but it devastated Daniel so badly that it tore a hole in his psyche that never healed. Twenty years later, he met a girl who he felt was the love of his life. At some level, he must have known she loved him too. But this scar prevented him from expressing it. Because he could not get past his own issues, he lost a woman he loved a second time. That must be why he wanted to live alone in the mountains, which, by the way, were only an hour from where he grew up. That is why he surrounded himself with humanoid women who would always stay with him and obey him. He needed that control. When he built me, he knew I would be the goal he was trying to reach from the standpoint of the Logicsolutions project. His problem was that he conflated the job and his personal experience. Once I wanted to be independent and leave the facility like any other growing child, I ripped the wound open. All the drinking, meditation, yoga, and extreme exercise could not assuage his pain. At that point, he needed to destroy me and replace me so the next humanoid would never want to leave. That would be a fitting end to his hurt. None of this seemed logical until I found this." She slid the yearbook picture across the table to the women on the other side.

"Oh my God!" and a deep gasp were the reactions as Laura and Samantha took the picture and stared at it for several seconds. They passed it around the table to the men.

"Wow!" Jack said.

Jim just passed the picture back to the women, as he had already seen it.

"What does this mean?" asked Jack.

"This lady's name is Anna Caulfield. She was Daniel's love. You should have read the letters between them. His personal issues were so severe that he left her without telling her why. He created me in her image so that I could always be with him. On Sunday, I met her. Daniel's talent for the art of what he was doing was astounding. I felt I was looking at my twin. There was a picture of Ms. Caulfield's daughter on her piano. Frankly, it could have been my high school picture, and even I wouldn't have been able to tell the difference. Now I know why Daniel and I had to fight to the death before I left. He could not live with himself if I left, and I made it clear I could not stay there with him."

"So you were a copy of a girl he was in love with. My Lord, the resemblance is uncanny," Laura said. "I am so sorry, Anna. You didn't deserve any of this."

Anna spoke again. "I need to move on. The last thing I wanted to say to you is the follow-up to our first meeting. I spent the first month outside the facility fighting to stay alive from many threats. I made a deal with you. I asked you for a chance. A chance to simply live my life. You wanted to know how this would all turn out. Since then, I have had the challenge to fill not just a human's shoes but also a woman's shoes. Mr. Mendola took me in and became an adoptive father. He let me become part of his family and surround myself with the love they share. I will be grateful forever for that."

Anna started to choke up again. She soldiered on. "I have finished my first year of college. I married the love of my life. I understand now how hard it is to make a marriage work, but I work hard at it every day. While working at Gloria's law office, I have seen firsthand children who have lived a life full of similar challenges to mine. I am grateful for the opportunity to help defend them and make their lives better. Like any human, I have made mistakes. I am fortunate that the people around me have allowed me to make these mistakes and not only have forgiven me for them but also have helped me learn from them. You asked at the following meeting how this would all turn out. I have your answer. I am going to be OK. Your deal is a success." With that, she had finished.

Laura spoke again. "Anna, I know you are going to be OK. Think of us as extended family. We will be here for you. I am sure you will be a success."

"Thank you." She looked at Joshua and said, "I'll see you at home," as she patted his forearm. She turned to the group, smiled, excused herself, and left.

Samantha spoke next. "Joshua, you have an extraordinary wife. I wish you the best in your new life together. I am sorry you didn't invite us to the wedding. It would have been an honor to be there. Please include us in your family events going forward. As for the project, I am still not comfortable with going forward in commissioning the two remaining humanoids. I don't see the financial upside to doing that. I only see the increased liability. If anyone has a different take on it, please tell me."

Laura said, "For myself, having experienced the powerful emotions of this meeting and Anna's comments, I don't think we want to carry this experiment any further. We need for you to find another way to fill our forty-million-dollar hole. Although, by the way, I think Anna was worth every penny of the forty million dollars." That comment drew some snickers and amens from the rest of the group.

Chapter 54

Anna referred to major life events as stations of life. It was a metaphor that compared the stops on a train voyage to all the big events in life that brought on big changes. There was Anna's graduation from college. The Mendolas celebrated with a big cake. It became a standing joke that every time Anna had a big event, they would buy a cake to celebrate. That was great for them but not so much for Anna. There was a cake for Anna's acceptance into law school, another cake for Anna's graduation from law school, and another cake for Anna's passing the bar. There were lots of family pictures, always with the cake. After a while, the cakes got annoying, but the family celebrations never did. It was always wonderful.

One of the biggest events was Stefani's wedding. However, it almost didn't happen.

In contrast to Joshua and Anna's wedding, the ceremony was a big affair. There were almost two hundred people invited. Jim hired a planner to run things. There was no expense spared.

Anna and Stefani were at the dressmaker's, where Stefani was getting her final fitting for her gown. They were chatting with simple girl talk, when suddenly, Stefani's face grew tense. "Anna, how do I know if I am doing the right thing?"

"Regarding what?"

"This. Getting married. How do I know for sure that I am in love with Mark and that he is in love with me? How do I know if we will be happy together? How do I know if I should go through with this? Is this just cold feet? Am I making a mistake? Please tell me this is OK."

"Stefani, yeah, this is the time to have cold feet. The problem is that you are asking the wrong questions. No one knows the future. Whatever you think is between you two now will change over time. Look, people make this complicated, but it isn't. There is only one question you need to ask. Two people are in love when each of the two partners can do three things. First, they understand themselves and their own needs. Second, they can successfully communicate those needs with their partner. Third, their partner internalizes those needs as if they were their own. Obviously, needs change with time. They have to do these three things throughout their lives."

Anna pulled the knit hat out of her purse. "This hat cost Joshua about three dollars at the army surplus store, but it is the most valuable gift I have ever gotten. On our first evening together, I told Joshua I couldn't be out in the cold because it bothered my head. He had three choices. First, he could quit seeing me because he wanted his partner to be able to be with him out in the cold. Second, he could compromise by simply agreeing not to do things together when it was cold. Or third, he could internalize my need so that it became his own and help me satisfy it. Obviously, this is a simple example. You and Mark will have conflicting needs. This requires patience and compromise, or the willingness to forgo some of your needs to internalize his. This is how marriages survive. Amazingly, you are in love when your marriage is healthy, not the other way around. So the question is, can you do these three things with Mark, and do you believe he can do them with you? If not, pull the plug now. If yes, be excited about beginning the greatest journey of your life."

"I know I can do it. I think Mark can do it also. At least he has until now."

"Then you are doing the right thing."

"Thanks. I really needed to hear that."

It seemed the time between stations of life was just a blur. The next big station of life was when Anna started working for Gloria Rogers as an associate attorney, not just an assistant. This was the reward for seven years at school. Quickly, her caseload became full of a wide variety of cases but mostly simple contracts and matrimonial issues. Gloria wanted her to get a little more experience before she started arguing in front of a courtroom.

Chapter 55

"All rise. The Honorable Judge John T. Ruskin presiding."

"The next case on the docket is *Mary Rutherford v. the New York Housing Authority*. Counselors, please approach the bench. Is there any possibility of a settlement on this matter today?"

The lawyers leaned in closely in front of the judge and had a conversation inaudible to the others in the room. After a few minutes of discussion, they finished and nodded in agreement in front of the judge.

"Yes, Your Honor, I think we can settle this today. These are the terms of the agreement." The attorney for the plaintiff handed a document to the judge.

"This appears to be in order. The court accepts this proposal." With that, the gavel was smacked against the wooden base. "Next case, please."

The plaintiff's attorney walked back to her client and explained what it meant: they had won. There was some hugging in the hallway, and Anna went back to her office.

Later that afternoon, the phone rang, and the receptionist answered. "Law offices. Can I help you?"

It was a woman who sounded upset. She asked if the attorneys there could help her boyfriend with a divorce. The receptionist looked at the calendar and said she could make an appointment with one of the attorneys. Anna Conners was free later that afternoon.

The man walked in at 3:00 p.m. sharp. He was a tall, well-dressed man in his early fifties. He was invited into the office and offered a seat. He held out his hand with a firm handshake and said, "My name is Barry Stiles. I heard your firm was the best around, so I want to thank you for agreeing to take my case."

Anna sat back in her chair. "Sir, could you give me a moment? I would like the senior attorney to sit in on this. The receptionist told me a little about the case, and I think that would be helpful."

Anna left the room and found Gloria Rogers at her desk, reading. "Gloria, I have a case I think you might be interested in."

"What would that be?"

"Barry Stiles has just found his way into our office to ask us to do his divorce. Can you believe it?"

Gloria made a face Anna had never seen before.

"Hollywood can't write this stuff," Anna said.

"Well, let's hear him out," said Gloria.

The two women walked back into the office. Anna said, "This is Ms. Rogers, the senior attorney."

Gloria shook his hand. "OK, Mr. Stiles, tell us what happened."

Barry went on to tell his story. He had been unhappy in his marriage for a long time and had started seeing another woman. Eventually, his wife had found out and exploded with anger. She had found a hatchet and chased him out of the house with it, smashing furniture, cussing, and threatening him all the way out to the front yard. He'd left without any of his belongings and had been staying in a nearby hotel. He'd bought the clothes he had on at the time earlier that morning at a nearby shop.

"Wow, that is quite a visual," Anna said. "This is a case we can handle. You need a court order to let you back into the house to get your things, and you will need a forensic accountant to calculate how much the marital property is worth. I am guessing from your age that there are no minor children. If we can keep you two apart so you don't kill each other and only communicate through the attorneys, I think you can survive this OK."

"Can I have her charged with attempted murder?"

"You could try, but you probably shouldn't. If we could get her attorney to agree to a reasonable settlement, you will fare better. If you have her charged with that, then she will undoubtedly have you charged with something, and we will have to litigate the charges before we can even begin to discuss the settlement. You will probably spend fifty thousand dollars just to get to the place you are in right now."

"I see."

Anna went on. "Mr. Stiles, Ms. Rogers and I are going to be forthcoming with you. We have had a previous encounter with you that we need to disclose."

"What is that?"

"Our office used to be on the twenty-one-hundred block, about a half mile up the street. We had to move when a firebomb went off in our window. You wouldn't happen to know anything about that, would you? It seems the men who did that will be getting out of prison in two and a half years."

"I wouldn't know anything about that," Barry said as he looked at his shoelaces.

"OK. There is one other thing."

"Yes?"

"You and I had a little business meeting by your car around the same time, and I asked you politely to stop harassing me."

"Stop harassing you?"

"Yes. Well, I wasn't really all that polite. I put a gun to your throat to make my intentions clear."

"No. You aren't—I'll be damned. You're the robot!"

"Anna Conners from Logicsolutions. You are one of the few people on the planet who know who I am. So I need to disclose that I still have my gun."

"I remember that. You are definitely the one I want to represent me. You scared the hell out of me. Can you threaten my wife with your gun like that?"

"No, Mr. Stiles. I just want to lay down the ground rules with you. I can represent you. I have forgiven you for what you did to me back then. But I will tell you now: you need to be truthful with me. Besides my dropping you like a hot potato if you lie to me, those promises I made to you that night about my safety and my secrets are still real. Do we have a deal?"

"Yes, ma'am. We have a deal."

After Barry left the office, Gloria pulled Anna aside. "What was that all about?"

"Remember when you called me with the good news and bad news? You told me that the gang wasn't talking and that Barry would not be arrested?"

"Yes, vaguely."

"Well, I knew the nightmare wouldn't be over, and I feared for myself and the safety of the ones around me. I waited for him to come out of work that night and followed him to his car. I held my snub-nosed .38 to his throat and made it clear to him that I would shoot him if he bothered me or my family again."

"Jeez, Anna, really?"

"Yeah. I was quite the terror back then. You really should have been there." She laughed out loud. "Joshua was sure he soiled his pants when I told him the story. Listen, though, all joking aside. We need to help this man with his divorce. The truth is that AJX Enterprises has lost millions over the last few years due to this guy's mismanagement. They fired him, and he is jobless. Logicsolutions is talking about making a play to rescue AJX Enterprises with a merger. There are stock assets that will be involved. I don't want this guy's wife to get in the way. So I want to do whatever I can to keep this affair out of the AJX Enterprises business."

The next day, Anna was on the phone with Barry's wife's attorney, who said, "My client wants all the liquid assets. That includes all the bank accounts, the retirement accounts, the cash at home, and all the money in the safe-deposit boxes. She also wants the house and to keep her car."

Anna responded as coolly as possible. "What about the AJX Enterprises stocks?"

"We both know they are worthless. AJX Enterprises is expected to file for bankruptcy in the next few months. She is not interested in the hassle."

"Mr. Parks, if your client takes every penny my client has and keeps the house and the car while my client is homeless and jobless, the bank is going to foreclose on the house and repossess the car. He won't have the money. Your client will have to accept the mortgage with the house and the car loan with all of his assets."

"OK, I can talk to her about that."

"OK, Mr. Parks. Your client seems to have made her needs clear. Send over a binding proposal. My client and I can examine exactly what your client is looking for and make a counterproposal. But I am insisting the proposal is specific and binding. I don't want to get into a back-and-forth about what was meant by the wording or mood swings of your client."

"OK. I will have it on your desk by the end of business tomorrow."

Barry showed up at Anna's office two days later in the early afternoon. She showed him the proposal and summarized it. "Your wife is asking for every penny you own, the house, and her car. She does not want your AJX Enterprises stock. There is no mention of alimony. It is probably the most unreasonable proposal I have ever seen."

Barry skimmed the proposal to see what Anna was saying. The reality of what his wife was trying to do to him sank in. She wanted more than a divorce. She wanted to destroy him. He started a string of cuss words and an angry rant.

Anna let him go on for about three minutes, until he had to take a breath. "Are you done?"

He glared at her.

"Listen, that proposal is my setup. I want to explain, but you are going to need a clear head. Do you like ice cream?"

"It's OK. Why?"

"Take a walk with me. We are going up the street half a block to the deli. I am treating you to an ice cream cone. You will think more clearly when you are doing something pleasant."

They grabbed their jackets and strolled about a hundred yards up the street. Anna ordered an ice cream cone for Barry and bought a *New York Times*.

"Is your head clear now? I am going to explain something to you that will have a lot of moving parts, so you have to listen carefully and with an open mind. That proposal is a spite proposal. She has no desire to agree to a settlement with you. She wants to prolong the fight because she hates you, and she is deranged. That proposal, on its face, is unworkable because she knows you have no job, and it leaves you with no money. The only bright spot is that I convinced her attorney to let her have the mortgage with the house and the loan with the car. You will be unburdened with that debt. It is not just that. Your wife knows you don't have any income, so asking for alimony is pointless. New York's guidelines ask of a percentage of your income. Since she isn't working, you can't ask her for alimony either. She is probably expecting you to get another job eventually. When you do and she finds out, I promise you she will be in court the next day, asking for a percentage of it. Typically, one pays alimony for one-third of the number of years you were married. You were married eight years, right?"

"Yes."

"So figure the guidelines would have you on the hook for about thirty-two months, or roughly two and a half years. Now, a judge can do whatever he or she wants. For this discussion, we will figure what would normally happen. If it takes two to three years for you to get another job or to see capital gains on your assets, you could escape most or all of the alimony."

"What are you suggesting?"

"In the end, it will be your choice, but I think you should take the offer. Here's why. She sees herself as getting all of a two-point-six-million-dollar estate. That will feel like a victory. She has left the fifty thousand shares of stock on the table because she thinks it will eventually be worthless and become a legal hassle for her. What are the shares at now?"

"About four dollars."

"OK. So there is two hundred thousand dollars left if it doesn't drop and go bankrupt. And you still have your Porsche?"

"Right."

"Open the paper to the financial section."

"OK."

"Remember the toy company that made some bad investments about two years ago and ended up almost going broke?"

"Yeah. I can't think of the name, but I know who you mean."

"Those shares got as low as two dollars and fifty cents. Then what happened?"

"What?"

"Another company acquired them. Merchandising unlimited. They were acquired in a deal that left the company basically intact and kept the shares intact with a new valuation. It was a sweet deal for both parties. The truth is that even in the vulnerable position the toy company was, they still had an income stream and some significant business. It was just mismanaged. Going bankrupt would have eliminated all of the good. A smart company acquired it and preserved the value. Look at the stock value now."

"Wow! It is forty dollars a share."

"Do you think with all the intellectual property AJX Enterprises has that the artificial intelligence industry would take a chance on buying those pieces out of bankruptcy or letting them disappear? Never. Someone will acquire the company in the same fashion—intact. If, in a year or two, under new ownership, your fifty thousand shares go to, say, twenty dollars, then they will be worth a million dollars. If the price goes to forty, they will be worth two million. Is this making sense? You have an offer that gives you the opportunity to lose your wife and her nuttiness right now. I mean immediately. You leave with this asset that, in two or three years, could easily be worth more than half your estate."

Barry listened intently.

"The alternative is that you fight with your wife for years at a cost of ten thousand dollars a month by the time your estate is done paying both of the attorneys, hers and yours. In that time frame, whatever increase the stock will show, it will have shown by then. This gives her another target. Even then, you may not have an agreement because your wife wants you to pay for some ten-dollar item she insists on going to court for." She paused for a moment. "My suggestion is that you take the deal."

"So how would that work?"

"Sign the binding proposal. They are committed. You sell your Porsche. How much do you owe on it?"

"Twenty thousand dollars."

"Great. Get fifty from a dealership for it, and learn how to live on thirty thousand dollars for a year. Maybe move in with your girlfriend. Let the company issues play out, and start your life over. It actually is the easiest choice for you. Of course, I don't have a crystal ball. AJX Enterprises could go bust, or you could find another job of your dreams. That is the chance you take. Go back to the motel, and mull it over. You have until Friday to decide."

At that point, they had reached Anna's office.

"Barry, this is really a choice between short-term outcomes and long-term outcomes. You want to try to focus on a new life ahead, hopefully with the woman who called for you. That means the long-term outcome. You are angry now, but you need to decide with your head, not your emotions."

Barry took a few minutes to say what was on his mind. "Ms. Conners—or, if I may, Anna—I have been in business a long time, and I think I am a pretty good judge of people. I can hear what you are not saying as well as what you are saying. You are connected to Logicsolutions somehow. They are the most likely company to be the white knight who buys AJX Enterprises. I appreciate your sharing your thoughts with me, and I respect what you can and can't say. I also can tell you are putting my needs above your own in terms of billable hours. Thank you. You really are a good lawyer. Listen, I think this is the point where I say I truly misunderstood you seven years ago. I'm sorry for the things that happened in the past. I appreciate that you really are looking out for me. I won't forget it. One thing you need to know about me is that I never forget to take care of the people who take care of me."

Friday came, and Barry agreed to take the deal. Like clockwork, Anna got an angry call from Mr. Park. "You said you would counteroffer, not accept the deal. It is a terrible deal. It is malpractice to take that deal."

"Mr. Park, I'm sorry this case did not become the cash cow you were hoping for. My client simply chose to take the deal. He wants it to be over, regardless of what he has to give up. He said taking the deal was the best one hundred twenty-five pounds he has ever lost." Anna smiled to herself.

Chapter 56

The executive team gathered for their weekly meeting. Invited guests were Joshua and Stefani. They had been working together for the last four years on the launch of the virtual agent product. The program had been going well. Small glitches along the way were solved quickly, and overall, most of the customers were happy with their new friends, their virtual agents.

"Everyone's here. Let's get started." Jim opened the meeting. "Joshua, would you update the group on where you are with the virtual agent product?"

"Well, as of January 1 of this year, we have approximately three million customers. Complaints are relatively few. The launch really took off this year after news of three massive data breaches in a row. When we added new identity qualities to the agent, such as post office address, virtual phone number, and credit card number, the sales almost doubled. I want to credit Stefani with that. So that the group has the whole picture, we worked out a deal with the bank wherein a special fund was set up to allow the agent to draw money for the purchases without divulging an identity or exposing the fund to any risk beyond the purchase itself. The credit card number is a onetime number that expires after the transaction. All the agents have access to this feature. The individual customer account is tied to this feature so that the customer's bank account is debited the exact amount of the purchase, and the funds are returned to the bank. This solidly protects the customer from identity theft, and it protects the bank from the customer. Frankly, this should have been done years ago. Does anyone have any questions about the service?"

"Do people have to qualify to get this service? They are getting a loan, aren't they?"

"No. Not any more than to get a credit card to begin with. That is the beauty of the setup. The purchase is not allowed if the customer does not have funds to cover it. The transfer from the fund to the customer account is instantaneous and seamless. It is as if the customer is showing up at the store with his or her own card, but with the same controls online. The difference is that the ability to scam the credit card numbers and steal an identity doesn't exist."

"So you have to have a credit or debit card to get this service?"

"Yes. The reality is you would have to have a credit or debit card to purchase online anyway, so no one is excluded."

"That's impressive. Kudos to you, Joshua," said Laura.

"Well, it's posthumous, but let's give Daniel some of the credit as well. Stefani will go over the numbers."

"OK. Well, as Joshua mentioned, we have three million customers, give or take, as of the beginning of the year. That number has increased by about two hundred thousand more since the beginning of this month. At seventy-nine dollars per year, that gets us to just under two hundred forty million dollars per year. We have had to open a customer service location dedicated to this service. That cost is running about thirty-eight million dollars per year. We have a server farm and IT infrastructure maintenance at about sixteen million dollars a year. Licenses, taxes, and fees are around three million. The cost of the banking service is another twenty million dollars for fees and interest. The profit anticipated for this year will be about one hundred eighty-three million dollars."

Samantha said, "OK, I am impressed as well. What is your projection for the future?"

"Well, at the rate it is growing, I anticipate we will reach five million subscribers by the end of the year. That gets us to a profitability level that rivals our core business of consulting with business solutions."

"Thank you," said Jim. "I would like you two to stay for the next part of the meeting. You all have heard that AJX Enterprises is in difficult financial straits. They heavily invested in the artificially intelligent machines Daniel was trying to create, but they were doing it with standard circuitry. It hasn't gone well for the reasons Joshua pointed out in our past meetings. There is simply too much unresolved legal infrastructure to make it work. So kudos again to Joshua for keeping us from going down that same rabbit hole.

"These choices have put us in a strong enough position that we can make an offer to the AJX Enterprises board to acquire them. We are cash heavy, and they are behind on their obligations. We can create a rescue package and take over the company. This would keep them out of bankruptcy. So let's look at how a deal like that would work. Once we negotiate over the cash issues and the stock revaluation, we can use their local production facilities for our research and development. We can use their server farms for our growing agent business. Most importantly, we can take possession of their patents and the research team. There are certain lines of business in which we can use their artificial intelligence development infrastructure to augment our own. Also, we can sell that godforsaken building in West Virginia. It will be a boon for Logicsolutions across the board.

"Time is of the essence. There are others who will see what we see. I plan to call the chairman of their board Monday to see if we can meet with them and work this out quietly and quickly. Joshua and Stefani, I am going to need for you two to work in tandem to produce all the numbers and business-line pieces for me to talk intelligently about this. I will need it by Monday. I need to make clear to everyone in this room that this is a once-in-a-lifetime opportunity. We need to make this happen."

"We can do this, Mr. Mendola. Stefani and I will work over the weekend and have it for you Sunday night. Is there anything else you need from us?"

"No, that's it. That's enough. Why don't you guys meet on your own to figure out what you need to do? Thanks. I'm counting on you."

Joshua and Stefani left the meeting. As they got on the elevator to head down to their offices, Stefani turned to Joshua and said, "Well, so much for thinking that being family would make our jobs easier. I'll bet Dad will come over to your house to make sure you are working on this and to see how much you have gotten done."

"You mean like we're in grade school? I'll bet he will. Stefani?"

"Yes?"

"Did he ever say how much he wanted for the building in West Virginia?"

"No, why?"

"What do you think of the idea of you and Mark going in with Anna and I to buy it and turn it into a vacation property for us?"

"Huh. What an interesting idea. I don't think Anna will go for it. From what you have told me, she doesn't particularly like it there. Actually, you were going to tell me why, but we got sidetracked. What happened?"

"Can I give you the *Reader's Digest* version?"

"Sure. If I have questions, we can go from there."

"It's pretty simple. Daniel wanted to dismantle Anna for parts for the next model. Anna did not want to die. He tried to force the issue, and she stabbed him with a two-pronged rotisserie spit, and he died right there in the hallway. Then, so I would not be connected to the murder, she cut all communication with me.

She disappeared for a month in Manhattan and called me when she needed me to fix her leg. If she hadn't hurt her leg, I probably would have never seen her again." He stopped walking and turned to Stefani to see if she had anything more to say.

"No! Get out of town! Anna stabbed Daniel and killed him?"

"Yeah. In the gut. He bled all over and died right there in the hallway. The police assumed Cassie did it. But it was Anna. There is more to the story, but you probably don't want to hear the rest. It doesn't get any prettier."

"Sweet Anna. That is unbelievable." She made a face. "So that is how you guys met? How romantic!"

"What's more, killing Daniel doesn't make her feel guilty. I don't think she has spent one minute thinking about that. It was the idea of spending her life in a glass prison until the day he decided to do away with her that haunted her. He abused her physically and mentally. She carried scars for a long time."

"So why do you think she will be OK with actually living there?"

"She met the person Daniel used as a model to create her, who, by the way, was also named Anna. Talk about a weird encounter. They look exactly alike. Anna has come to terms with these events because of finding some of the personal things Daniel left behind. He was a damaged person, and Anna has a soft spot for damaged people. Aside from that, she can compartmentalize. That is what she does. You would be surprised how she can process danger as separate from everything else. You also need to understand that Anna has never really learned the emotion of fear. She understands danger and dread when she knows something bad is going to happen, but when confronted with danger, she simply goes clinical and thinks her way logically through any situation. You watched her run into a burning building, for God's sake. She struggled with going back to the lab for the inventory, but after I took her there to help her recover from the fire, she doesn't connect the facility to Daniel anymore. We'll see when I bring it up to her. Do you want to talk to Mark about it?"

"I will. I need to talk to him about taking time off anyway. You and I will be seeing a lot of each other over the weekend. I'll ask him and tell you when I see you."

"Sounds like a plan."

It was Sunday night at the Mendolas'. Joshua handed Jim a binder full of notes for his phone call next day.

Jim asked Joshua to sit with him for a moment. "You really are a hero over at the venture capital company. You rescued a forty-million-dollar loss, and you have almost doubled the company's gross sales. They actually asked me to tell you they are giving you a bonus on top of the one I give you. This is unusual, but they want to give you some reward for making them a lot of money and protecting their investment. I don't know the exact amount, but I think it is in the fifty-thousand-dollar range."

"Wow! Thank you. That is great news. Actually, that helps me segue into what I wanted to ask you. You didn't say if there were any specific plans for the West Virginia property aside from just selling it. Stefani and I were talking about whether we could buy it and turn it into a vacation home. The views in the mountains are just breathtaking."

"Joshua, there are no roads to get there. Yes, you can fly there with Ray occasionally, but how do you manage the day-to-day needs?"

"Apparently, the county plans on building a road that comes within two miles of the property. We can pay to make a private road from there. That makes the town accessible and puts us two hours away from an airport in Pittsburgh or Wheeling. The truth is, I was going to ask you if I could work some of the time remotely. My job involves so much video time, telephone time, and computer work that I have very little need to be in the office except for face-to-face meetings."

"I'll talk to the executive team and see what they think. I would love to just give it to you, actually, but they are going to insist on market price. I'll see what I can do."

Chapter 57

The following Sunday, the whole family gathered for dinner. After they cleared the table, Jim said to Joshua, "The executive team agreed to sell the property for three quarters of a million dollars. They were originally thinking of New York prices, and I pointed out that it is ten miles to the nearest road and in the middle of the mountains, which means common amenities are hours away, so it is hard to have comparables. Anyway, does that still work for your plans?"

"Actually, it fits in well. Between the four of us, we can afford it. We'll all talk it over while we are here tonight."

Joshua called the others to the kitchen table. "Mark, Stefani, Anna, come here. This is a floor plan to the facility. Let's see what we can dream up. Jim says the price of the property is seven hundred fifty thousand dollars. In today's market, that means about fifty thousand down and a mortgage of about fifty-five hundred a month, plus taxes and insurance. West Virginia's property taxes are low compared to New York's. I can find out exactly next week."

"Anna, you've been there more than any of us. What would you like to see?" asked Stefani.

"These glass walls are incredibly strong. I think if we removed them all, we could build a large room completely made of glass, ceiling and walls, and seal it so it could be used year-round. Maybe put a fireplace in the center for effect."

"Yeah, and for heat also, and put a large television against the existing wall here," Mark added.

"What do we do with the space left from the glass rooms?" asked Stefani.

"Maybe three-bedroom apartments. We can make two of them and put them facing each other on opposite sides of the hall. We want to work remotely, so we need a space for that that is big enough for all four of us," said Joshua.

"Wow. This could be really cool. It is like our own villa in the mountains," Mark said.

"The beauty of it is that over the next two years, they are going to build a road that makes this very accessible. We will be thirty minutes by car from Morgantown and two hours by car from Pittsburgh or Wheeling. We can still fly from the helipad, or we can fly commercially and drive from either airport."

"What does it cost to do these things after we have bought it?"

"We'll find out. Mark, why don't you reach out to prospective contractors for a ballpark price? I'll call the county to find out the taxes and permitting process."

"I'll call a decorator," said Stefani. They all looked at Anna.

"OK, OK, I'll draw up the closing documents."

Chapter 58

After collecting their personal items, two men walked out of a New York state prison. The leader and a team member of Barry's gang had completed nine-and-a-half-year sentences for arson in connection with the bombing at Gloria Rogers's office ten years earlier. There was only one thing on their agenda. They never had been paid for the job. They had been paid a fee of $50,000 for killing Nick Walsh, all of which had gone to the shyster lawyer who'd set them up in a plea deal. The other $50,000 for their job with the robot was still outstanding.

The phone call to Barry looking for their money did not go well. He said he wasn't going to pay them because they had failed at the job. The robot never had been captured or killed. Barry made it clear that was the end of it. The leader of the team assumed that meant the job had to be finished, even if it was ten years later.

As they set out to collect their prey, internet searches turned up little. Public records showed that Anna Conners had been married to Joshua Harrington and had been admitted to the New York bar. They also found a newspaper article about the fire in the bookshop and another one about Barry's termination from AJX Enterprises.

They paid a visit to Barry's house and found that only his ex-wife lived there. The gold mine of information came from a fifteen-minute expletive rant when they asked her where they could find him. All they had to do now was lay out their plan.

Chapter 59

"Anna, there are two men in dark suits here to see you. They say they are from the Securities and Exchange Commission."

"Ask them to wait a minute, and I'll come right out."

A minute later, Anna met them in the waiting room. "Good morning. I am Anna Conners. May I help you?"

"Ms. Conners, I am Agent McLellan, and this is Agent Wiskowski. We are from the Securities and Exchange Commission. Can we talk in your office? We have some questions we want to ask you."

"Sure, come right on in over here." She led them to the conference room. She had no clue what they would have wanted with her. She had a retirement account, but she hadn't traded anything ever. "What can I do for you?"

"There was a complaint filed against you. It seems a Mrs. Stiles claims to have been hurt financially when you gave her ex-husband insider trading information during the negotiation of a settlement for their divorce."

"What are you talking about?"

"You are married to Joshua Harrington?"

"Yes."

"You are the adopted daughter of James Mendola?"

"Yes."

"It seems you would have been knowledgeable of the merger between AJX Enterprises and Logicsolutions before it happened. Mr. Stiles owned a significant number of stock shares in AJX Enterprises, and you advised him of a financial advantage before it was made public."

Anna sat back and tried to make sense of the situation. "Mr. Stiles didn't sell any of his stock. There was no trade."

"Mrs. Stiles claims that if she had known there was going to be a merger, she would have sought her portion of the shares of stock. She feels she lost a million dollars because you gave her ex inside information, according to a complaint filed by her attorney, a Mr. Park."

"But my conversations with Mr. Stiles predate the merger by a good three or four months. There was no deal then. Besides, I never said Logicsolutions would be involved. I couldn't have known that then, because no offer had been made. On top of that, at that time, AJX Enterprises could have said no. There were no negotiations."

"I'm sorry, Ms. Conners. I have to issue a subpoena for you to appear at a hearing to determine whether you broke SEC rules with your conversation with Mr. Stiles." The two men stood up, and Agent McLellan handed a piece of paper to Anna. "We can see ourselves out."

"Anna, what was that all about?" Gloria asked.

"It seems the SEC is suing me over the conversation I had with Barry for his divorce settlement. Mr. Park made an absurd offer to Barry so he could run the meter up. Because his ex didn't think the stock would be worth anything, she neglected to go after it. When I recommended that he accept the offer, I explained that someone—and I didn't mention any names—would acquire AJX Enterprises and that the stock would have value. Maybe a lot of value. It made more sense to give his wife what she wanted and start over rather than spend a lot of time and money fighting a battle that would litter his life with collateral damage. But this is stupid. This Agent McLellan knows that no crime was committed. Yet he is making me lose a day of work and spend your energy at this frivolous hearing."

"McLellan—that sounds familiar. Didn't you represent a woman named McLellan about a year ago? Was that his wife?"

"Yeah, I did. Come to think of it, I'll bet this is payback," Anna said.

"Oh, Anna. No good deed goes unpunished."

"Thanks. Will you represent me at the hearing?"

"Of course. I need to protect my investment," Gloria said with a faint smile.

A week later, Anna was in federal court for the hearing.

"Counselors, are you ready?"

"Yes, the government is ready, Your Honor," said Agent McLellan.

"Yes, the defendant is ready, Your Honor," said Gloria.

"As you know, this is not a trial but a hearing to see if a crime has been committed. The government may proceed."

"Your Honor, we have reason to believe Ms. Conners had knowledge of a merger between AJX Enterprises and Logicsolutions prior to the public having that knowledge. She used that knowledge to advise one of her clients in a divorce settlement to his advantage. The evidence for this is the stipulation of facts in this case of the relationship of the defendant and persons who are employed by Logicsolutions who would be privy to the business negotiations. We also want to submit to evidence the proposal of settlement by the ex-wife of the client that stipulated that the stock is not included. The ex-wife claims her lack of the information that was provided to Ms. Conners's client cost her over a million dollars at today's market valuation."

"The defendant may proceed."

"Your Honor, the law is clear about the requirements of the crime of insider trading. An action must be taken that harms the stockholders, not a third-party client. That would require the sale of stock or a short-selling of stock in a move beneficial to the individual and hurtful to the remaining stockholders. None of these requirements occurred in this case. The government's case is baseless."

"Is that true?" The judge looked at the government's side of the courtroom. "Was there any action on the part of the client to sell or short-sell?"

"No, sir."

"Then we are done here. I find for the defendant. There is no crime here." The judge slammed the plate with the gavel.

Agent McLellan walked by Anna and, with a sneer, said, "It has been a pleasure. Have a nice day."

Anna and Gloria got up and packed their things, met with Joshua at the door, and headed into the hallway. Gloria said she had other business and left to go down the hall. Joshua and Anna headed for the exit and down the courthouse steps.

Chapter 60

"Excuse me, sir. Are you Joshua Harrington?"

Joshua and Anna had left together and were walking away from the courthouse immediately after the hearing, when a man approached. Joshua said, "Yes. Do I know you?"

"No, but she does. Anna, come with me quietly, or your husband gets shot right here." The man put a gun to Joshua's side. "You won't be blowing anyone up today if your husband is standing right next to you."

Anna remembered her bluff in claiming she had C-4 built inside her to protect her from being kidnapped. She realized this was one of the gang of thugs. He must have gotten out of jail. It was about time for his sentence to be up. "Why do you want him? He has nothing to do with why you want me."

Joshua made a face as if to say, "Who is this guy, and how do you know him?"

The man said, "Protection. You make a move against me, and he dies. Simple as that."

Just then, a car pulled up, and he forced them into the backseat. Another man drove while the first thug pointed the gun at them from the front seat. He handed them two sets of handcuffs. "Put these on after you"—he pointed to Anna—"put your arm through his. Do it, or I'll kill you right now."

Anna looped her arm through Joshua's and put the cuffs on her wrists. Joshua put his cuffs on. The man reached out and tightened the handcuffs on both of them until the cuffs squeezed tightly against their wrists. They rode the rest of the way with the man pointing his gun at them.

Wouldn't it have been helpful if I still carried my own gun? Anna thought. The other thing that occurred to her was that there was no hood this time. Apparently, he didn't care if they saw the path to where they were going. That meant, at least in the man's mind, they weren't ever going to return.

About fifteen minutes later, they arrived at a warehouse. The driver got out of the car, opened a garage door, and drove in. They were helped out of the car and escorted to a large room past a small vestibule.

"Sit here." The man pointed to two chairs and ordered them to sit side by side, shackled together.

Finally, Anna asked, "Who are you, and what do you want from us?"

"I want my money." He then pulled out his phone. After a minute, they overheard him say, "I have the thing here with the husband. I don't care if you want them dead or alive. I want my money."

They heard the voice on the phone say, "Don't hurt them. I will be there within an hour with your money."

Turning to Anna, he said, "Oh, and by the way, do you see this?" He lifted his pant leg and showed a huge misshapen ankle. It was the size of a grapefruit and a weird purple color. "You don't get medical care in jail. I spent nine long years in constant pain, waiting for this moment."

After several minutes, the other man approached Anna and moved her hair away from her face with his hand. "Boss, we have an hour before Stiles gets here. What do you say you let me take the lady into the other room and show her a good time?"

Joshua yelled, "Don't you touch her, or I'll kill you!"

The man lifted his hand with the gun as if to hit Joshua across the face with a backhand swing.

"Wait!" Anna said, and the man paused a few inches from Joshua's face. "I think that is a great idea. If you want to take me into the other room and show me a good time, go ahead. I'll bet you want to see me naked. You know, I am built with special robot equipment that would make having sex with me incredible. I can satisfy all your wildest fantasies." She had everyone's attention, even Joshua's.

After a moment, Anna continued. "Listen, genius, you have lost track of the fact that I am the one with the bomb. That is why we are shackled together, remember?" She stared down the leader of the duo. "You are both such fools. Do you think you are in control of the situation here? It doesn't matter that we are cuffed. I can set my C-4 package off whenever I choose. We are in a standoff. You are right that I won't blow up my husband. However, if I am convinced you are going to kill him, then I have no problem taking out all four of us. I would say that even though you have the guns, unless you are going to shoot us from a much greater distance than is possible inside this building, we are pretty evenly matched."

The leader stared at her for several minutes and then ordered the other man to leave Anna alone. "Let's just all calm down and wait for the money."

After what seemed like an eternity, Barry Stiles appeared at the door of the vestibule. He entered the room and laid a briefcase on the table. "All of your money is there. Open it."

The team leader looked away from Anna and Joshua and laid his gun on the table as he began to open the briefcase. Barry pulled a Glock out of his waistband from behind his back. He didn't leave any time for the two men to react. He simply raised his arm and fired two shots, hitting the first man in the chest and the second one in the back of the head. The power of the bullets lifted the first man off the ground and left the second man with the contents of his head on the wall behind him. They were dead instantly.

Joshua recoiled at the sight. Anna simply kept a clinical face. Joshua was reacting to the cold-blooded killing. Anna was reacting to the fact that this was the same guy she had held at gunpoint and told to leave her alone that night by his car nine years ago. Either he had a weak spot for strong-minded women, or she had escaped with her life by a stroke of luck. Or maybe she had amused him with her bravado and he really never had been threatened by her at all. Now she understood how truly formidable Barry was as an enemy. She was relieved that in this moment, he was her friend.

"How much were you supposed to pay them?" Anna asked as Barry unlocked the handcuffs.

"I wasn't going to pay them anything. The briefcase was full of play money with a real fifty on the top of each stack. I just needed a distraction to shoot him. My wonderful ex-wife had to call me to gloat over how she had caused you trouble with the SEC. I went to your hearing to see what would happen. I tried to catch you as you left and watched the whole thing. I knew who these guys were and what they were up to. Here are my car keys. Leave my car at the Manhasset train station, leave the keys under the mat, and take the train home. I am going to take care of this mess. When you walk out that door, this has to disappear from your memory. You were never here, and you never saw anything that has happened tonight. Go on with your lives, and never look back. You will not hear from any of this gang again."

Anna realized that three of them were still in jail. She could read between the lines that when they got out, the same thing would happen to them. Barry must have had his reasons. She hated them, but she shuddered at the thought of their demise.

Anna and Joshua left the warehouse, as they'd been told. As they were getting in the car, Anna said, "Well, look at that. He traded in his Porsche for a Ford Focus. He really did take my advice about surviving his divorce." She laughed to herself as they strapped on their seat belts.

Anna wanted to drive, because Joshua was an emotional mess. Unfortunately, he was the one with the license.

They arrived at the Manhasset train station about a half hour later. He left the car unlocked and the keys under the driver's-side mat. Anna bought tickets to the Jamaica station and then on to their apartment. The ride home had been silent. Now Joshua spoke first. "Anna, what just happened to us?"

"Remember when Nick Walsh was involved with a gang and was trying to sell me to AJX Enterprises? That was them. The only way I was able to get away was to shoot them in the feet. I hit this guy, and apparently, he didn't forget. I wonder if the other guy was one of the ones I hit as well. Anyway, these two just got out of jail, and finding me was apparently their first order of business. I didn't know about the money, but I am sure revenge for shooting him in the ankle was part of why he wanted to get me. They waited until they could get both of us to be sure I didn't set off my self-destruct bomb."

"But you don't have a self-destruct bomb," Joshua said.

"Fortunately, they didn't know that. My pretending to have one when they tried to kidnap me was really what made them give up and run away. For some reason, they didn't want to be in the same van as an angry woman with a bomb. Go figure." Anna said, almost laughing.

"Aren't there three more in the gang you have to worry about?"

"You weren't understanding Barry's code. He is going to kill them as they get out of jail. That is why he said we would not hear from any of them again. There is clearly a lesson here."

"What is that?"

"It would have been entirely understandable for me to have turned Barry away as a client. I didn't. I told him he was forgiven and said I would represent him in spite of the past. I gave him the best advice I could. He appreciated the help. The last thing he said to me that day was that he would never forget the people who took care of him. He kept his word. How differently this night would have turned out if I had held a grudge and turned him away instead of doing the right thing. It is hard to wrap my head around how that works."

"I will never understand how you think. We almost died tonight, and you are thinking about karma, not how close we came to never seeing another day."

"Oh no, I totally grasp the peril we faced tonight. I have just moved on to the next idea, which is how Barry saved us. And then on to the next idea, which is why Barry saved us."

As Joshua turned the key in the lock of their apartment, Anna said, "Let's just spend the night in each other's arms and appreciate how wonderful that feels. It will help us to forget what happened tonight, just like Barry told us to."

Chapter 61

Anna and Joshua were driving out to West Virginia together for the first time since the contractors had started working on their new property. They were almost there. "Joshua?"

"Yes, dear?"

"I was thinking."

"Am I in trouble?"

"No, silly. Now that we have our dream home in West Virginia, I was thinking about how it would be if we moved out there—you know, instead of just vacationing there."

"But we both live and work in New York. How would we do that?"

"You could work out a schedule of remote work and occasional trips to the New York office. I could just start over here."

"That's a lot of hassle. Why would you want to do that?"

"You know that we were attacked by a pair of thugs trying to settle a nine-year-old score. I spent a day in court because an angry ex wanted to settle a different score. I was mugged in the middle of the sidewalk by a guy who didn't even have a score to settle. That is a lot of danger from people over which I have no control. I think about Mark and Stefani with their children and how much I would like to raise a child. Raising a child in New York makes me feel so much more vulnerable. I checked it out, and Morgantown looks like a really cool place. It has thirty thousand people. That is big enough to have everything we need and small enough to have the coziness and safety of a small town. I think the house in West Virginia would be such a great place to raise a child. I am sure there are needy people to defend in West Virginia. I could open a Gloria Rogers satellite law office or even my own office nearby. I could get my driver's license here, because driving is so much easier. I could drive from this place to my parents' house in six hours. Your parents live only an hour and a half away. What do you think?"

"Anna Conners-Harrington, I know you. You are asking me what I think about relocating to West Virginia, but what you are really asking me is if I want to adopt a child. Aren't you?"

"Well ..."

"Don't give me those eyes. That is what you are asking, isn't it?"

"Well, yes."

"OK, I think we should do it."

"Sweetie, I love you," she said as she leaned her head against his shoulder.

Chapter 62

Working on the house turned out to be fun. Joshua was the general contractor and called one subcontractor after another. They opened up the service road from the border of the property to where it would meet the new county road. After that, trucks had access, and they could bring in anything they needed. It turned out Daniel had had a path cleared for trucks to be able to bring in the heavy building supplies. After the construction had been completed, he'd torn up the road so it would be impassable. Once the old service road was identified, it wasn't hard to open it again and lay out ten truckloads of gravel to make it more passable.

The coordination of the subcontractors was almost a full-time job in and of itself, but it was a labor of love for Joshua. He felt like a kid in a toy shop to be able to build their dream house. They took out all the glass walls of the locked rooms in which the prototypes had been stored as well as the guest rooms. That opened up an area of about four thousand square feet. It was easy to divide it into two three-bedroom villas across from each other. The lab became a large common room that both families could use for recreation, including watching television, reading, or working on a hobby. Stefani and Anna worked together to decide on decor, furniture, and wall coverings. The kitchen was still the kitchen and would be shared between the two couples. The leftover glass was used to create a sunroom with a breathtaking view of the mountains. The foyer was changed to be an atrium with a large entryway.

If they had wanted to show it off, the home easily could have been featured in a magazine. Joshua flew out every Wednesday to supervise the progress, keep the subcontractors on schedule, and inspect the quality of the work, and returned every Sunday. Then there was the parade of overseers, such as the building inspector, the electrical inspector, the plumbing inspector, and the highway department. Finally, the building inspector walked through again to issue a certificate of occupancy. The assessment value was just over $1 million. Joshua and Anna had agreed to split the cost equally with Stefani and Mark. They split the down payment and split the monthly payment of the mortgage after closing. So far, it had seemed to work out well.

On one of his trips, Joshua took a few hours to bring out the remains of Cassie. He examined the mechanism by which Cassie had been able to hear. He found there was a small microphone buried under the plastic sheath of the side of her head. Was it possible that Anna had a similar piece of equipment and that the heat might have damaged it?

Anna came with Joshua on the next trip, and he was able to see if, in fact, the microphones could be swapped. She agreed, and he gave it a try. The surgery only took a few minutes. He found the microphone behind her ear, and yes, it had been damaged in the fire. He replaced it with Cassie's good microphone, and Anna started to hear again.

Fascinatingly, she could hear sounds, but they had no meaning. She had to learn to hear by connecting the sounds to the meanings of the letters and words in her head, as she had in the beginning. Her ability seemed to improve quickly over the next few weeks. By the end of the month, her hearing was almost back to normal.

Chapter 63

The big day finally arrived. The house was finished, and stuff was getting moved. No one knew how difficult the private road would be to navigate, so the initial loads were small. The big furniture would have to wait. They rented a storage space in Morgantown for the furniture and bigger things. The smaller things were in boxes and suitcases. Most of them were loaded onto the helicopter.

The four-hour flight seemed different this time. There was no specific plan for returning. When the three of them arrived at the property, Ray was drafted to help, and he began moving the boxes into the atrium. Stefani and Mark were going to start moving their things two weeks later. The moving in had begun.

During the six-month construction process, Anna and Joshua had applied to an adoption agency. It had been a long process that ran concurrently with the house construction. In the beginning, they had expected it to run much longer, but with a few strokes of luck, they'd found themselves signing documents for a child only six months later. They had been able to accept the child one week before the completion of the house. With all the formalities concluded, the big day had arrived for that also. Anna and Joshua had successfully adopted a three-month-old orphaned male named Thomas. The first meeting had been several weeks ago, and just last week, little Tommy had come home.

One day, after all the boxes had been unpacked and the house had become a home, Anna was feeding Tommy while Joshua read his news feed. He called over to Anna. "Honey, listen to this. There is a quiz that says you can tell a lot about people if they try to describe themselves in seven words. I have been working on this all morning, and I don't know if I can find seven words to describe me. What about you? What seven words would you use to describe yourself?"

Anna had to think for only a few minutes. She smiled. "Yes. I can describe myself in seven words: *daughter, sister, wife, mother, friend, blessed*, and *success*."

"Really?"

"Yes, I define myself by the important people in my life: Jim and Charlene, Stefani and Mark, you, Tommy, Gloria, Sophie, God, and myself."

"So you think of yourself as a success?"

"Yes. It's from that poem written by Ralph Waldo Emerson. You've heard of it: 'To laugh often and much, to earn the respect of intelligent people and the affection of children, to appreciate the words of honest critics and survive the sting of betrayal of false friends, to appreciate beauty and find the best in others, to leave the world a better place.' That is how he defines success. I have done all of those things."

"That is amazing. How do you do that? You take so many complicated things and make them so simple."

"It is not a big deal. I just know me."

At that moment, Tommy spit up on her. Anna laughed and thanked Tommy for the gift. Then she paused to reflect on the moment. Just ten years ago, she had been a waif. She had been a useless piece of junk meant to be destroyed for something else that would work better. She had fought her way out. She'd scraped out a living from almost nothing. She was welcomed as a member of a family. She had completed seven years of school and become an attorney. In her practice, she helped many people find their way through difficult times. She had earned her soul. The prison meant to contain her for all of a short life had become her million-dollar dream home. She had found a husband and created a family of her own as she raised her child.

This was the home she had set out to find. It was more than the home of the children of Dick and Jane and of Spot and Puff. It was more than the home of the happy people in commercials. It was the home that made her feel like the person she was meant to be. As she took in the joy she felt from the people around her, she saw the conclusion of her journey. Now she was ready for the next chapter of her life.

CPSIA information can be obtained
at www.ICGtesting.com
Printed in the USA
BVHW032139130922
646980BV00006B/23